Saranne didn't know how it happened but she found herself in Neville's arms, held tightly there, her heart pressed close to his while he showered fiercely ardent kisses upon her bewildered, upturned face. She shivered for a moment, her first instinct to recoil, then surrendered herself to the warm spell of his embrace. Raising shy, tremulous lips to his, she answered his kisses with her own. "Oh, Neville!" she breathed at last. "I did not dream that you could ever love me."

His gaze narrowed, grew calculating as he gazed down at her open innocent face and her red hair flaming in the candlelight. It troubled him not a whit that she believed he loved her, and he did not bother to dispel the illusion that would make his conquest of her delightfully easy.

Accessory to Love

Maureen Wakefield

WARNER BOOKS

A Warner Communications Company

WARNER BOOKS EDITION

Copyright © 1979 by Maureen Wakefield
All rights reserved.

ISBN 0-446-84790-9

Cover art by Walter Popp

Warner Books, Inc., 75 Rockefeller Plaza, New York, N.Y. 10019

 A Warner Communications Company

Printed in the United States of America

First Printing: July, 1979

10 9 8 7 6 5 4 3 2 1

Accessory to Love

Chapter
1

Kensington, in the year 1812, was merely a small village near London dominated chiefly by the mellow, old-brick royal palace across the fields, sheltering coyly behind its tall elms. It consisted mainly of one long straggling street given over on either side to a line of poor shops and even poorer dwellings.

In one of those tiny houses lived a young woman with her only child, a daughter, Saranne. "Mrs. Markham," as she was known, although she had no legal right to the title, was understood to have "seen better days." She kept to herself to a remarkable extent, mixing little with the humbler folk all around her, holding herself aloof from the neighbors. In reality she was a "kept woman," mistress of a rich city merchant who was Saranne's father, a certain Mr. Paton.

To Saranne herself, it was all so much water over her red head. Life flowed on smoothly and sweetly, without a care in the world. Her mother doted on the child, which was hardly surprising. To Phoebe Markham, clinging to this child she had produced like a drowning man clutching at a straw, Saranne was her sole grasp on sanity in a world of shifting quicksand. A poor, weak-willed creature at best, Phoebe found her whole existence wrapped up in Saranne.

For Saranne, shielded against the harsher, colder facts of life, Kensington was an enchanting village in which to dwell. She was content, awakened sleepily each morning by Debbie, their one domestic, with a cup of sweet, rich and creamy hot chocolate. It was Debbie who had shortened her two names, "Sarah" and "Anne" into one, Saranne, and it stuck.

Birds sang in the apple orchards at the back of all the buildings in the High Street. Cows mooed from the dairy shop on the corner, patiently waiting to be milked in the yard there. There were fields, winding country lanes beyond Holland House, haymakers, plying their craft, wielding their long wooden rakes. Stretching all the way to Windsor Castle in the west, hedgerows were aflame with wild dog roses in summer, pink and delicate as a maiden's blush, yet heavy with the dust that lay everywhere. In autumn there were ripe berries to be picked, carried home in a pail to

Debbie, who made them into jellies and preserves.

The stout gentleman who often came out to visit them, riding down from London and stabling his horse in the local livery establishment for the night, she addressed diplomatically as "Uncle." He, on his part, did not often address his remarks to her at all.

Indeed, he tended to disregard her altogether as if he felt her to be more of a hindrance than an asset, an unwanted by-product of his illicit association with Phoebe Markham, one of his work-girls.

"Reading your book well, miss, cyphering your sums, heh?" He stood before the fire in the sitting room, staring down at her and wearing the fashionably smart riding clothes, admirably tailored, molded over his plump figure. He rattled keys, small change in his breeches' pockets, turning to Phoebe. "Have her learn fine sewing, too," he ordered. "Never know when it might come in handy, later on, heh?"

Thus directly appealed to, the hovering mistress simpered obediently. She was like a lovely waxen doll, a puppet strung on wires, ready to do his every bidding, pulled by the strings he manipulated. She glanced in timid anxiety at her lord and master, as if striving to read his mood aright, fathom what was in his mind at that moment.

As if in response to something she read there, a secret signal, she suddenly bundled Saranne and Debbie out for a walk in the park. But then, Saranne and the old servant were used to this treatment on the occasion of his visits. Nor did she think it strange that Uncle should share her mother's bed.

And then disaster struck the little house in Kensington's High Street. Out of the blue, as such things so very often do. Drainage was not the main preoccupation of the authorities and open sewers ran in the streets in the poorer quarters. First Mama, then Debbie fell ill of the dreaded typhoid fever, although by some miracle Saranne herself escaped. The two women nursed each other as best they could, in turn. But while Phoebe survived, Debbie died.

To Saranne, this first brush with death was like the pulling of a front tooth. It left a gap that it seemed nothing would ever fill again. Debbie was not replaced. And now a subtle wind of change, of which Saranne was hardly aware, began to blow with an icy chill, a cold foreboding, through their affairs, hers and Mama's.

Like a dark blight over everything, a cloud across the face of the sun in a summer garden, Phoebe lost most of her looks in the aftermath of illness, becoming pinched looking, plain. This had its repercussions in a falling off of both her allowance and Mr. Paton's visits to Kensington. Inexplicable delays in the remittance on which they lived, hitherto arriving so punctually on the first day of each quarter, through Mr. Paton's lawyers.

"'Tis the fever, love, he is afraid of catching it," the poor young mother sought to make her excuses to the child.

Saranne, playing with her dolls upon the carpet in the living room, was indifferent to the fact that Uncle did not ride down from London to see them in those days. But tradesmen, the small local shopkeepers, began to grow restive as bills went unpaid.

The child knew little of all this, Phoebe keeping the worst from her daughter. Phoebe daily grew more desperate, thinner, paler, her face pinched with starvation, stinting herself to feed Saranne, selling bits of jewelry, trinkets, her better clothes.

"You will be paid all in good time, sir!" she told the importunate tradesmen, around her like sharks now, scenting the kill. She drew herself up, gathering the last tattered remnants of dignity about her like a cloak, saying wildly: "There has been a slight delay in my dividends—"

On the morning of the last day, when she went up to town with Mama, Saranne waited on the front porch, already dressed while Phoebe made herself tidy. When Phoebe presently came out to join her daughter, Saranne noticed that Mama's red hair, which was always so nicely dressed, was rough and tousled looking, as if she had not run a comb through it that morning.

"You ready, Saranne?" she asked gently. The scarlet stuff she smeared upon her lips and cheeks to make them healthy looking, was all smudged, ugly, as if she had dashed it on in a hurry, carelessly.

"Yes, Mama."

"Let's go, then," Phoebe said.

All that Saranne could think of at that moment was the cool, silky feel of the new petticoat Mama had made her out of one of her own; the clean white hose upon her feet. And if Phoebe's hands trembled as they presently went into the apothecary's shop in the High Street the child never noticed. Phoebe asked the chemist almost in an apologetic whisper for some rat poison.

"But, Mama—?" Saranne tugged at her mother's arm. "We have no rats, Mama," she objected in some surprise.

"Hush, child!" Phoebe managed to look both confused and determined at once and ran a vague hand across her white forehead under the red hair, biting her lip. "I—I thought I saw one yesterday, by the woodshed in the orchard," she said weakly.

Saranne did not reply to this, quickly losing interest. Her mother was well liked in the little hamlet of Kensington. Despite her reputation, there were many folk who smiled at Phoebe Markham that morning, curtseying or doffing their hat, according to sex. But she returned their friendly courtesies unsmilingly, like an automaton, as if she did not see them clearly.

Afterwards they waited by the corner where Kensington ended and Hyde Park began, its wildest stretches still the haunt of footpads. A hackney coach came by eventually and Mama hailed it, giving the Jehu an address in the city. Phoebe stopped the vehicle outside an imposing building in Cheapside given over to women's fashionable gowns.

Telling the jarvey to wait, Phoebe grasped Saranne's hand and hurried her across the sidewalk and into the Emporium, for such it was. As if she knew her way about very well, indeed might have worked here sometime herself long ago, Mama led Saranne up through the maze of rat-infested passages and workrooms to her Uncle's office on the top floor.

"How dare you come here?" he roared, rocking on his heels. "And to bring that brat here, too!" Wrath overcame him.

"Quite easily." Phoebe raised a scared yet somehow resolute face to his, finding the courage from somewhere, steeling herself. "I had to see you," she went on wanly, glancing at him briefly with all the old return to subservience and timidity he had come to expect from her. "I have no money, Sam," she said softly. "We are destitute."

"Oh, go to the devil, woman!" he snarled. Testily he turned his back on her, staring out of the window at the unappetizing vista of chimneypots and roofs of the city before him. He mumbled almost shamefacedly, without turning around to look at her: "I am now a married man. I married Miss Adeline three days ago. A quiet, private ceremony—" His listener heard him in stunned silence, blenching.

Phoebe hesitated for a moment, staring at his unresponsive back. He was standing in his favorite attitude, hands thrust deeply into his pockets jangling keys, money, whistling under his breath.

She drew a deep, ragged breath. "Please, then, will you keep her for a short time, at least?" Phoebe pleaded as a last resort. "I have business in the city to attend to, but I will be back by twelve o'clock."

It did not occur to him to wonder or even

question what this poor creature was doing, what possible business she could have in town.

With an oddly despairing gesture, Phoebe turned and kissed her daughter, then went out without another word or glance, her frail shoulders bowed. The fragrance of the perfume she ways wore lingered on the fusty air of that dingy office long after she had gone. At the same time that Phoebe left, a tall, beautifully gowned and elegant lady came in, stopping dead upon the threshold as she caught sight of Saranne, standing forlornly there.

"What is she doing here?" the newcomer demanded in a loud, shrill voice, nostrils distended and quivering with ill-temper. "Did—did that woman bring her? Send her away at once, Sam, I insist!"

The finely-drawn brows on the hard, pale blue eyes, were raised as he swung round at her entrance, pivoting eagerly upon the heels of his highly polished smart riding boots. It was plain even to Saranne that he sought to placate this lady.

He seemed to shrink in upon himself, become smaller in stature somehow, altering his appearance. His solution, as ever, was to pass the responsibility on to someone else, in this case the forewoman of the workshops below, Miss Hanley. Going to the door of his office and opening it a fraction wider in order to bawl into the void beyond—"Miss Hanley?"

"Yes, sir?" She came running at once in obedience to his call, wiping her palms upon her work apron as she appeared.

It was to her employer she spoke, but she smiled at Saranne as she did so. A grin—big, friendly, enveloping—that embraced the child like a warm hug. Saranne's drooping spirits, a moment ago sagging to a dangerously low level, perked up at once.

"Take the brat and keep her amused until midday, when her mother returns," he muttered sulkily.

Miss Hanley took Saranne's hand as bidden and led her from the room. The door closing behind them, she dropped upon one knee and took a fold of Saranne's miniature green gown in one workworn hand. She fingered it knowingly, head on one side.

"Mama make it?" Miss Hanley asked casually.

"Yes." The child's vivid face lit up. "From one of her own," she explained truthfully, eager to confide in this new friend.

"Ah!" Miss Hanley said mysteriously, sighing, adding under her breath, almost to herself: "Poor Phoebe Markham's hand hasn't lost its cunning, then!"

Miss Hanley was dark and short, round and plump as a ripe apple—"cosy" was the word that leaped most readily to Saranne's mind. The workshop into which she ushered the child was filled by many women and girls of all sizes and ages, busy at the long tables, plying their needles. The room was badly ventilated and exeedingly hot from the heat of many flatirons needed for pressing and smoothing the finished garments, set upon a big stove in the middle.

Miss Hanley, in her role of forewoman, wore a gown of some nondescript material of dun color, as became her position of minor authority. It was fastened at her throat by a brooch of such dazzling brilliance as to hurt the eye. She caught sight of Saranne's wondering upward gaze and chuckled.

"They ain't *reel*, silly," she confided to her new charge in a strong Cockney accent, twanging like a lyre, reading Saranne's mind like a book. Her expression suddenly changed, became serious, almost wistful as she gazed thoughtfully at Saranne. "Only imitation, dearie —the *reel* diamonds of life aren't for the likes of yours truly, duckie! Your poor Mama, maybe —and Mrs. Paton certainly! But Mamie Hanley, no!" And she sighed deeply, as if at some memory that hurt.

"Oh," was all that Saranne could find to say at this. Her new friend smiled again.

"Well—" Miss Hanley squared her shoulders, as if throwing off a burden that irked. "What say to me finding you a piece of material now, some silk perhaps, for you to make a best dress for your dolly, while you're waiting for Mama? I will cut it out for you, show you what to do."

"Oh, yes, please!" Saranne said eagerly, perking up at once, all her troubles temporarily forgotten.

Brightening, she accepted the offer gratefully, in the spirit in which it was given. Miss

Hanley was so easy to get along with, she thought, surrendering her heart.

Saranne presently shared their midday meal with the seamstresses, the rough coarse hunks of meat and thick slices of bread, the rank poisonous pickles they had brought with them, and all washed down by tankards of weak ale. There was even a sweetmeat or two, and some fruit as a treat for Saranne. They were kind to her because like all poor women, they had a soft spot in their starved, beaten hearts for children. And partly because—well, wasn't she their late workmate Phoebe's "little mistake," her love child?

In the midst of this repast her father passed through the workroom again, starting when he saw that Saranne was still there. He was not alone; the beautiful lady Saranne had seen before was with him. His eye darkened, his face flushed angrily as he beheld his daughter sitting like a small queen holding court amidst her willing subjects. But he said nothing, passing on.

Presently they heard the church clocks striking all over the city, the sound floating in through the open windows. Clear, sonorous, bell-like came three strokes—no more—and then silence. So there could be no mistake; it was now three hours past the time Mama had promised to return. Miss Hanley cast a troubled look in Saranne's direction, sitting quietly sewing her doll's robe.

"Your Mama's kind of late, isn't she, love?" she said gently to Saranne at last.

17

Saranne looked up, alarmed. "Yes, ma'am," she said worriedly, nodding.

At this moment, as if in response to a hidden cue, her father reappeared in the doorway, with the beautiful woman like a chilly, watchful wraith at his side. He scowled once more as he saw Saranne, his brow clouding over. She was a little less bright now, more apprehensive as she gazed solemnly back at him, laying down her sewing. His eyes darkened anew but he ignored her, turning his attention directly to Miss Hanley.

"Her mother not back yet?" he said sharply.

Miss Hanley shook her head. "No, sir— and it's getting kind of late." She laid down her own needlework, staring anxiously up at him.

Saranne created a diversion at this moment by suddenly starting to cry, hopeless tears torn from the depths of her small being. She sniffed, wiping them away childishly with the back of one hand. Mama had never done anything like this to her before, left her alone and undefended, as it were, in the midst of the enemy's camp.

"Here—" Miss Hanley rummaged within her capacious reticule and came up with a big, newly washed and ironed gentleman's handkerchief. "Blow!" she commanded.

Smiling through her tears, the child took it and did as she was bid, and dried her eyes. Mr. Paton meanwhile caught the disdainful glance of his haughty companion, who stood by the door while all this was going on, glowering in utter contempt. She wore an exquisite summer gown of cornflower-blue silk in the long Empire style, which clung to her tall willowy figure and set it off superbly.

It brought out the Nordic iciness of her pale blue eyes too, under the thinly penciled, superciliously arched brows. Her abundant golden hair was piled high on top of her head in the style of the day. One artificial contrived-looking blond curl drooped coquettishly, falling over one shoulder. The tight red lips curled into a sneer as she briefly contemplated Saranne before turning sweetly to Mr. Paton.

"Coming, my love?" was all she said, however. Yet the underlying threat was there, implicit in her voice, a hidden menace, like a whip cracking through the air. And he jumped to its bidding. "In a minute, my dear."

"Very well," she said coldly. "Do not be long."

He drew a handful of assorted coins from his breeches pocket, among them a gold guinea, and flung them upon the workbench in front of Miss Hanley. They rolled and scattered and some of them fell to the floor, where Saranne busied herself picking them up.

"Get a hackney coach and take her home," he ordered. "And you had better remain there until the mother returns." He added an afterthought, viciously, sneeringly: "If she ever does!"

"Yes, sir," the forewoman said woodenly.

As he vanished into his office, thankfully closing the door behind him, Miss Hanley stood up. She thoughtfully scooped the little pile of coins into her purse of knotted string, stowing this safely away in her reticule. Then she took down her shawl from its nail on the wall, draping it about her shoulders.

Her last task was to hurry Saranne down the stairs and out of the building into the street, after tying on the child's bonnet, with its long, green satin ribbons, firmly under her chin. This time Saranne did not object, but accepted the irksome bow meekly.

The brightness of the day outside with all its earlier promise seemed to have evaporated when they emerged from the Emporium and stepped across the sidewalk of the street below. The warm sunlight of early morning had given away to a dull, leaden gray tinge in the atmosphere, dark and sullen. The sky was overcast, cloudy over the skyline, gloomy with the look of a coming storm.

"Come on, love," Miss Hanley said kindly.

She led the way to the hackney coach stand on the corner of the street and hired one, briskly giving the driver his instructions. But she did not talk much as the vehicle rumbled out of the city over the cobblestones. Saranne was silent, too, enjoying the unprecedented treat of no less than two coach rides in one day.

She was a little tired now, yawning in the semi-darkness of the vehicle's interior, all the excitements of the day proving too much for her. They passed by Hyde Park and were entering the environs of Kensington before she spoke again. She tugged at Miss Hanley's arm anxiously.

"Ours is the house with green shutters," she said timidly. Miss Hanley nodded, smiling.

"I know," she said gently. She added grimly under her breath, so softly that Saranne could not hear her: "I know your poor Mama's little love nest, child!"

When they stopped before the cottage Miss Hanley paid the driver off, but prudently told him not to go too far away—she might need him soon for the return journey. Saranne noticed how forlorn the house looked somehow, empty without Mama there. The windows with their half-drawn drapes stared at them blankly, like dead unseeing eyes.

Miss Hanley paused with her hand already on the wicket gate, about to push it open. Staring up at the front of the little house, her brow wrinkled into a puzzled frown. "That's odd, pet," she murmured.

The windows were all firmly closed save one, which was opened a few inches at the bottom. A strip of curtain had managed to squeeze itself through the gap and was fluttering gaily in the breeze with all the abandon in the world. Saranne's eyes followed the direction of Miss Hanley's gaze wonderingly.

"What is odd, ma'am?" she asked.

"That window, dearie—your Mama's room, I take it? Does she often go out and leave windows open like that, for every petty sneak-thief and pickpocket to walk in and help himself?" Miss Hanley pursed her lips wisely, dropped her voice instinctively, shaking her head. "Such a poor neighborhood, too, near to the Park—worse than Vauxhall and its infamous Pleasure Gardens any day!"

"Yes, ma'am," Saranne replied dutifully, completely befogged.

"Well—" Miss Hanley straightened her back, taking a firmer grip on Saranne's hand. "What say we go and take a look-see, eh, round the rear of the place?"

Saranne was quite agreeable and so, suiting the action to the word, her new-found friend led the way to the back of the cottage. Miss Hanley found the spare key, as Saranne said she might, under an earthenware flowerpot beside the kitchen door, placed there for just such a contingency as this. As they stepped across the threshold of the kitchen, a warm friendly air rose up to greet them, enfolding them in a welcoming embrace, an air redolent with the many good meals cooked there in Debbie's day, of Saranne eating her bowl of curds and whey at the well-scrubbed table. The copper warming-pans and other utensils hanging upon the wall winked ruddily at them in the firelight of the stove. Saranne was all eagerness now that her new friend and her Mama should meet without further delay.

"We could all have a dish of tea together," she suggested happily. Using the best china, the treasured silver teaspoons, in honor of the cherished guest.

Perhaps Mama had got home ahead of them? Saranne went out into the hall and called up the stairs with a rising note of anxiety, as she always did when she came home from her Dames school every day.

"Mama—?" she called, experimentally.

Nobody replied and the brooding silence of the tiny house remained unbroken, became enhanced, rather. There was no sound save their own loud breathing, minute noises from the kitchen, the hiss and soft crackle of the fire as the coals fell in.

Miss Hanley did not follow Saranne immediately. She paused in the parlor in order to indulge her burning curiosity, gazing about her inquisitively, yet with native good humor. Her homely face a mixture of awe, wonder, and respect, as if the aura of poor Phoebe's sins had rubbed off a little onto her possessions.

Her shrewd, not unkindly glance swept over the few remaining items of silver and glass. The pictures in gilded frames on the green-tinted walls were mostly watercolors of Kensington and its vicinity, and the furniture was fine without being luxurious. There were flowers everywhere, for it was obvious that Mr. Paton's discarded mistress had the proverbial "green thumb" with plant life.

But it was Horace, Phoebe's beautiful big, black tomcat on which her facinated gazed finally stopped. The cat lay stretched out fast asleep upon the cushions at one end of the sofa, with all the feline's disdain and contempt for human tragedy or comedy, ignoring it. He balefully opened one topaz eye as they came into the room, disturbing his slumbers. Tail twitching, he lay there for perhaps thirty seconds more, without otherwise moving or giving any sign that he noticed them. Then, in

23

one lithe movement he uncurled and leaped soundlessly to the floor. He, stalked over the carpet to Miss Hanley and rubbed against her skirts, clearly asking to be picked up, purring loudly.

"Oh, you lovely thing, you!" she exclaimed, stooping to gather him up and cradle him in her arms admiringly.

Still holding the cat, she then followed Saranne out of the room. There was no particular reason why Miss Hanley, a mere casual visitor at best, should follow suit as Saranne began to climb the stairs. But that is what she did—automatically, without thinking, Horace twined about her neck and shoulders now like a soft black fur stole—yet in a more leisurely fashion than Saranne's own hop, skip and jump approach to the upper regions of the house.

Again Saranne called—"Mama?", and as before there was no reply. A glance in passing into her own room showed her that Mama was not in there, the curtains round her little white bed looped back, just as they had left them that morning.

The door to Phoebe's room, with its pretty china handle, was closed, blank looking. But the slightest pressure of Saranne's hand was enough to send it swinging inward noiselessly on well-oiled hinges. The doorknob held firmly in her fingers, she stepped into the room beyond, her feet sinking into the deep, creamy pile of the India rug.

This room had always been a holy of holies to her, a place into which one did not venture without invitation or command. There were many things there, pretty, frivolous things, that were plainly labeled "don't touch." The pink satin coverlet upon the wide, low double bed was tumbled and awry, the pillows dented as if someone had lain there.

That is not like Mama, she thought, troubled. Saranne frowned, hesitating upon the threshold. But eventually she took a step forward, thrust out a hand instinctively to tweak the disarranged counterpane into place. It did not respond immediately to her action, something obviously holding it down on the far side, nearest the wall.

Miss Hanley had reached the open doorway behind her now, with the cat held in her arms, watching. Saranne went round the foot of the bed to detach the coverlet from that angle. At first, she did not see Mama lying there sprawled in the narrow aisle between wall and bed.

Her blue, innocent eyes were wide open, staring straight at Saranne without seeing her. Clasped in one hand she held the round, sinister, dark-blue poison bottle she had bought from the apothecary that morning. It was intact, the stopper still in its narrow neck. The aftermath of illness, pain, despair had taken their toll at last. Death had come for Phoebe Markham before she could take her own life.

Mama was quite, quite dead.

Miss Hanley came to the pathetic little funeral in Kensington's cemetery, one of a mere handful of mourners there. She dropped a modest posy of cheap flowers onto the coffin lid, tribute from the seamstresses—her former workmates—before Phoebe was buried out of sight forever.

Mrs. Paton was at the funeral, too, in her official capacity as representative of Paton's Emporium. She was splendidly gowned that day in a magnificent creation of black velvet trimmed with bands of rich sable fur. Her bonnet and cloak were of the same material, framing the cold face with its fair hair. Conscious of the stray onlookers present, she gripped Saranne's hand tightly, until the child cried out for the pain of it.

"Please, ma'am, you're hurting my fingers!"

Adeline Paton scowled beneath the veil which hid her sharp features so well.

After that Saranne was taken for a short period into her father's new house, as nobody seemed to know what to do with her. After some strong prodding from that lady he had, at Adeline's orders, purchased a large mansion in a quietly fashionable London street, where they were now residing. It had many unoccupied rooms.

The new Mrs. Paton had the sleek, self-satisfied, not to say smug look of a cat that has just lapped up the saucer of cream meant for the pet next door. Yet in successfully disposing of her rival, as she saw her, she still found herself left with a reminder of Phoebe Markham, in the person of Saranne. Infuriated, perhaps not unjustly, at having this undesired, "difficult" stepdaughter foisted upon her, Mrs. Paton took a subtle revenge.

Soon after Saranne took up her abode in

their household, quarrels between her stepmother and father began in earnest. Saranne was the cause, the main bone of contention, the rope used in the marital tug-of-war. Before Adeline banished her to an attic room under the roof, she lay awake next door to the conjugal chamber, listening to them, for the walls were thin.

"She will have to go, Mr. P., I am warning you! Why must I put up with her, forever watching everything I do, listening to whatever I say, hanging round my neck like a noose?" Mrs. Paton demanded heatedly. She laughed, a short brittle bark without any mirth in it. "I didn't bargain for *this* when I married you, Samuel Paton!"

"I am sure she doesn't mean to annoy you, my love." This was Saranne's father, trying to placate his bride, conciliate her. Caught like a heavy, bumbling fly in a web of his own making, but too besotted with Adeline at that point, too stupid to escape, he went on in a wheedling tone: "We could go away for a trip if you like, my dear, take the waters at Bath or Harrogate Spa, if that would please you."

"And have her waiting for me when I got back?" Adeline laughed again, scornfully. "No, thank you! And besides," she flared anew, going off at a fresh tangent, "she has red hair—and you know how I detest folk of that coloring. You can never trust them, my old mother used to say."

"The brat can't help the color of her hair," he argued with unexpected spirit. He added imprudently, without thinking, "She gets that from her mother."

"And Phoebe Markham's eyes, too, I presume?" she riposted dangerously, as if her teeth were on edge. She snorted. "If you think I am spending the rest of my life, Samuel Paton, with a dead woman peering out at me from her daughter's eyes—" She paused, breathing hard, and Saranne cowered in her little bed next door.

It sounded like the knell of doom to her. Desperately she tried to make herself small, insignificant, hoping in this way to escape Adeline's notice. Uncle—she never learned to call him "Father"—never took her side in these arguments; that was the hardest to bear. And in the end Saranne had to go.

Mr. Paton remembered, after some prompting from his wife, that he had on his books the proprietors of a girls' boarding school in Surrey, who were experiencing some difficulty in settling their bills. He got in touch with the Misses Patterson at their Academy for Young Ladies in Epsom, a small country town famous alike for its green Downs and the races held there.

"Although the pupils of The Limes," they were swift to point out in their brochure and their interviews with parents, "have nothing to do with *that*."

They agreed to take Saranne at greatly reduced fees and no questions asked, in return for certain adjustments to their account at the Emporium in Cheapside. Nor did it cost Mr. Paton much in the end. He sold the love nest he shared in Kensington with Phoebe for a nice profit and put the money this brought into gilt-edged stock, the dividends of which more than paid for Saranne's schooling.

They would pay, too, for any other extras she might incur in the way of books, clothes and doctor's bills until she was sixteen years old, when all such payments would cease, as she would then be old enough to stand on her own feet and earn a living.

Moreover, he arranged with his chief clerk, Mr. Soames, to board Saranne and lodge her with him and his wife during the school holidays, in their little house south of the Thames. Miss Hanley turned out to be her adopted "Aunt Bertha's" sister! Even the cat, Horace, was there, purring on the hearth as if he had never lived anywhere else, Miss Hanley having rescued him after the funeral.

It was just like coming home. . . .

All fees that changed hands were remitted, as before, through Mr. Paton's lawyers. He did not appear in it at all, thus removing all onus of responsibility from himself, and, indeed, congratulated himself on his benevolence in the matter.

"After all," Adeline pointed out sweetly, "she might just as easily have been sent to an orphanage. Or gone onto the streets, ending up in a gutter!"

The Principal of the school in Epsom and her assistant, her sister Abigail, who was a faint carbon copy of her elder, were mildly vexed with their patron for foisting this unknown, unwanted pupil upon them, but they could hardly refuse. Aside from the financial consideration,

Saranne's sad gray eyes made a bigger impression than they cared to acknowledge even to themselves. Romance may still have blossomed in some dim, half-forgotten corner of their withered, dried-up old hearts. Miss Abigail herself popped Saranne, her red hair gleaming in the candlelight, into a beautiful, hot steaming bath of shining porcelain set before the fire in their own private sitting room.

"Because, after all, Lou," Miss Abby said earnestly to her sister, kneeling upon the hearthrug with a cake of soap in one hand and wiping away a stray wisp of damp hair from her forehead with the other, "she has come from that rather dubious part of town! Also—" Miss Abby dropped her voice to a dramatic whisper, "her ancestry, my dear—one of her father's work people, rumor has it."

Miss Patterson merely grunted in reply, bending her head low over her task, correcting a pile of smudged and inky copybooks from the lower forms.

Yet when Saranne was presently dressed in the school uniform for all ages, —a demure gray woolen gown right down to her ankles, a white apron, a neckerchief draped about her thin shoulders—she looked no different from any of the other children there. Her gray eyes alert with intelligence, her red hair curling naturally around her small, piquant, heart-shaped face, she was so slenderly fashioned as to appear tall for her age, with delicately tapering fine slim hands and feet.

"Which shows," Miss Abby remarked wisely

to her elder, pursing her lips, "that there must be good blood in her, somewhere."

And so Saranne took up her residence at The Limes. Life, thereafter, became mostly an affair of taking great care with one's clothes and remembering at all times where one was—and one's Ps and Qs; of mending one's gloves and darning one's hose and above all, never, *never* resting one's elbows upon desk or table—because, apart from being most unladylike, it wore out the sleeves of one's gowns. This incurred the risk, ever present, of bringing Miss Abby's, or worse still, the Principal's wrath down about one's luckless red head.

No, it behooved her to tread warily, like a cat. And like a cat she walked mostly alone and from choice, holding herself slightly aloof and giving her confidences to none, in all that teeming hive of schooldays among richer, more fortunate girls.

The years sped swiftly by and then Saranne was sixteen. She was a pupil-teacher at The Limes now, all fees from her father ceasing to flow dating from her birthday. And there arrived at the school a rich banker's daughter and heiress in her own right, one Miss Arabella Crale.

A girl of about Saranne's own age or a fraction older, Arabella had been sent to The Limes to be "finished" in all those arts and graces so necessary to one of her station in life, the key to which only the Misses Patterson and their like possessed. Preceded by an imposing coach with the Crale family crest upon the panels, piled high with an enormous amount of luggage—

"—Out of all proportion to her needs," poor Miss Abby stormed.

—Arabella descended upon an awed school. She "took" to Saranne on sight—her own confession—an honor that the recipient of it accepted with some reservations. Saranne was conscious of the vast financial and social gulf that yawned between them, if Arabella was not.

But, as time went on, Miss Crale would have none of this, overriding Saranne's scruples. The ill-assorted friendship ripened by leaps and bounds, culminating that summer in an invitation to join the heiress for part of the long vacation at the latter's family home near Bath, Crale Court.

Bath! Saranne's heart leaped in joyful expectation at the very name of the place, signifying as it did all the very best of society; a city in the West Country where virtue rubbed shoulders with vice, lodestone of wit and fashion and beauty, good and bad mixed hopelessly, and all drawn toward it like moths to a candle flame, there to singe their wings. It was the haunt of high living and seedy adventuring alike.

Most of all, she thought, Arabella's invitation would enable her to escape from the jaded stuffiness of London in midsummer, and the Soames's little house in particular, where she normally spent her holidays from school. Town was so crowded then, heavy with the dust of horse-drawn traffic everywhere. Even the open spaces, the lungs of the city, snatches of greenery amidst all that wilderness of bricks and mortar, were inert, stifled. Arabella's invitation will save me from at least a month or six weeks of *that*, ran her grateful thoughts.

Instead, she would spend the holidays savoring the almost legendary delights of Bath. And yet, strangely enough, it was Arabella's glowing accounts of the countryside surrounding her home that Saranne found herself dwelling on most: those lonely stretches of West Country moorland, empty and untouched by the hand of man, lying for miles in every direction, a world of nothingness, dark and somber, bounded by a range of distant hills.

A huge area under the Wessex sky, with only the ling and gorse, the wildflowers to clothe its nakedness above the underlying granite. The "kissing bush," the country folk called the yellow gorse bush, and said that when that plant was in bloom, so was kissing! But that was only a rural superstition, to be ignored, Arabella said artlessly.

It was like a living flame, as Saranne imagined it, a lambent gold so fierce in hue that one fancied one could warm one's hands on it as at a brazier. The moors around Arabella's home were untrammeled, free, and she envied them with a sigh. The winds blowing above them had a life of their own under the empty roof of the sky, flecked with billowing white clouds like the sails of ships . . . skies under which she, alien outsider and stranger that she was, might yet hope to find a measure of peace and happiness at last.

Early one morning in the spring of her seventeenth year, Saranne emerged from the rear of the main school building on her way to the kitchen gardens, executing an errand for the Principal. There was an unusual sparkle in the air that day, light refracted from every blade of grass, each single leaf in the hedgerows in a million tiny diamond points.

Under the hard clear blue of the April sky the whole earth had become transfigured overnight, enchanted as if tipped by Merlin's magic wand. A slight, warm breeze was blowing, potent as wine. It ruffled up her silky red curls, put a welcome touch of color in her always too pale cheeks, suffusing them with a becoming, wild-rose pinkness.

Taking a short-cut round the back of the mansion, where the walled gardens, her destination, lay, Saranne was startled to come face to face with a smart phaeton drawn up behind the laurel bushes, a fine specimen of horseflesh between the shafts, pawing the ground impatiently.

"Oh!" She halted dead in her tracks at the sight, taken by surprise.

She could not understand what such a showy vehicle was doing in the blameless vicinity of The Limes, hiding in its shrubbery. An assignation with one of the young ladies? No, that was unthinkable. The glittering paintwork and metal harness of the horse were so well-kept shining in the strong sunlight, that they hurt the glance. She instinctively raised one slender white hand to shield her dazzled eyes.

34

It was then she saw, with a further shock, that the vehicle was not unaccompanied. A young man stood there, leaning casually against its side, completely at ease. Beneath the impudently tilted brim of a peaked cap, such as jockeys, postillions and amateur gentlemen drivers wore in those days, he regarded her confusion with amusement.

Saranne frowned, nonplussed. His tight, fashionable trousers were the exact shade of soft gray of the breast of a ringdove, and he wore a blue coat adorned by expensive silver buttons. At his throat a high cravat of snowy linen was speared by a golden pin. As their eyes met, she experienced a disturbing tingling sensation such as she had never known before in her short life. Her heart missed a beat and then went on again, galloping uncomfortably fast. She blushed and was angry with herself for doing so, biting her lip.

Striving to recover her lost dignity, she felt flustered and ill-at-ease. None of these telltale, give-away signs were lost on her companion, who smiled slightly at the sight of them. It was a battle of wits between man and girl, a subtle fight of two strong wills. And her gray eyes fell first, before the bold overmastering challenge in his blue ones.

As they did so, a slight fugitive smile flitted over his handsome features and was gone. "I say—don't go." He spoke abruptly, smiling in winning fashion as Saranne seemed about to depart, turning on her heel. Overcome by shyness, a sudden emotion she did not understand, she was inwardly seething with indignation. "I won't eat you, you know," he went on lazily, in a mildly humorous way, smiling once more disarmingly.

His voice was as prepossessing as his whole person, low, thrilling, cultured. In her ears it sounded like music—"a manly voice," she thought innocently. Pleasantly charming now, he set himself to gain her approval and succeeded, eyes twinkling slyly under long dark lashes that were just a little too luxuriant for a man. Thawing under his scrutiny, Saranne drew herself up to her full height of five-feet-nothing.

"I had no intention of running away," she said loftily and untruthfully. She glared at him, breathing hard as if she had run a long distance over hard going, trying to still the trembling of her voice.

"Splendid." His glance slid down in calculating fashion over her slim figure, taking in the gray stuff of her gown with its ornamental white apron used as protection against chalk and slate pencils during class time, the apple-green ribbon woven in the lustrous glory of her red hair. And finally, the smoldering gray eyes regarding him suspiciously in turn, as he surveyed the bundle of books she carried under one arm. "You *look* like a schoolma'am—?" he began doubtfully, staring enquiringly at her.

"I *am* a schoolma'am, as you term it," she retorted tartly, stung by the question. She tapped one small foot in its neat shoe upon the gravel path. "What can I do for you?" she demanded crisply.

"Ah!" He heaved a sigh of theatrical relief,

rolling his eyes comically. And suddenly, something in the turn of his head, a fancied resemblance to someone she knew, outlandish as it might have seemed, struck Saranne with the force of a blow. So that she was not as surprised as she could have been when he continued blandly, "I am Roderick Crale, one of Arabella's many long-suffering brothers." He leaned toward her conspiratorially, dropping his voice dramatically: "Tell me," he begged, "I mean, is there any chance of meeting Arabella on the strict Q.T., eh? Are those twin she-dragons, Lou and Abby, anywhere about?"

Saranne dimpled at this despite herself. All her best efforts at appearing cool and dignified, in charge of the situation, failed in the face of his impudent self-assurance. There was an engaging brashness about his approach that rivaled Arabella's own.

"Those twin she-dragons, as you call them," she said demurely, "happen to be my employers, the Misses Patterson. Still—" Saranne laughed outright now. "They can be rather dragonish, at times!" she admitted ruefully.

"By Jove!" It was his turn now to start, to look surprised, if only for an instant. "Then you must be Miss Saranne Markham, Arabella's best friend at The Limes?" he said slowly, with a quickening interest, and Saranne blushed.

"I believe I have that honor," she agreed dryly.

All of a sudden she was aware of a new, overwhelming emotion in his presence such she had never known with another human being before. She had heard the saying "like a

Greek god come to life" but had not really grasped its true significance until now.

He had clear, laughter-lit blue eyes set in the tanned oval of his handsome face, eyes bright as the sea or a summer sky. And his hair, as he removed his cap, was a helmet of pure gold, fitting tightly to his head. Yet she could not help thinking wistfully, It is a proud face, though, as if its owner, like Lucifer, were thoroughly aware of his own good fortune, his outstanding good looks.

He knew, too, of the power of sheer physical attraction their possession gave him over lesser, more ordinary mortals.

However dazzling Roderick Crale was to Saranne, Arabella took the visit in her stride, greeting him coolly—Almost guardedly? Saranne thought, puzzled—with a sangfroid, a casualness that matched his own. On Saranne's advice, diffidently given but accepted eagerly enough by brother and sister, Roderick was persuaded to approach the Principal by more orthodox channels, obtaining an interview with that lady and extracting permission from her to take the two girls out to tea in the nearby town of Epsom. For Saranne, to her gratified astonishment, was included in his invitation.

"Always providing, young man," the Principal said warningly, "that you promise to bring them both back at a reasonable hour."

He promised readily enough, a girl already on either arm. But then, Saranne mused shrewdly, no doubt he would have promised anything glibly enough at that juncture, in order to gain his own way. They turned in presently under the low doorway of Ye Olde Englishe Tea Shoppe in Epsom's High Street, with its charming bow-fronted window overlooking the passing scene.

Over tea and the most delicious French pastries—Arabella enjoying a chocolate éclair and unashamedly licking her fingers afterwards—Saranne learned that Roderick had been abroad on the Continent making the Grand Tour, a tour that was now cut short for some reason not vouchsafed to the two eagerly listening girls.

Chapter
2

Arabella seemed to have got over her initial marked coolness of manner toward Roderick, her offhand acceptance of his appearance. She now listened at least as eagerly to the recital of his travels as Saranne herself.

"Coming up from the coast this morning, after landing at Newhaven in Sussex," Roderick confessed charmingly, "it occurred to me as a very good idea to break my journey to London at Epsom, for the purpose of calling on my sister at her finishing school. And," he added with a little bow in her direction, "make the acquaintance of Arabella's very good friend, Miss Saranne Markham—of whom Arabella's letters home are full!"

"Arabella's letters?" Saranne blinked,

startled. "I thought she never wrote any," she demurred.

"Enough," Roderick retorted significantly. "Enough for us to know how kind you have been to her, showing her the ropes, etcetera, at The Limes!"

"It was nothing," Saranne said quickly, conscious nevertheless of a glow of happiness, delight suffusing her whole being at his words. Once more that wayward heart of hers, which had already misbehaved once on his account earlier that day, missed a beat then went on, thumping loudly within her ears. She caught her breath, bending her red head low over her plate to joyfully hide the sudden rush of color to her cheeks. I am not wholly a stranger to Roderick, then, she thought happily. Or he to me!

She had seen Roderick Crale ere this, she realized. Or rather, his likeness. Those pupils at The Limes who were rich enough to afford to do so enjoyed a room of their own while living under its roof. And Miss Crale, naturally, was in this category. The rest had to make do with a quite comfortable shared dormitory, divided into cubicles.

Among the many knickknacks and souvenirs brought by the heiress from home and dotted about her room was a picture of the family residence, Crale Court, down at Bath. A badly executed watercolor by some amateur painter, it showed a view of the mansion with a picture of the whole Crale clan in front in various poses, as the fashion of the era dictated. Arabella, as the only daughter, was seated upon a rough rustic bench between her parents, Sir Joshua and Lady Crale.

Both ladies were in sumptuous formal costume as the age demanded, all silks and satins and furbelows, fine feathers and lace and ribbons. The males were different, some of the Crale sons being pictured on horseback, others leaning against trees in the background, a favorite sporting dog or two at their feet. All very blond, all very handsome to a degree. Trying to remember which one was Roderick was an almost impossible task.

But Saranne managed it—or thought that she did, eventually. A matter of luck rather than judgment, she admitted later, back in Arabella's room. Yet she found her gaze straying more than once to another figure in the family group. A tall, dark, saturnine looking man who stood head and shoulders above the Crale boys, his coloring in marked contrast to all that blondness.

"Who is he, Arabella?" she asked frowning inquisitively.

"Oh, him?" Arabella squinted at the watercolor Saranne still held in her hand, then shrugged carelessly. "That is Jerome DeLacey," she said coolly, with real or feigned indifference, Saranne was not sure which.

"And that," Saranne retorted crisply, with an ironic smile, a curl of the red lips, "tells me all, I presume? I only asked you who or what he was, Arabella," she said reproachfully.

"Well—" Thus directly appealed to, Arabella had the grace to blush slightly and look a little ashamed of her laconic manner. She tossed her fair head. "He is a lawyer, if you must know," she said grudgingly, sulkily. "An attorney who handles all Papa's legal affairs down in Bath. As indeed he does for most of the important County families around there. How he got into our picture I don't know—I guess he must have been visiting at the time." And Arabella shrugged again.

"Oh." Saranne shook her red head doubtfully, staring down at the dark one in the picture. "He looks—formidable," she said slowly.

"Jerome formidable?" Arabella looked genuinely surprised. She went on chattily—apparently once having started there was no stopping her: "Of course, he is not only a lawyer. He is a landowner, too, who lives at Lacy Place and is a neighbor of ours."

But Saranne was no longer listening or even interested in Mr. Jerome DeLacey. She strove to banish the image of the dark-haired, stern-faced lawyer from her mind, concentrating instead, as if it were a talisman against Arabella's verbosity, on the limned picture of Roderick in the little watercolor. Poor and bad as that scrap of pasteboard was, it was doubly, trebly precious now.

Before Roderick had taken them both safely back to the haven of The Limes that evening, depositing them on the gravel drive just inside the gates, and given a cheery wave of the hand in farewell, then driving off at a spanking pace to take the corner literally on one wheel, she had fallen wholeheartedly in love with him.

As wholeheartedly in love, that is, as it is

possible for a girl to be with a young man of whose existence, up to a few short hours before, she had been in blissful ignorance. And because of that fact, the Crale watercolor became of great import to her now, whenever Arabella would allow her to examine it. And whenever that happened, as before her glance was drawn back, again and again, to the painted likeness of the laywer, Jerome DeLacey.

"Oh, bother the man!" she thought crossly.

He had no business to affect her so, this stranger who shared a family portrait with Roderick Crale. It was a strong, forceful face that stared boldly up at her, a fine one that could be deemed strangely handsome even, when in repose. She conceded that unwillingly. The countenance of a Conquistador of old from the Spanish Main, a pirate. The dark eyes watched her enigmatically, with lofty indifference. Some instinct, a disturbing sense of warning, told her that this man could also be a dangerous enemy, given the chance, and the necessary circumstances.

If one were unlucky or foolish enough to cross swords with him, that is! And she shivered at the idea. But Roderick's sister was frankly amazed when Saranne mentioned something to her of her troubled doubts about Mr. DeLacey which vexed her still.

"Jerome proud, cross, ill-tempered?" Arabella echoed, wide-eyed. "Why, whatever makes you think that, my dear? You are joking, of course—Jerome is a perfect lamb, if you know how to handle him!"

"And you, I suppose," Saranne retorted crisply, "are in the latter category, miss?"

Arabella merely giggled at this, good natured as ever, and slow to take offense. She refused to be drawn further on the topic of Mr. DeLacey. Saranne, at that, felt her fingers tingling with a wild desire to slap Arabella, hard! Instead, she changed the subject.

She suddenly shivered again, an ice-cold shudder running down her spine. It was like what Aunt Bertha, back in London, called "a goose walking over your grave, dearie." She decided then and there never to speak or even think of the odious lawyer ever again.

She turned instead to the far more agreeable task of overhauling her wardrobe in preparation for her forthcoming trip down to the West Country, to Arabella's home. The latter's big, blue, somewhat empty eyes were bubbling over with mischief, and something else, an emotion Saranne couldn't name, when a few weeks after Roderick's visit to Epsom she danced into Saranne's cramped little cupboard of a room one morning, and thrust an envelope into the other girl's hand.

"Go on, read it!" Arabella urged impatiently as Saranne still hesitated. "It's for you."

Saranne withdrew from the big white envelope the single sheet of notepaper it contained. The letter was addressed to her in a handwriting that she did not recognize. She wrinkled up her nose in appreciation at the faint odor of potpourri which emerged fragrantly with the letter from its outer covering.

45

Staring at the ornate letter c surrounded by fat, chubby pink Cupids flinging garlands of flowers to each other which headed the note, she frowned—such *billets* were a rare occurrence in her short life. For one blinding, intoxicating moment of sheer happiness, she wondered if, somehow, it might not be from Roderick himself. The next minute, however, she chided herself hotly for thinking any such thing. Silly! she thought scornfully. Why should he write to you, of all people?

To hide this temporary lapse into the realm of sheer nonsense, utter madness, Saranne returned to her examination of the letter. If not from Roderick, it was from the next best possible source, his mother. Lady Crale "begged the pleasure of her daughter's friend, Miss Markham's, company at Crale Court during part of the summer vacation—"

Saranne hoped that Arabella's oddly intent gaze, fixed upon her own face, had not noticed that pause, her hidden confusion. Lady Crale's note, its stiffly worded invitation, was like a cup of cold water dashed on her cheeks.

"B-but—?" she stammered dazedly at last, raising bewildered gray eyes to Arabella's dancing blue ones. "I—I don't understand, Arabella?"

"Don't look so alarmed!" Arabella scolded her, chuckling. "It is only the official version of the invitation *I* gave you!" Arabella paused, staring at the other with an oddly calculating look upon her round pink face. "It is all Roderick's doing, really," she crowed, watching

Saranne. "It was *he* who persuaded Mamma to ask you formally."

Arabella drifted light as thistledown, like some woodland elf dressed in pale blue satin to match her eyes, around the foot of Saranne's narrow little white bed, and perched upon its foot, ruffling the counterpane there, hugging her silken knees. It was her brother, she insisted to the still doubting Saranne, who had asked their mother to add her, Saranne, to the houseparty at Crale Court for the forthcoming season, for the almost endless round of balls, trips to the races, soirées and parties—some around the gaming tables, at the Assembly Rooms in Bath—next month. All of which made up the daily and nightly occupation of that famous (or infamous) spa resort. But once again Saranne was not listening, busy with her own excited thoughts.

"Roderick asked?" she echoed in awed tones. And then, "Oh, Arabella, how wonderful!"

"Umph!" Arabella threw her a curious glance, one that suddenly made Roderick's sister look older than her real years, tart and old-fashioned, so full of malice was it. The next instant, however, she was her usual sunny self again. "Oh, forget Roderick—he can wait, my dear! Let us think instead of what we are going to wear, eh?"

"Yes," Saranne agreed slowly. "I was intending to ask your advice. What should I take with me, Arabella?"

"Now, let me see—" Arabella looked wise

almost owlishly so, then she brightened. "You will need a few simple print gowns for mornings, it's in the country, don't forget. Something more elaborate for afternoons, and oh, a ball gown or two! But above all, don't forget your riding habit. You must bring that with you, Saranne. We will enjoy our gallops over the moors every day!"

Saranne's heart sank. How could she tell this daughter of society that far from possessing a habit, she could not even ride? Well, she decided, she would jump that hedge when she came to it.

As she had grown older and more useful to them, the Misses Patterson paid her a salary of sorts, in return for her considerable services as pupil-teacher in their establishment, the allowance from her father having ceased. By exercising care, she could keep herself decently clad for school, but she had not been able to save much.

And then one morning, out of the blue, fate, destiny—call it what you would—took a hand in her affairs again. In the midst of teaching a class of ten-year-olds, she was called away to the Principal's sanctum. She went in some trepidation. But once there, Miss Patterson, in the beaming presence of Miss Abby, nodding like a China mandarin in approval at the rear, handed the girl five brand-new golden guineas.

"A slight—er—token of our esteem, my child," Miss Patterson began formally.

Saranne's gray eyes filled with tears of grati tude as she took the proffered gift. "Oh, thank you, ma'am—and you, too, Miss Abby!" she exclaimed, trembling a little in her happy excitement.

"Not at all, child—our pleasure," the Principal murmured grandly. She cleared her throat dryly, polishing her eyeglasses with an old silk handkerchief yellow with age, kept for that particular purpose. "To live with money, I am afraid you will find that you *need* money," she warned darkly. "As I understand it, you are to spend part of the forthcoming long vacation down at Crale Court, Arabella's home? And Arabella, of course, is one of our wealthiest pupils!"

"Yes, ma'am," Saranne said humbly.

"Whether she is also one of our *best*," Miss Patterson went on, "is a moot point!"

"And mind you spend it wisely, Saranne," Miss Abby put in before her sister could speak again.

"I will, Miss Abby, indeed I will!" Saranne promised warmly, from her heart.

She escaped from the room then. Small as the sum might have appeared to many, Arabella for instance, to her it seemed like a miniature fortune. Each newly-minted coin was like a golden key to her future.

Adding her own microscopic savings, she bought a warm woolen traveling cloak, sober in cut, in a dark gray material, she considered befitting and practical for one in her position of life. Clever at needlework, inherited from Phoebe, she now made over her old gowns, refurbishing them until they were as good as new again.

But what will I do for the ball gown that Arabella suggested? she thought, worried. There was no dressmaker in town; she hadn't time to sew it herself; she would have to see if she could afford an adequate ready-made gown. Feverishly she planned to buy the simplest that she could find, and alter it for an elegant fit. Yet the saleswoman in the gown shop she finally timidly entered persuaded her instead into something different, a gown beyond her wildest dreams, so stiff in all its silken folds that it stood away from her slim body like the petals of a flower, some bizarre Oriental blossom of the night.

"Ye-es?" She would have loved this gown, she mused wistfully, but it would cost too much . . . Tempted, she whirled this way and that before the tall pierglass in the dim little shop, while the saleswoman shrewdly watched her. Light rippled and flowed over the skirts of Chinese blue, richly embroidered.

My very first ball gown, she thought, enraptured by the sight. Humbly she hoped that *he* might like her in it, applaud her taste. The saleswoman, who had been regarding this prospective customer as a goose ripe for the plucking, now intervened. A worldly-wise smile upon her sallow face, she tactfully drew Saranne's notice to a minute spot of faded fabric on the bodice.

In an effort to minimize the damage, she said smoothly, "Must have stood too long in the window, miss, and the sun caught it."

"Oh, what a pity!" Saranne's face fell, her spirits tumbling right down to her shoes. She did so want this wonderful gown, she thought miserably!

The longing for it was almost like a physical ache. The saleswoman smiled once more, in an understanding way, as the girl's gray eyes filled with tears of vexation. Saranne made as if to step out of the gown then, take it off, with a deep, woeful sigh that she could not suppress. But the other stopped her.

"Wait!" she cried, laying a detaining hand upon Saranne's arm, entering into the mood of this customer by some species of sales magic of her own. As Saranne obeyed wonderingly, the woman took down off its shelf a large cardboard box filled with flimsy tissue-paper. She rummaged amidst this for a moment, then emerged triumphantly flourishing a spray of artificial red roses made of silk. She held this up against Saranne's gown.

"Look—this will do the trick!" she exclaimed excitedly, almost as involved as Saranne herself now. "It will hide that patch on the shoulder, so!" She paused cunningly. "And Mademoiselle can have the gown at a greatly reduced price because of that," she finished softly, naming a sum well within Saranne's slender means.

Saranne made up her mind in an instant.

"Then I will take it!" she cried impulsively.

It was thus she acquired the gown of her dreams. And barely for the cost of a new pair of gloves. Gazing at her new purchase, the saleswoman's deft fingers adroitly pinning the corsage into place, she felt well satisfied with her morning's shopping. With that and her new cloak, the rest of her wardrobe refurbished, she felt all set now for Bath and the West Country.

Until the morning of the day of their departure from The Limes, Arabella and she. Too late, then, she saw her mistake. Many of the pupils had already left, whisked away in the private family coaches that had rolled up to the Queen Anne mansion all day long, the day before. Those who had long distances to go over bad roads, that is. The rest would leave this morning.

Saranne was standing ready dressed and waiting in the foyer for Arabella long before that young lady put in an appearance, listening idly with but half an ear to the Principal's famous last words, such as she invariably addressed each year to those pupils who were leaving for good. Saranne was half amused, half irritated, having heard it all many times before.

Arabella burst into her friend's sight with all the impact of a mild bombshell. Unaware of all the sartorial magnificence which now intruded upon her stunned senses, Saranne could only stare in petrified silence at the sumptuous fur-lined cloak of blue velvet Arabella wore, the fashionable "shovel" bonnet in a matching material. Her small hands were hidden in a coquettish sable-fur muff. Saranne gasped, turning red, then white, taking in the air of wealth and sophistication Arabella exuded like an invisible aura.

"Why, Arabella!" Saranne could only stare at her erstwhile schoolfellow in consternation, in a stupor of utter misery. "You have turned into quite a swell," she said tonelessly at last.

"Like it?" Arabella asked eagerly, pirouetting to set the wide hem of her fur-lined cloak swirling wildly. "I wanted a *whole* cloak of fur," she pouted. "But Mamma wouldn't let me—not till I'm grown up and a married lady, she says!"

"And quite right, too," Saranne said wearily, a trace of bitterness that she could not quite quell creeping into her voice. "I shall be cleaning out dirty inkwells then—or trimming quill pens!" She sighed heavily. "You are a lucky girl, Arabella."

"I know." Arabella shivered, suddenly sobered by the thought. "I should die if I had to be a schoolma'am like you or—or earn my own living, when we left The Limes," she declared passionately, her small piquant face scared. Saranne smiled.

"You would, if you had to," she said grimly.

All at once the brightness of the day seemed clouded over. The sunlight gone, the sky became overcast, gray, full of ominous storm-clouds. Where a moment before—with the appearance of Arabella in her finery—the world had been sunny, bright, full of hope, the earth had suddenly gone dark, chilly, for Saranne.

She felt out of her depth with the Crales and their kind now, floundering about in waters that were too strong for her, longing for her feet to touch solid bottom. A sense of panic seized her, a feeling that events were fast slipping out of her grasp. She felt tired, disillusioned and, yes, not a little angry with Arabella. A tiny, dawning flicker of resentment, too, that Roderick's sister should have led her into this trap.

For trap it was, she saw it all now. Her own room at The Limes was some distance away from Arabella's and on a different floor altogether. She had no way of knowing how many packages, parcels, hatboxes, with the names of famous London fashion houses on their labels, had been arriving almost nonstop for the Crale heiress during the past few weeks, to burst now, in all their glory, upon Saranne.

While they were both under the roof of The Limes, they had been deemed equals, more or less. There was nothing to show the difference between penniless orphan, a veritable little Miss Nobody, and rich banker's daughter. It came to Saranne, with a further shock, that henceforth this equality might not exist, that *she* would be forced to drop back in the race to the place where she belonged, in the ranks of the working girls.

For the first time she faltered, drew back in spirit from the brink. She knew so very little, really, of Arabella and her background, except by hearsay. Or of hers, if it came to that, for Arabella had never seemed interested. Perhaps she had been extremely foolish to accept that invitation. Yes, even if Roderick wished it too. She sighed.

Well, it is no use crying over spilled milk, she thought resignedly. The die is cast now! She reminded herself for perhaps the hundredth time: And Roderick *did* ask me!

At this point she realized that the Principal

was beckoning to her and hastened to obey. Miss Patterson asked her to go up to their private rooms and fetch her reading glasses, which she had left on the desk there. Saranne went at once, leaving Roderick's sister surrounded by a small bevy of admirers.

"Just write a farewell message in my album, please, Bella," they pleaded, knowing that she was finally leaving.

"Me too!"

"And I!"

Arabella obliged, smiling. It was obvious that Saranne was the last thought in her mind at that moment. Saranne secured the Principal's spectacles, finding them easily as directed upon the desk. There was something else there too, a large white envelope propped up against a paperweight upon the blotter. It was addressed in Arabella's weak, spidery handwriting, to Miss Patterson.

This did not surprise Saranne, concluding it to be a farewell note or some such. She returned to the lobby below to find that the crowd of girls there had considerably thinned in her absence. Of Arabella herself there was no sign. It became manifest soon, to both Saranne herself and the few pupils still remaining, that Arabella had already left.

"Has anyone seen the Crale coach call for Miss Crale?" the Principal demanded briskly, hiding her inner dismay with a display of authority.

Nobody had, it seemed. "No, ma'am," they all chorused dutifully, curtseying.

The shattering implications of Arabella's

flight was at last borne in upon even Miss Abby. She promptly had a fit of shrieking hysterics, from which she was brought back to life —her sister being cruel to be kind—by a resounding slap on each cheek in turn by the Principal. This created a minor diversion, true, but it was only that.

"Pull yourself together, sister, do!" Miss Patterson hissed tersely. "This is no time for histrionics."

It was not, indeed. Soon, the very last of the pupils had left. And it was then that Saranne remembered the envelope in Miss Patterson's room in Arabella's handwriting, ran to fetch it and so learned the worst. Arabella had gone, shaken the dust of The Limes, Epsom itself, from off her pretty heels forever.

Yet even this was not fully brought home to them until one of the elderly maids on the staff, coming in from the town on an errand, reported breathlessly that she had seen one of the young ladies driving off along the London road, she said excitedly, in company with a flashy, fair-headed young man whom she had called "brother," hoodwinking them all.

"But why?" Miss Abby wailed through her tears, looking utterly bewildered. She dabbed at her wet eyes with a handkerchief. "Why should any girl run away with her own brother?"

"Oh, be quiet Abby, do!" The Principal lost her temper at this point. "He *wasn't* her brother. Oh, that poor, poor girl!"

Nobody called for or took away Arabella's trunk, standing ready corded behind a potted plant in the lobby. (Later, it was discovered to be full of bricks, Arabella having smuggled her clothes out of The Limes earlier). For its owner, it transpired, had eloped to Gretná Green, that romantic smithy in Scotland, haunt of clandestine marriages, to be united in wedlock there over the anvil by the blacksmith himself. To "Roderick," who was not Roderick at all, but someone named George Bellemy.

Saranne did not find Arabella's letter to her until later that night, when she at last was able to escape to the temporary haven of her own room. In thus blotting her own copybook, as it were, Arabella had also successfully managed to burn every bridge behind her irresponsible self. She had planned her escape so well, either with or without the help of her lover, that they were confident it could not fail. He had had a light, fast carriage and a good pair of horses waiting around the corner from The Limes until such time as Arabella could slip away. They thus had a good head start on any pursuers. All this and more Arabella artlessly explained in her letter:

"Darling Saranne," she wrote, apparently contritely and with no suspicion of a tongue in her plump pink cheek, "I was *forced* to enmesh you in our schemes out of *direct* necessity, my dear." She continued, in the same vein: "It was the only *possible* way in which I could get in touch with George in the *flesh,* under the circumstances, Papa and Mamma being so *tiresome* about him.

"The Misses P. would never have allowed me to go out from The Limes alone, without some kind of chaperone, a *responsible* person in attendance. So that is where *you* came in, Saranne. I had to deceive you, for which forgive me, and George begs your pardon, too. Yours devotedly as ever, Arabella.

"P.S. I *do* have a brother called Roderick, but he is only twelve years old. We had to borrow his identity for George, to throw everyone off the scent."

The Misses Patterson's first instinct, born of necessity, was to look around them for a suitable scapegoat. They found one unexpectedly close to hand in the person of Saranne, their pupil-teacher, and the problem was immediately solved. They naturally had sent word of the disaster to Crale Court at once on discovering Arabella's flight, and now awaited, with some trepidation, the reaction of the bereft parents.

Hurt and angry by turns, bewildered and humiliated in their tenderest spot—pride in their establishment—they could now only wait with such patience as they possessed for the arrival of Sir Joshua or Lady Crale, or both, in person. Or worse still, the representative they might send to investigate the affair in the place. The finger of suspicion was now firmly pointed in Saranne's direction.

"Is she not the likeliest suspect to have a hand in Miss Crale's defection?" the Principal demanded hotly. "Pulling the wool over all our eyes!"

Saranne Markham had been the missing girl's closest friend and confidant at The Limes, had she not, the Principal demanded logically. It stood to reason then that she had known all along what was going on. Caught a whiff at least of the trouble that was brewing in the wind, surely? Further, and most damning of all, was she not the recipient of that most unsuitable invitation to Crale Court, Arabella's home?

It was all highly suspicious, adding up to a formidable sum of guilt, whichever way one looked at it, Saranne agreed listlessly. Arabella's new clothes, the velvet bonnet, the fur-trimmed cloak, were all part of the trousseau she had boldly ordered for herself, to be paid for later by her father the baronet, Sir Joshua, settling his daughter's bills for her for the last time.

Meanwhile, Saranne stayed on at The Limes at the Patterson's request—orders, until such time as the Crale's emissary might arrive to question her, hold a court of enquiry. She wondered at first if she should go home to London, to the Soames's little house on the south bank.

There is nothing to keep me here now, at the school, with the pupils all away, she thought wretchedly.

And certainly there would be no holiday trip now down to Bath with Arabella! It was a distinct shock to her, therefore, when she timidly sought out the Principal and put the suggestion before her, to be coldly told that on no account must she leave The Limes just then. She was a key witness in what might be termed the case of the missing heiress and could not be spared at that time.

"You must be on hand to give evidence if need be," Miss Patterson said frostily. She laughed hardly, cynically. "No doubt you will be able to throw some light on the matter!"

"But I know nothing of Arabella's plans or her whereabouts!" she protested in dismay. "What has happened to her?"

"That is as may be." The Principal shrugged. "But you were the last person to see her, to speak to Arabella before she left The Limes," she pointed out frigidly, with icy clarity. Poor Miss Abby, in the background as usual, looked unhappy at this disclosure that her idol had feet of clay. "You were seen together in the lobby not five minutes before she disappeared."

Saranne forbore to remind the Principal that she herself had sent their pupil-teacher on an errand at the crucial time, to fetch her spectacles. And during Saranne's absence Arabella had slipped away. It had given the banker's daughter ample time in which to make her exit, unnoticed by all.

What is the use, anyway? Saranne asked herself dispiritedly. Least said, soonest mended, was the only line of defense she could take now with any hope of success. She did not take her meals any more with the Pattersons in their private apartments. The separation cut her to the bone, hurting deeply.

She was banished instead to the school dining room, where she sat in solitary state, a lonely figure at the head of one of the long refectory tables—which seemed longer than usual now, with all the young ladies gone. Dwarfed by her surroundings, she was waited upon by the remnant of household staff still there, who seemed to resent the extra work her being there entailed— As well they might, she mused ruefully.

"Will you be wanting anything more, miss?" The chilly distance in old Sarah's voice was not lost upon the girl, who winced. It was icy enough, almost, to freeze the water in Saranne's pewter drinking goblet.

"No, thank you, Sarah," she muttered meekly. The aged servitor sniffed as she whisked away the victim's plate from under her nose. Saranne sighed.

She crept like a thin wraith, a pale ghost of her former self, about the school in the days that followed. The Limes was all but empty now in this, its off season, its windows shuttered and with the iron bars drawn across them, blotting out the sunlight without. Furniture was swathed in dustcloths as with a winding-sheet of the dead, the carpets all rolled up. Her hollow, echoing footsteps followed her from room to room, matching her mood of heartache and despair, disillusion with living.

She was summoned one morning to the parlor the Misses Patterson kept for their own exclusive use, in which to interview important visitors, such as the parents of prospective pupils.

There was no sign of the Misses Patterson this morning, however. Instead, a man stood in one of the window alcoves, staring out over the garden.

He swung round at her entrance, the sound of her slight footfall alerting him, awakening him from his reverie. Bareheaded, his hair was dark as night, the intense deep blue of his eyes seeming almost black in the dim room, most of whose shutters were still closed. That strong saturnine face with its high cheekbones and gipsylike swarthiness she knew well, she thought.

"Miss Markham?" He spoke first, in an ambiguous tone, formal to a degree, bowing slightly.

"Yes, sir?" Saranne raised a puzzled, frowning face to his dark and glowering one.

She was sure they had met before, that she had seen him somewhere else. But where?

And then it all came back to her with a rush, the color draining from her face. Of course—it was perfectly obvious to her now! He could be none other than the Crale attorney, Mr. Jerome DeLacey. The man she had stigmatized in Arabella's family picture as "formidable." She saw it all now, only too plainly. The Crales could not come themselves for some reason, so had sent their lawyer instead.

And so it transpired. Lady Crale was too prostrated by grief and shock at her daughter's downfall to travel; Sir Joshua, apoplectic by nature, transported by rage, was on the verge of a stroke. The physicians had had to bleed him with leeches for relief.

Mr. DeLacey, it would appear to all but the inexperienced trembling girl before him, knew all the tricks of the legal trade, and meant to use them in questioning this witness.

Without speaking, all his movements curiously deft and competent for so tall a man, he went over and fetched a highbacked chair from a line standing in a row against the wall, like prim young ladies. He placed this beside the round table in the center of the parlor and briefly gestured to Saranne to sit.

She took her place there meekly, after a slight hesitation, and sat looking the very picture of dejection and misery. Now that her sight was better adjusted to the poor light of the room, she saw that he must have traveled a long way from the West Country in a very short time. His riding cloak, thrown over one shoulder, was dusty and travel-stained, but that did nothing to diminish his air of authority.

There were some men and quite a few women, she knew even from her limited experience of life, who radiated that almost mystical power of sheer animal magnetism in whatever company they were or however placed, to the detriment of their fellows; able to draw all eyes to themselves, to become the focal point of attention whenever they wished. Mr. Jerome DeLacey, she was sure, was one of that small, select band. And furthermore, knew it.

For his part, searching her face from under lowered brows, in a disgruntled mood, he felt that there was little about this young wench of which he could approve, try as he might— and he would not try very hard, he thought grimly. He had already had a few words with Miss Patterson in private, and had learned something of the girl's history, which only served to confirm his opinion of her now.

He felt only contempt and disgust for the part she had reputedly played in Arabella

Crale's disgrace and fall from virtue. His own acquaintance with young women such as this one was surprisingly rare. But his sisters had been in the charge of a succession of governesses in their childhood.

He recollected them as a series of meek, humble gentlewomen who would not have said "Boo" to the proverbial goose, let alone connive at the moral and social ruin of their charges. This girl puzzled him; she did not seem to fit into that category at all. And this both irritated and antagonized him against her from the first.

To begin with, he thought, going off at a tangent as Saranne's stepmother had done in the past, she has red hair!

In some obscure way this incensed him. He disliked people with that particular hair coloring, he told himself firmly; they were not to be trusted. One in her lowly position in society, he felt dourly, should have had mousy locks, primly arranged, instead of flaunting hair the hue of copperbeech leaves in autumn, a living, vivid flame. However, ignoring the vexing question of her hair color for the nonce, he got down to the task at hand: questioning her part in the Arabella affair.

He watched her face closely as a hawk as he spoke, his dark eyes searching for clues, signs of faltering, confusion, evasion in her replies. There were none, although he swept aside her feeble denial of any complicity in her friend's elopement with a scornful laugh.

"Oh, come, of course you must have known,

even had a hand in this disgraceful business, if the truth be told," he insisted coldly, his eyes like blue steel, so hard were they. "Were you in the pay of this scoundrel, Bellemy?" he shot at her suddenly and had the satisfaction of seeing the arrow find its mark—or so he imagined. "A willing partner to his schemes?"

"Bellemy?" she echoed stupidly, knocked off balance temporarily by the sheer absurdity of his suspicion. She put out appealing, helpless hands as if to ward off a blow. "Arabella's lover?"

"Yes." He nodded curtly, still with that chill, cynical look of stern disbelief on his dark, brooding face.

She stared silently at his hands, gripping the back of the chair before him until the knuckles showed white. He would destroy me, she reflected wildly, given half a chance!

"Come, don't play games with me, miss!" he said sharply. "Don't pretend that you don't know what I mean. George Bellemy is a notorious card cheat, a gambler well known at Bath, Brighton, Harrogate, any haunt of vice that you care to name! He is a common fortune hunter too, on the lookout for a plump pigeon, a well-to-do heiress to cajole into marriage. And your so-called bosom friend, Arabella Crale, had to be the chosen victim, falling to his wiles!"

"No!" She covered her ears with her hands, refusing to listen any more. "It isn't true, I won't believe it!" she cried.

She could bear it no longer, she thought, this blackening of the character of George Bellemy, Arabella's George, she reminded herself forlornly, Arabella's lover, not hers. The man she had fancied herself in love with, in all the strength of her youthful, untried heart. The "Roderick" who had shared all those sweet daydreams and who had now changed back, as if in a nightmare, to the man he had always been in reality. A rogue, a liar, as this lawyer said he was.

The figure of her lovesick fantasies did not exist, had never existed, except in her romantic mind. *She* had given him life, no one else—and what had she in common with Arabella's George now? Nothing! One word was written across her heart—*betrayal*, in burning letters of fire, hurting deeply, searing her soul.

This was what Arabella and George Bellemy had done to her in return for her unswerving loyalty and unquestioning devotion to their cause. Anything that this hateful man, Mr. DeLacey, did to her now, his worst efforts to harm her, were as nothing compared to that. And yet she was torn by anxiety for her erstwhile friend.

"Have—have you any knowledge of Miss Crale, sir? Do you know where she is now?"

"None whatsoever," he returned shortly, shrugging. "There has been no word of her since she left." He continued grudgingly, relenting a little: "Rumor has it that they are on the Continent, honeymooning, if you please! It seems to have swallowed them up."

"I see," Saranne looked even more dejected than before at this meager scrap of news.

He threw her a curious glance, contemplating that downcast red head.

"Did you know," he demanded abruptly, his voice sternly accusing now, "that she met this man Bellemy over a year ago, at some soirée or evening party down at Bath? That her parents then sent her to The Limes for the express purpose of separating them and so protecting her from his unwelcome attentions?"

No, she did not know, Saranne told him in a quiet, muffled voice that was barely audible. How could she make him understand by mere words, tell him that she had known nothing of this? That she, too, had been hoodwinked by Arabella, that she was an innocent victim twisted, like so many others, round that aristocratic young lady's little finger? He would never believe me, she thought dismally, or concede that I might be telling the truth!

But he was speaking again, almost hissing in a low, vehement tone: "Rest assured, miss, that the matter does not stop here! I will make it my business to see that you never get another chance to corrupt a young person given into your care. You will be dismissed from your present post here at The Limes, of course— I can promise you that! You are not fit to be in charge of the pupils." He had seen Arabella grow up, he said passionately, watched her progress from babyhood to youth—only to see her ruined through the criminal negligence of a wretched schoolmistress who should have known better!

Saranne would never have deemed it

possible that hope could change so swiftly to despair, a brightly glittering secure future into one without light. She, who had been so full of happy plans, expecting to revel at Bath on Arabella's invitation, had less than nothing. She felt she would never rise again.

She left The Limes fortified slightly by the comforting belief that she had seen the last of Mr. Jerome DeLacey, that their paths would never cross again in this life. Henceforth their two ways would diverge in widely different directions, she hoped. This was some small grain of consolation to her, hugging the knowledge to her breast like a talisman. He has made his devastating mark upon my fortunes, she thought ominously. Is that not enough?

The Misses Patterson had had no alternative but to dismiss her, she knew only too well. They were as helpless, as much victims of the system, as herself. The Limes survived on word of mouth; the Crales could ruin them.

And at the final count, in the dilemma they were in, the Pattersons took refuge in an appeal to Saranne's better nature.

"We are sorry to lose you, my child, you must know that. But you do realize the awkward position in which we are placed. For you to remain at The Limes, under these circumstances, is out of the question."

Yet at the end she and the sisters parted amicably enough. Benignly waving aside the generous tip they had already given her, standing very much upon their dignity, the Principal paid Saranne the tiny residue of salary still owing her. After all, they might have argued in some dim, private corner of their own minds, we, too, fell under the spell of that archscoundrel Bellemy in a way in accepting him as Arabella's "brother." They also gave Saranne a more than adequate written reference if not glowing, at least in warm terms.

"Why not try and seek a post as governess to children, my dear, in some nice family? Or go as a lady's companion? As you live in London, your home is there, we can give you the address of an excellent employment bureau that specializes in such things, if you wish."

Saranne did wish and accepted the suggestion eagerly. She tucked the slip of paper bearing all the necessary information into her glove for safety: it was her lifeline for the dark future. Her heart was filled with a bitter choking hatred for Jerome DeLacey, as the author of her misfortunes and present predicament. Arabella's part in it she discounted. Because, when all is said and done, at the best Arabella is only a silly, empty-headed girl! she thought forgivingly.

Saranne was conscious of no great feeling of regret as she drove away from The Limes for the last time, only of a sweet, lingering nostalgia, a sort of homesickness for the old house that had sheltered her so long. Henceforth, that safety might not exist.

She took her seat in the dark interior of the London stagecoach and stared out the window in a sober frame of mind, eyeing without really seeing the flying vignettes of English countryside, as they flitted swiftly by.

Nothing, she discovered when she arrived there at last, had changed in the little house on the south bank of the Thames in London. It was as she had always remembered it, her room undisturbed, unaltered, her memory not playing her false. The narrow white virginal bed was waiting there, her favorite doll lying there, wearing the same gown of green silk she had made for it long ago, on the day Mama died, out of the scrap of material given her by Miss Hanley. The doll smiled widely up at her, glassily, in a fixed grin, as only wax and sawdust can.

"Oh, Belinda!" she said softly, gathering up the limp, lifeless bundle of rags and holding it for a minute against her hot, wet cheeks.

Chapter
3

There was a certain quality about Saranne Markham at this time, a lack of aggression amounting on occasion to excessive meekness, which made many people, and older folk in particular, rush to her aid. Recognizing that innocence, that vulnerability, they had the urge to protect her.

And so it was on the morrow, when she walked with some hesitation into the office of the employment agency whose address had been given to her by Miss Patterson. There were several older women, quietly dressed, and a sprinkling of younger ones in her own age group waiting there in an outer lobby. Hunting a post like myself, no doubt? she decided ruefully.

Naively, she had not counted on competition. And despite the fact that she had spent the previous night, well into the small hours, standing at the kitchen table with a heavy smoothing-iron, pressing her clothes into pristine freshness, she suddenly felt very shy, youthful, and inexperienced, immature in contrast to this metropolitan poise all around her in the city streets.

She wore the plainest of her gowns that day, in a soft dove-gray, with bonnet and a light summer shawl to match. Her only concession to smart London fashion were the new gloves of kidskin from Vienna, a gift last Christmas from the Soames to their beloved adopted "niece." The apple-green fichu at her neck was part of the finery she had bought for her ill-fated trip to Bath.

They all look like fashionable ladies of society, she thought, eyeing her fellow female travelers upon the sidewalk. Or heiresses in search of a rich beau, an eligible marriage!

And then it was her turn and she was called into the agency's inner office at last. She had been so busy summing up her possible rivals, assessing their chances of success, that time had positively flown. Saranne sat down by a desk on which was a bowl full of summer flowers, scenting the air with their sweetness. The light from the one window behind the clerk sitting there, falling on her face and her red hair clothed her in a shimmering aura of eager hope.

Before she quite knew what had happened, she found herself unburdening her wants, and needs to the pleasant-faced mature woman behind the desk, who took down all her particulars in full. As the laborious writing in longhand came to an end, Mrs. Larkins laid down her quill and stared hard at Saranne.

"Are you certain you wish to become a governess or companion in a private family, Miss Markham?" she began doubtfully. "It is a difficult life at best, my dear. Far less freedom and remuneration, into the bargain, than teaching in a school, say, as you have been doing."

"I am quite sure, thank you, ma'am," Saranne said earnestly. "I—I need a change for my health's sake, among other reasons." She stared hard at the clerk in turn. "And I would like a post where I could travel, see the world," she ended firmly.

At this, the woman looked really hard at this young client. Most of the women and girls who came to the agency seeking posts wanted nothing more, in her experience, than a warm room in winter, a fairly tolerant employer, and a quiet life allied to a minute salary—this last was always the final consideration. In an over-crowded profession they were not in a position to demand more.

She sighed, replacing a file she had already lifted from the drawer at her side. A bulging folder that Saranne could not help seeing was labeled "Vacancies." It did not seem the sort of post that would suit the child opposite, she mused grimly! Aloud, she finally said, looking Saranne over with a kind of gathering uneasiness:

73

"You are very young, my dear. To travel abroad, I mean—even if I am successful in placing you in such a post! Wouldn't your parents or guardians object to such an arrangement?"

"I have no parents, as I told you," Saranne repeated patiently, with a trace of weariness now in her voice. "So there could be no refusal on that score, ma'am. And I am sure my adopted uncle and aunt will agree. They as good as told me so, before I came out this morning."

"I see," Mrs. Larkins said slowly, thoughtfully, at last. "I *do* have a post that might suit you, Miss Markham, as it happens! Companion-secretary to a wealthy old lady who wants someone to read to her, handle simple accounts, go shopping. Do you think you could handle that?" Mrs. Larkins paused at this point, her face more serious, registering uncertainty for the first time. "There is one difficulty, though—"

"And that is, ma'am?" Saranne interupted eagerly, unable to contain herself. It was an appeal for help, for understanding, and Mrs. Larkins shrugged uneasily.

"She wants someone older, more experienced than you appear to be, my dear," the clerk said slowly. She hesitated. "How old did you say you were?"

Saranne gulped. "Seventeen, ma'am," she said quickly, hopefully. "My birthday was January last."

"You were born under Saturn, then? A Saturday child who works hard for her living,

74

eh?" Mrs. Larkins retorted gently. She smiled, hesitating no longer. "I am going to take a chance with you, Saranne," she continued kindly. "Will you wait over there for a minute, please? I have some writing to do." She indicated with her quill pen a row of straightbacked Windsor chairs along a wall at the far end of the office.

Saranne went over and sat down as directed, sitting there as upright as the chair itself, gloved hands tightly clutching her reticule in her lap, lips compressed in an effort at selfcontrol. Her feet, in their neat little boots, were pressed firmly upon the floorboards. Mrs. Larkins finished her short bout of pen scratching and beckoned to the girl to come near once more. She shuffled through some papers upon her desk as Saranne approached.

"Now, please listen carefully," the clerk began when Saranne was once again seated beside the desk, the flowers at her elbow scenting the fusty air with their fragrance. Mrs. Larkins took a card from a rack bearing the agency's heading at the top, copied most of Saranne's particulars onto this. "At least you can go for an interview," she said cheerfully then, "and no harm done!"

"Yes, ma'am." Mrs. Larkins smiled indulgently, noting this unusual client's eager face, slightly flushed with anticipation, red lips parted.

The clerk relented enough to explain: "Mrs. Arundale is an elderly lady, very rich, who wants a companion to spend part of the year with her down at her country house near

Bath. The rest of her time is generally spent traveling on the Continent or resident in a villa she rents there. Her late husband was in the diplomatic service, I believe, so she is well used to foreign parts."

"It sounds wonderful!" Saranne exclaimed enthusiastically, clasping her hands in delight. Her gray eyes were like twin stars now, with excitement. Mrs. Larkins smiled faintly.

"Yes? Well, that is as may be," she replied more cautiously. "The salary is quite good," Mrs. Larkins went on primly, consulting her ledger. "And there is plenty of free time for you to go sightseeing on your own when abroad."

Saranne interrupted for the second time at this, to announce simply that it sounded remarkably like heaven to her. Heaving a sigh of sheer bliss, she held out a hand for the note Mrs. Larkins had written to Mrs. Arundale in the meanwhile, to go with the agency card. Her eyes were shining—filled with the romantic starlight of ignorance, the clerk mused cynically. Aloud, she said: "This is the address and give the note to Mrs. Arundale when you get there, please. I should hire a hackney coach if I were you. Have you any . . . enough money to get one?"

"Yes, ma'am, thank you. Ample," Saranne said simply.

"Off you go, then," Mrs. Larkins murmured. "And Miss Markham—?"

"Yes, ma'am?" Saranne paused, already at the door, the card and note Mrs. Larkins had given her in her hand.

"Good luck," the clerk said softly, with a smile. But a moment before she left the agency, Saranne asked suddenly, hesitating: "Why did Mrs. Arundale's last companion leave, ma'am? Do you know?"

"The lady in question got married, "Mrs. Larkins replied with some asperity now, a touch of frost in her voice that bade Saranne to be wary of probing further. Adding significantly, with a hint that Saranne was treading upon thin ice, and that the girl could not ignore: "She spent nearly twenty happy years in Mrs. Arundale's service, if you must know, having gone into her employ at an early age. As a matter of fact," Mrs. Larkins said dryly, with an air of finality, "she married an ironmonger in a good way of business!"

"Oh," was all that Saranne could find to say to this piece of information.

Mrs. Arundale, Mrs. Larkins told her, had been staying over in London during the past few weeks while she tried to find a suitable companion, having opened up part of her townhouse in Nightingale Square with a skeleton staff brought from the country to run it. The mansion stood in one of the Belgravia squares being opened to the west of the city by speculative builders, who had taken over the marshes there, lately the haunt of wildfowlers and other sportsmen.

The house in Nightingale Square proved to be a tall narrow building wedged in between its twin neighbors on either side. A flight of stone steps ran up to the ornate front door with a curved Georgian fanlight over it. It was guarded on both sides by curved iron handrails leading up to the sconces fixed to the wall for extinguishing flambeaux, the torches so necessary in the ill-lit streets of the time.

Builders' rubble lay everywhere, the broken sidewalks knee-deep in it in places. In a boom of jerry-building, houses were being hastily erected to catch the expanding tide of population spilling over from the city proper. The driver pulled up at the entrance to the square and she eyed the scene of disorder with a frown, alighting from the coach hesitantly.

"No. 28?" she begged, turning to him. "Do you know which it is?"

"Just along there, miss, a few doors down," he said sourly as Saranne paid him. He had refused to venture his vehicle further. A moment after that he had whipped up his horse again and driven away.

Saranne found No. 28 at once, however, picking her way daintily through the debris festering upon the sidewalk. The number was written upon the front door in raised figures, above the great brass knocker in the form of a lion's head, a ring of the same brightly glittering metal in its mouth. She seized this with her gloved hand and let it fall timidly once or twice.

The door was opened by a middle-aged woman with graying hair and an open, honest face. She wore a dark gown, very plain, the severe touch of lace at her throat caught back by a cameo brooch. A sober enough dress that yet managed, by some alchemy of its own, to look like a livery, a scrap of an apron, more ornamental than useful, over her skirt.

"Yes, miss?" She had a strong West Country accent still, a burr to her voice, not unpleasant, despite long years abroad spent globe-trotting with her mistress.

Mrs. Janet Dawson, the old lady's lifelong friend and faithful housekeeper—for such she proved to be—gazed enquiringly at Saranne, her strong work-a-day hand upon the door still, ready to slam it and retreat into the safety of the house should the occasion warrant it.

"My name is Saranne Markham. I have been sent by the agency in regard to the position as Mrs. Arundale's companion, please?" Saranne said by way of introduction.

"Ah!" Recognition dawned upon the other's good-natured face and she relaxed her unconsciously suspicious stance, smiling. Mrs. Dawson laughed. "And it is about time they sent someone suitable, too!" she laughed. "Will you step this way, please, Miss Markham?"

As she followed the housekeeper into the entrance hall beyond, the door closed behind them, shutting out all sounds from the busy street outside. The noise of carpenters' hammering, the metallic click of bricklayers' trowels, all the noise and stir of building died away. Saranne paused in the lobby in which she now found herself to stare about her. Several doors, heavily paneled in mahogany, with cut-glass handles, led off it in all directions.

The wave of warmth, sheer luxury in living, struck her full in the face like a deliberate

79

blow, as she stepped across the threshold into this, the Arundale home. Facing her was the grand staircase of the house, curling round and out of sight to the upper regions of the place like a gleaming, highly-polished interrogation mark. Opening one of the many doors, one on her right, Mrs. Dawson ushered Saranne into the room beyond.

"A young lady from the employment agency, Madam," she announced. "She has a letter of introduction."

As Mrs. Dawson signaled her to do so, Saranne stepped shyly forward, blinking uncertainly in the transition from the dim hallway she had just left to the brightness and height of the room in which she now found herself. There were flowers everywhere, or so it seemed, masses of them scenting the air, and costing a fortune, she was shrewdly aware. Tall silver vases, terracotta bowls upon low sidetables, the tops of the bookcases, the shelf of the pink marble mantlepiece from Italy which dominated the room, all bore their burden of loveliness.

Being her mother's daughter she was drawn to the blooms at once, great sheafs of roses, the delicate pale green of maidenhair fern, all a feast for the tasteful eye. Final luxury of all, a real log fire burned upon the open hearth, piled high with wood, even though it was midsummer, keeping life in old bones still, the delicate aroma of apple smoke drifted out into the room.

It was an instant or two before she saw the

aristocratic looking old lady, sitting very up-right beside the fireplace in a highbacked chair with wings. Snow-white hair piled on top of her head in a bygone fashion, she presented a distinctly awesome sight to Saranne. One thin old hand, wrinkled and nearly transparent with age, grasped the knob of a stout black-thorn stick, silver-topped, which partly sup-ported her as she sat there.

Her old fingers were ablaze with diamonds and yet more of the precious stones shone and sparkled in the valuable brooch pinned to the lace neckerchief at her ancient throat. Round the scraggy neck was woven a slightly dis-colored rope of pearls, falling to her knees.

At the far end of the room was a pair of open glass doors, giving onto a small balcony overlooking a panoramic view of the distant city of London, shimmering in summer heat. A man and girl stood there and as Saranne en-tered, the young lady turned round and smiled. It was a simple, friendly gesture; Saranne's heart glowed in relief.

Tall, slim, and quite plain, the girl none-theless had a certain quality, an unmistakable sympathy for others, which drew Saranne to-ward her at once. I'm going to like Clara Arundale! she thought.

Clara was dressed that day in a simple print morning gown, sprigged with rosebuds, cool and comfortable, a gown which served to enhance its wearer's healthy out-of-doors look, her traditional peaches-and-cream complexion of the West Country.

Although her mouth was too wide for real

beauty, her hands too large, she had sincere, truthful, eyes, her long, fair hair caught back in a knot at the base of a soft, white neck Saranne noted. Which is just as well, Saranne mused, for such a severely classical style suits her—and I cannot imagine Mrs. Arundale's granddaughter with a mass of frizzy little curls!

Then Clara's companion at the open French windows turned toward Saranne. The blood drained from her face, leaving her pale as death and trembling—Mr. Jerome DeLacey! She shuddered as their glances met across the width of the room with an impact like clashing, naked steel, in a challenging struggle.

As icy and implacable as his manner had been down in Epsom, it was outclassed now by the outraged amazement, the horror and astonishment with which he regarded her appearance.

I am ruined! she thought wildly, gazing around her for some way of escape. He will never let me get this post!

Freezing her to the very soul, inhibiting her every thought, every hope, draining away all her energy, he stood looking at her furiously, glaring, his brow dark. Taking in, without being conscious of doing so, the soft gray stuff of the gown she wore, the cheap little bonnet and shawl. And finally coming to rest upon dear Miss Hanley's non-diamond brooch of long ago. Which she had pinned upon Saranne's bodice just as the girl was leaving the house—"For luck, dear," she had said.

Remembering, Saranne felt her terror turn to rage. How *dare* he—? Her small chin rose.

Gathering together all her resources of courage, her hands clenched, she decided to meet his challenge boldly, defy him.

It was at this crucial moment that the old lady by the fireside created an opportune diversion, having apparently noticed nothing of all this. Smiling, she beckoned to Saranne to come closer. It was then, as she obediently approached, that Saranne became aware for the first time of another person present in the room.

A tall young man in the scarlet tunic of an officer in a crack Guards' regiment of the army was lounging there, completely at his ease, in an armchair opposite the one occupied by Mrs. Arundale. Remembering his manners, he began to rise hastily to his feet, displaying his full slim height, as Saranne almost fell over him.

"Oh, I am so sorry—I beg your pardon, sir!" she exclaimed in some confusion, halting.

It was thus she met for the first time, as he hurriedly withdrew his long legs from danger, the other man who was to figure in her life for good or ill, for some months to come: Clara's brother, Captain Neville Arundale, of the Brigade of Guards. If Clara was plain, it was as if all the good looks of the junior branch of the Arundale family, at least, were concentrated in him.

Saranne could only stare in wonder. His clear-cut features bore a becoming suntan, telling of an outdoor soldier's life in no uncertain terms, allied to his gallant military bearing, as upright as his grandmother. His bright blue eyes flashed under level brows; between the brilliance of his smile and the brilliance of his eyes Saranne was quite dazzled.

"So you are Miss Markham?" It was his grandmother speaking now, breaking in on Saranne's reverie with a jarring note of practical reality. Mrs. Arundale finished reading the note the girl had brought with her from the agency, folded it meticulously, and put it away in a pocket in her wide skirts. "Well, let me have a look at you, child." She had a high, clear old voice, like a bell, a little cracked now with age, but still full of authority. "So you think you would like to enter my employ as a companion, eh?" she murmured thoughtfully, eyeing Saranne up and down amusedly.

"Oh, yes, please, ma'am," Saranne said eagerly without thinking, and the old lady smiled again.

"Umph! We shall have to see," old Mrs. Arundale went on more slowly, less impulsively than Saranne. "You realize, young woman, that it entails living abroad for the best part of the year? In a few weeks, even days' time I shall be crossing the English Channel I hope, en route for Italy. Do you find that very short notice, my dear?"

"Not at all, ma'am," Saranne replied quickly, her heart a mixed jumble of excitement and hope. "I should be happy to accompany you, Mrs. Arundale, if you wish," she said earnestly.

"'Mm." Mrs. Arundale still looked and sounded a trifle doubtful, undecided as she searched Saranne's face. "You look very young," she said. "Before I engage you, I would first like to make sure that your uncle and aunt, your legal guardians I understand, are willing for you to travel so far afield. I really wanted someone older, you know—" Her old voice trailed away, uncertain.

"Oh, but I am sure they will agree," Saranne put in swiftly, choosing to ignore the latter remark. She added with more conviction than she really felt, "In fact, I *know* they will, ma'am!"

"Very well." Mrs. Arundale suddenly appeared to make up her mind, sighing with relief. She signaled her satisfaction at the outcome of events by gazing triumphantly around the room at her assembled visitors, catching the eye of each in turn. "And now," she said briskly, "if you are going to become a member of my household, Miss Markham, allow me to introduce you to my family! This is my granddaughter, Clara, and her brother, Captain Neville Arundale. And last but not least, let me present my lawyer, Mr. DeLacey, who looks after all my legal affairs and gives me good advice—not that I always take it, of course!" the old lady finished tartly, chuckling, with a mischievous glance in his direction. He bowed.

"This young woman and I have already met," Jerome DeLacey said suavely.

"Have you, indeed?" Mrs. Arundale sounded surprised, taken aback, staring from him to Saranne and back in turn.

He had not moved since Saranne first entered the room. He still stood there in the window alcove in that same watchful, curiously grim attitude beside Clara, who had apparently noticed nothing. Saranne herself had felt too wound up, tense, anxiously intent solely on securing the post upon which her whole future rested, to spare any further time for Mr. DeLacey just then. Hoping to make a good impression upon her prospective employer, she had had no time to spare for him, or fear what he might do to her hopes.

Yet she was acutely conscious of him now, as Mrs. Arundale addressed him by name, abruptly aware again that her whole fate depended upon the whim of this man. Of the enormous harm he could do to her now, had he the mind to, she had little doubt.

She cast a wan imploring glance in his direction, silently begging his aid, forbearance. In vain, it seemed. His granitelike face did not alter the stern grimness of the glance he cast upon her from under dark brows. It was like bracing oneself to meet the impact of a cup of icy water dashed in the face, she reflected gloomily.

Not for the first time since they had encountered each other so disastrously at The Limes down in Surrey, Saranne critically examined the outward appearance of this attorney-turned-landowner from the West Country. Although above average height, he lacked the lithe grace of Neville Arundale and so looked almost stocky by comparison, broad-shouldered as he was. His eyes were so dark a blue that they appeared black in some lights, as she remembered, glowering at her now.

Jerome DeLacey stood there completely

at his ease, hands clasped behind his back in a distinctly judicial manner, and in complete command of the situation.

He looks too well groomed, she thought resentfully. Yes, even better than the military smartness of Captain Arundale!

And then he turned slowly, deliberately, away, addressing his remarks solely to Mrs. Arundale and pointedly ignoring Saranne.

"Don't you think you are being a little premature in your hiring of this young person, Isobel?" he suggested coldly to his client, his brow raised. "After all," he pointed out icily, "there are still certain important preliminaries to be gone into first, in a case like this." He paused, a warning light of battle in his eye.

"What case? What preliminaries, as you call them?" the old lady demanded testily, in her high old voice. She tapped the arm of her chair with those heavily beringed fingers, breathing hard. "Really, Jerome, what do you mean?"

"References to begin with," he retorted. "They must be gone into, you know, thoroughly investigated before you go one step further."

He looked straight at Saranne now. "Would you mind waiting outside in the lobby, for a few minutes, Miss—er—Markham, please?" He added with a deadly emphasis that finally killed all hope in Saranne's mind: "I wish to have a short talk with Mrs. Arundale. In private."

Not being in a position to do otherwise, as she was ruefully aware, she obeyed. To her pleasant surprise, Captain Arundale, perhaps to make amends for his earlier bad manners, sprang to the door and with a courtly bow held it open for her to pass through. She smiled in recognition of his gallantry and went out into the lobby beyond, her feet, as before, sinking soundlessly into the rich, deep carpet.

It did much, she reflected gratefully as the door shut behind her, to make up for Mr. De-Lacey's churlishness. She sank nervously down upon a frail, gilt-backed chair she found there beside a console table holding a big bowl of flowers. Exquisitely arranged, she thought dreamily, like all those others in the room I have just left.

She wondered if they were Clara's handiwork and admired the girl's good taste. And as she waited there, her fate hanging in the balance, she tried to be fair, to see things from the attorney's viewpoint. Of course Mrs. Arundale's legal adviser had every right to protect his client's interests, had he not? But the rancor, mistrust, she felt toward him would not go away.

She bit her lip in the comparative privacy of the hallway, savagely forcing back the tears that sprang to her gray eyes despite her efforts to conquer them. But now a new factor entered, adding to her discomfort, sending her thoughts off in a new direction.

In closing the door, Neville Arundale had, he imagined, effectively cut Saranne off from the sound of conversation within the room. And so it might have been but for an oversight, something overlooked by all concerned, which put a different complexion upon things.

Like many houses of that age, the main reception room of the mansion in Nightingale Square ran from back to front on the first floor and was divided halfway down by wooden folding doors. Doors that could be folded back to make a larger space, should occasion warrant it, or be kept closed if a smaller one were required. Mrs. Arundale and her family were now clustered in the front half, overlooking the square outside. But Saranne had already noted that the door in the rear portion leading into the lobby, was slightly ajar.

"Oh, dear!" she said to herself in dismay, as voices from the drawing room floated out to her. She sat up straight, wondering what to do.

Once she realized where they were coming from, what they were uttering, she did not want to hear any more. But she had no choice. The paneled walls and high ceiling of the lobby acted as a sounding-board, amplifying sound.

"The illegitimate daughter of a Cheapside haberdasher!" the lawyer's voice came out scathingly through the door panels. "Why, she hasn't even the saving grace of being heiress to his riches, for he has disowned her, I understand!"

There was a respite as he dropped his voice for a moment. Then old Mrs. Arundale's high tones came sharply on the heels of an uncommonly down-to-earth, ungenteel laugh that sounded remarkably like a derisive snort.

"Arabella Crale, that silly flibbertygibbet of a girl?" There was a cackling hoot of cynical laughter. "Like mother, like daughter, I say, for Lady Crale is an idiotic creature, if ever there were one, too!" Mrs. Arundale paused here to sniff scornfully, evidently unimpressed by his arguments. "If it hadn't been that George What's-His-Name, it would have been someone else," she said darkly. "So don't talk of that gambler and Miss Crale to me, please," she ordered him sharply.

Mrs. Arundale defying her attorney, taking Saranne's side against him? Her low spirits began to rise accordingly.

"She is young, raw, wholly inexperienced in every way," he pointed out with a passionate intensity unfitted to his theme, Saranne thought. "Immature and certainly not qualified to be even your hired companion, Isobel. Remember your reputation, position in society."

"Pshaw!" Mrs. Arundale brushed this objection aside contemptuously, as she had dismissed all the others. But if the paralyzed girl, listening against her will, imagined that this would demolish his arguments, she discovered the next minute that she had been woefully misled.

"A real little Cockney sparrow," he went on scathingly. "Do you want a young person like that around you, to show off to your friends, escort you to dinner parties, soirées? What is the fashionable world going to say about you behind your back, Isobel?" he asked, an almost pleading note in his voice now. He paused. "That you have taken leave of your senses!" he finally exploded. "I beg of you, implore you to reconsider this folly, before it is too late?"

"Fiddlesticks!" his opponent retorted rudely. "She has time on her hands to grow older, wiser, in the meanwhile." Mrs. Arundale's autocratic wilfulness rose to the surface at this challenge to her plans. "She can be taught the things she needs to know, can't she, Jerome?" Her tone became conciliatory. "I like her, Jerome. There is something about her that appeals to me. Call it an old woman's whim, if you like, but please don't try and make me change my mind!" She suddenly chuckled wickedly. "You'd be wasting your time, anyway, for it's already made up! I am going to engage her."

"Yes?" he drawled. "And 'whim' it certainly is, Isobel." He gave a hard, short laugh, without any mirth in it. "I just hope you are not mistaken, that's all," he said. "That you don't live to regret it! And when that time comes—well, I hope you won't forget that I warned you?"

"I won't," she promised meekly—with her tongue in her cheek, Saranne surmised.

"Anyway—" Clara's clear voice came through the panels at this point like a ray of cheer to the listening victim. "We don't have a choice, Jerome," Clara pointed out logically, pouring a soothing libation of oil upon much-troubled waters. "Or rather, Grandmamma hasn't. The agency hasn't sent us many suitable young women to interview, up to now. The others were willing to spend six months of the year in sunny Italy, but jibed at living the rest of the time down in the West Country in winter."

"Being 'buried alive in a damp, gloomy

mansion' was the graphic way one damsel described it privately to Mrs. Dawson, as she went out," Captain Neville put in lazily at this point.

There was a long pause, then: "Very well," Mr. DeLacey said at last, curtly, while Saranne waited breathlessly. "But I shall certainly delve thoroughly into her history, background," he warned. "Acting as your attorney, even if you won't, Isobel."

"You do as you like," Mrs. Arundale agreed sweetly, unimpressed.

He cleared his throat. "In any case," he pointed out suddenly, going off abruptly into what seemed like a tangent, "have you stopped to think that her—er—legal guardians might not want to allow this girl to go abroad with you? And so I intend to settle this question once and for all, hear their side of it, by interviewing them in person! And now, Neville, if you will be good enough to ask that young person to step inside once more?"

Saranne had just enough time at this to readjust her features to something like the blank expression of innocence before Captain Arundale appeared in the doorway again.

He beckoned to her with an impish smile, showing the gleam of white teeth beneath his fair mustache, laying a lean, well-manicured finger upon his lips conspiratorially. She smiled, dimpling, shaken out of her usual shyness by his very obvious admiration.

"Time to go back before the judge again," Neville said, lowering his voice for her ears alone. "His Honor, Mr. Justice DeLacey! The jury has brought in a verdict of 'not guilty', so you are to be set free, more or less!"

Saranne laughed then, won by his sheer ease. A little of it rubbed off upon herself. She rose from her chair obediently and followed his tall figure back into the room to hear her fate.

She was never quite sure afterwards, looking back to that fateful day, how she presently came to find herself in a hackney coach with the odious Mr. DeLacey, speeding as fast as the horses could carry them over the cobblestones of the busy London streets, muffled now by summer dust. A stray gleam of brilliant sunshine penetrated the dark coach, lighting his stern, cold face. He sat bolt upright, his hands —strong hands, she noted not for the first time —clasped firmly over the silver knob of his walking cane.

Hands with an inordinate amount of character, she thought. She turned her face away and huddled as far away from him as she could upon the narrow seat. He appeared not to notice.

Since they first boarded the vehicle in Nightingale Square, he had seemed preoccupied. He had commanded, rather than suggested, that she accompany him back to the Soames's little house in Battersea, there to seek their permission for her to go abroad in her new capacity as Mrs. Arundale's paid companion.

"What do you think of Captain Arundale?" he shot at her suddenly.

"He is very nice," Saranne stammered, off guard. "So—so gentlemanly and gallant." De-Lacey laughed—a harsh sound.

"You little fool," he said coolly, almost casually. "What possible interest do you imagine he could have in you, apart from an attempt on your virtue? Be warned—a girl like you and a man in his position, of some importance in the world!"

She fell silent; the attack was so unexpected, bizarre, coming from such a quarter. Why should he care if she did indeed fall victim to such a fate? Not, she thought swiftly, indignantly, that she accepted for one minute the vile, wicked aspirations he attributed to Captain Arundale! He turned to stare at her then, frowning as if at some fresh idea that had just struck him.

"I suppose someone will be at home in your—er—uncle's house?" he demanded. "I mean," he drawled in his dry, precise lawyer's voice, "they won't be out at their work or anything?"

"No." Saranne shook her red head in its gray bonnet. "My uncle might have been," she conceded with quiet dignity, "but he has been suffering an attack of the gout lately. So he will be there, as will my aunt. Also Miss Hanley, her sister, who lives with them."

She offered the information wretchedly, trailing off into silence again as she realized that he was apparently not listening. She sighed, reflecting that she did not want this taciturn man to see and perhaps sneer at the Soameses' modest home.

They presently crossed one of the many ancient bridges leading to the South Bank, the Thames below glittering in the sunshine like a vast, torpid snake curving lazily. Yet it was a busy scene, too, light craft of all kinds scuttling to and fro upon its smooth surface like so many water beetles. The coach turned into the poor road which led to the Soames's humble abode, the driver following the directions she gave, conveyed to him via Mr. DeLacey.

And Myrtle Crescent, she was only too ruefully aware, was not looking at its best this morning. Ragged urchins with bare, dirty feet were playing at football in the street, kicking an old tin can noisily. Girls sat huddled in mean doorways, tending the family baby or else playing with ragged, nondescript dolls. Untidy, dispirited-looking women, old before their time, stood about in groups on street corners, gossiping.

They turned suspicious heads to stare silently, disapprovingly, as the coach went by. And it was midday by the time they reached the tiny house and were ushered into her front parlor by a flustered Aunt Bertha. This room was only used for high days and an occasion such as this—a distinguished visitor.

"Won't you please take a seat, sir?" Aunt Bertha begged politely.

As she described it herself later, "all of a twitter," Aunt Bertha dusted one of the hard, horsehair-stuffed chairs with her apron and offered it to the attorney. A needless operation, really, Saranne reflected, for the room was kept dusted nearly every day.

He declined it politely, as well as her offer of refreshment of some kind—tea, a glass of wine—? Mrs. Soames subsided into the background after that and Saranne stole a look at that proud, handsome face, haughty and unyielding as he plunged straight into the business on which he had come.

They discussed her future as if she were not present. In stiff, stilted tones he spoke of his client, Mrs. Arundale, the post she offered their ward, if they were so willing.

In turn, he offered formal references and accepted theirs. Bowled over by his masterful personality, allied to the sight of the hired coach still standing outside the door awaiting his return and which they hoped the neighbors duly noted, they had little objection to anything he might say.

"I'm sure you know what's best for our lass, sir," Uncle Henry said, sitting in an armchair—for which he apologized to the standing attorney—with his ailing leg stretched out upon a footstool before him. He continued earnestly: "I hope you will treat her kindly, for she is a lucky young woman to be offered such a place as you mention! Seeing foreign places and all, traveling—"

"She will be well looked after, never fear. Then it is all settled?" DeLacey cut him short impatiently. "Mrs. Arundale's family is one of the oldest, most respected of landed gentry in the West Country. You need have no scruples in allowing your adopted niece to enter into her service."

"We cannot keep our pretty bird caged up forever, sir," Miss Hanley agreed wisely. "She must try her wings, spread her feathers to the sun some day!"

"Oh, quite." The lawyer nodded curtly.

There were a few further exchanges after that. But Saranne was no longer listening. She had switched her mind off into an entirely different direction altogether. To, in fact, Captain Neville Arundale of His Majesty's Brigade of Guards, whom she had met that morning in his grandmother's household.

Tomorrow I will be free, ran her joyful thoughts, as if a heavy weight had been lifted from off her shoulders. To go where I will, do as I like—within reason, of course! Now she could spread her wings, as dear Miss Hanley had said. Existence, as Mrs. Arundale's companion, promised a far wider horizon.

It was, she reflected dreamily, like reaching a green oasis at long last, after struggling, sick and tired at heart, through the desert. . . . There remained only the last niggling details to be settled and then he was gone, after coldly telling Saranne to be packed and ready with her trunk by ten-thirty o'clock tomorrow morning.

"Someone will be sent to pick you up," he added. "Either a hired coach or Mrs. Arundale's own private coach—unless she needs it herself."

"I will be ready, sir," she promised quietly.

They had been talking of her salary, how much she would be paid per annum and how, the time she would have for herself to follow her own pursuits. The notion of paid vacations was a joke, she thought, brimming over with inward laughter like a beaker of foaming, heady champagne.

My whole life is going to be one long holiday from now on, she thought lightheartedly. So being *paid* for it too is just silly!

She was too excited to eat any of the midday meal of bacon and boiled greens that Aunt Bertha had prepared before the lawyer's arrival and left heating upon the kitchen stove. She pushed aside her plate and escaped up to the privacy of her room as soon as she decently could and began her packing.

When it came to the crunch, as now, it was forcibly borne in upon her how little she really owned in the way of worldly goods. A battered doll or two, including the favorite Belinda, a few precious books, the unworn ball gown she had bought with such high hopes, and some ornaments—that was all. She put them away at last, ruthlessly, in a large wooden tea chest smelling strongly of Orange Pekoe, which Miss Hanley helped her carry up from the cellar below. Saranne wanted to be done with her past.

Her room looked curiously empty, bare, after that—*impersonal,* she thought, gazing about her. The windowsill was bereft of her books now, and the cheap knickknacks she had gathered over the years. The marks where they had lain were still there, however.

For years the undemanding Miss Hanley

had slept upon an old dilapidated sofa in the livingroom-cum-kitchen downstairs. Now retired from the Emporium, earning her meager living by taking in a modicum of plain sewing, it was understood that she was now to be promoted to Saranne's room. She was looking forward to this with much unconcealed relish—and Saranne felt that she could not blame her old friend.

She lined the tea chest with some old newspapers and put her treasures away with the awful feeling that she was laying them to rest forever. She put a few more pieces of newsprint on top and closed the lid down firmly. Uncle Henry would carry it down eventually, when he felt less unwell. And there it would stand, upon a shelf in the cellar next to the homemade ale, slowly gathering cobwebs and dust.

Saranne owned but the one ancient trunk, which Uncle Henry had carried upon his shoulder across that bridge, so long ago, when she was little. Woefully inadequate now for a grown-up young lady. Saranne, in the midst of her packing, looked about desperately for something else. And then, as always, Miss Hanley came to her rescue with the offer of another trunk, equally battered, which Saranne accepted gratefully.

"It looks kind of—bare, doesn't it?" her old friend commented, looking around her domain-to-be. And then, abruptly going off at a tangent, Miss Hanley said sharply: "That was a very handsome gentleman who came with you this morning, Saranne." Her eyes narrowed as she continued with a casualness that deceived nobody: "Is he married, my dear?"

"Who? Mr. DeLacey?" Saranne stared at her in astonishment, pausing in her packing. She frowned. "How should I know?" she said shortly at last. She went on with a studied lack of interest that made Miss Hanley glance at her with a sudden intentness. "I have other, far more important things to do, think of, than Mr. DeLacey! Personally," Saranne said coldly, folding a petticoat and putting it away, "I found him most unpleasant!"

"What—Mr. DeLacey?" It was Miss Hanley's turn to look surprised, bridling, a little displeased even. She tossed her head. "We all thought he was such a nice gentleman," she said. "So polite and pleasant."

Saranne allowed this to pass without comment. *You would!* she thought.

Saranne was ready the next day long before the time specified by Mr. DeLacey. As a special treat in honor of the occasion, she was allowed to wait in Aunt Bertha's pride and joy, the front parlor. Peeping through Aunt Bertha's cherished Nottingham lace drapes, waiting for the vehicle to carry her away, the two trunks at her feet, Saranne felt as ill-equipped as ever to face reality. It was, she thought, unpleasantly like the time she had first entered the little house in Myrtle Crescent as a homeless waif, a lost child. Her spirits fell. And then she heard the clatter of hooves, the jingle of harness, and rumble of wheels as a carriage rounded the corner and entered the narrow street to draw up before the Soames's door with a final flourish.

It was not the hired coach that Mr. De-Lacey had promised, nor the Arundale private carriage with a cockaded manservant on top. No, it was a smart two-wheeled vehicle, very fast-looking and high off the ground, with its hood folded down. A sporting gig, much affected by the young bloods of the town, with Captain Neville Arundale in the driver's seat holding the reins, a long whip in his gloved hands.

He was bareheaded that morning and the sun glinted on his fair hair, turning it into a helmet of pure shining gold, matching his mustache. Saranne's undisciplined heart missed a beat, then went on again, fluttering uncomfortably fast with pleasurable excitement.

Half pleased, half nonplussed, she turned away, overcome by a sudden shyness that she did not understand. She recoiled from the window and its concealing drapes in some confusion, hoping that she had not been seen. To gain time in which to partly recover her lost poise, calmness of manner, she stooped and pretended to be concerned with the locks of her trunks.

At the same instant there was a loud knock upon the front door. She straightened up with a heightened color—only to hear someone, probably Miss Hanley, rush forward to answer it.

"Good morning, is Miss Markham ready?"

she heard him ask, no doubt with a winning smile, she thought fondly, hearing Miss Hanley's response.

"Yes, sir, all ready and waiting for you," Miss Hanley replied eagerly. And then, warmly, "Won't you come in, sir?"

Chapter
4

And then it was all over and they were gone, out of Myrtle Crescent, that little street, leaving Miss Hanley behind. Yet she had a feeling of happy excitement, of hopeful expectation to buoy her up, raising her spirits in timely fashion. Now she could go to the ends of the earth if needs be, subject only to Mrs. Arundale's whim of the moment, with nobody to say her nay—

"I am free," she said softly, and was not conscious that she had spoken. Nor that he had heard her, until this glorious Greek god of a man by her side chuckled outright.

"Free to do what, my dear?" he asked her teasingly, in a frankly flirtatious tone, glancing at her sideways with those remarkable blue eyes. He laughed again, lightly, but also more seriously this time. "Just so long as my dear Grandmamma does not work you to death in the meantime!" Neville said warningly. He cast a meltingly ardent look at the downcast red head. "We must see that she doesn't, eh?"

She was thrilled by his voice, more so by his near proximity, scarcely taking in the sense of what he was saying. His use of that intimate "we," slipped in so artlessly, apparently without thinking, betokened a dawning warmth between them, a closeness that made her feel all-glowing inside, wanted in a way she had never known before.

She felt relaxed, able to sit back literally and enjoy to the full this lovely summer's morning with him. It had turned out a lovely day, she perceived, a sparkling one to match her hopes.

"Oh, but you are going the wrong way, sir," she exclaimed suddenly, clutching his arm. She glanced around her at entirely new surroundings. "This is not the direction we took yesterday, with Mr. DeLacey."

"Is it not?" he said genially, smiling at her anxiety. "Yes, I know," he went on easily, his hands resting lightly upon the driving apron before him. His blue eyes were intent on the dusty roadway ahead to the exclusion, it seemed, of all else. "I thought we would take a drive down into the country somewhere or else out by the riverside," he suggested. "You would like that wouldn't you, my dear? We could have a meal there, at Barnes or Richmond."

"It would be very nice, thank you—but what about your grandmother, Mrs. Arundale?" Saranne asked quickly. "Isn't she expecting me?"

"Neither Barnes or Richmond are far from London, as the crow flies," Neville continued with a quick grin. "My grandmother is not expecting you until this afternoon, she told me. So why look so anxious, Miss Markham? I told her before I left that I would be taking you out to dine with me somewhere. She was quite agreeable—in fact, she rather encouraged the idea. And I know a splendid little place overlooking a quiet reach of the river."

She allowed herself to be persuaded, of course.

He drew up at last in the courtyard of an inn, ordering dinner in the hostelry itself. While it was being prepared, they went for a stroll over the fresh green grass along the bank of the swiftly flowing Thames, unsullied by the dust and mire of town.

There was so much to see, so many new things to discover in his company, that the time simply flew by for Saranne. Although the air was as languid as in London itself, here by the waterside it was cool with its invisible fine mist of spray, the softest of breezes wafting gently to and fro. Eyes shining like stars, she did not remember much of that walk along the river-bank of the rural Thames, nor the meal at the inn which followed.

Dining with Captain Neville Arundale, sharing a table with him for the first time, was a dream of bliss. He was not in uniform that day, but wore civilian clothes that did nothing to hide his magnificent form. Nonetheless, the waiters seemed to know him as an old and valued customer, greeting him respectfully, apparently recognizing him as one of "the Quality," to be treated as such.

Bowing them to a seat in the curved bow-window overlooking the flashing Thames below, one of the servitors deferentially handed Neville the bill of fare. Saranne was impressed. She shyly commented upon their surroundings when they were seated, trying to hide her desperate ignorance of such matters by making conversation. Neville laughed.

"Oh, I come here quite often when I am not on duty in town," he said carelessly.

"At the Palace, guarding the king?" she suggested, round-eyed.

Neville grinned again. "Something like that," he agreed offhandedly. Then he busily attacked his plate of boiled mutton with dumplings that a waiter brought him. "Of course, I am not on call all of the time," he relented at her obvious burning interest, helping himself to mustard. "None of us are, come to that! What I would like," Captain Arundale said suddenly out of the blue, a faraway look of longing in his eyes, "is to be able to live down in the country, out of town, to manage the family estates at Bath!" He sighed heavily. "But I am afraid that must wait—"

"Wait for what?" Saranne asked softly, in her deep, infatuated curiosity about his affairs.

"My mother lives with Grandmamma down at The Grange," Neville went on, almost as if he had not heard, "both being widows. My father is dead, you see, so I suppose I am really the heir to everything."

"Is Clara your only sister, do you have any brothers, then?" Saranne queried, toying with a bread roll.

Neville shook his fair head. "No, we are a pigeon-pair, Clara and I. Only the two of us. Clara has been betrothed for years to a local squire, a gentleman farmer near us in Bath, Giles Fairley. They have known each other since childhood." He sighed. "But they won't be able to marry for ages," Neville said lugubriously.

"Oh? Why is that?" Saranne asked again. Some comment seemed sought of her, she deemed.

He sighed once more, then said slowly, heavily: "Because they were waiting—we are all waiting—to inherit Grandmamma's money, that's why! Not a pretty situation, is it, Miss Markham? She holds the purse strings, we none of us have a penny to call our own, except what she chooses to dole out to us!" And he laughed again, sounding bitter.

Saranne was silent. But she was not thinking of Captain Neville Arundale's self-confessed financial straits. He does not add, say, if he himself is also engaged to be married? She longed for this vital piece of information. He was, she decided. How could he not be?

The inward gloom she felt now settled down over her features, darkening the day. Her dismay gnawed at her heart, and their conversation faltered until, after the meal, Neville drove her back to his grandmother's house in Nightingale Square.

Her new home, she reminded herself, her spirits rising again, as the grand butler, Starn, in charge of all Mrs. Arundale's household, came out upon the steps to greet them.

He was an imposing-looking figure in his green livery with gold braid, his white stockings showing off his bulging calves—of which he was inordinately proud, if Neville's mischievously muttered aside were to be believed!

Starn, with a gesture that Saranne felt could be described as "lordly," waved a white-gloved hand at a young footman hovering nearby.

"Take Miss's baggage upstairs, there to await further instructions."

"Very good, sir." The underling cast an impassive glance at her two shabby trunks and Saranne felt that she would die of chagrin. Wholly unworthy of the Arundale mansion in Nightingale Square, they sat forlornly, a silent reproach to her. Even though she had just dined on a basis of equality with the grandson of the house, she thought, the vastness of the step she had taken by entering into Mrs. Arundale's service was too much for her timid feet.

She gulped, trying to swallow the lump which had suddenly arisen in her throat, threatening to choke her. The trunks looked poor, out of place in these splendid surroundings—as, no doubt, I do myself, she thought wildly.

But the sidewalk did not open up in answer to her earnest prayer, nor the trunks vanish. The young footman merely stepped forward and with cool indifference hoisted one trunk onto his shoulder and picked up the other by its strap. Ignoring her agitated look—if, indeed, he noticed it at all, he strolled up the steps and into the house, dumping them outside the door of Mrs. Arundale's living room.

His job done, the footman strolled away to melt into the shadows at the end of the lobby, whistling softly under his breath when he was sure that he was out of earshot of that petty tyrant, Starn. The latter knocked respectfully on the door panel, his summons being answered by Mrs. Dawson, still in her black silk gown and tiny, useless apron. She smiled as she saw Saranne and Neville, her broad good-humored face crinkling up.

"Good afternoon, Captain—and Miss Markham, too," she said warmly, beaming. She added kindly to Saranne: "Madame is expecting you, miss."

In this world of stiff formality into which she had moved, Mrs. Dawson's greeting made a welcome change, Saranne thought. Her heart warmed toward the homely housekeeper with her red, honest countrywoman's face and simple manner.

Abruptly, this adventure upon which she had embarked so enthusiastically, unthinkingly, did not seem so terrifyingly strange to her after all—yet it was still full of alarming dangers and pitfalls. Unlike Clara and Neville, who had been born to it, she was merely a paid attendant, one of the staff. She could be instantly dismissed, Saranne reminded herself, if she lapsed from grace in any way.

But there was no time to dwell on any such contingency now. For without further ado, that practical West Country woman, Mrs. Dawson, picked up the two trunks the footman had dumped and slid them neatly out of sight under the console table there. That done, she ushered Mrs. Arundale's grandson and his companion into her mistress's presence.

"They've arrived, ma'am," she announced unceremoniously. "Master Neville and the young lady you were expecting."

Again, as she had experienced on the occasion of her first visit to the house, Saranne was conscious of a room wide as it was long, with high ceilings, and, like yesterday morning, also filled with people. Yet an instant later she noted a new member of the company present.

He was a tall, rather clumsily built young man with a distinctly bucolic, out-of-doors, even *raw* look, she mused. A man who looked as if he would have been more at home on the back of a mettlesome horse, rather than straddling awkwardly one of the fragile, gilt-backed chairs in the drawing-room of his fiancée's grandparent. This, she decided, must be Clara's prospective husband, Giles Fairley.

She was proved right when he was presently introduced to her by Miss Arundale, glowing with pride. Clara and he were only too obviously very much in love, exchanging hopelessly fond looks when they imagined themselves unobserved, tenderly holding hands as they sat side by side upon a large sofa.

"Giles," Clara explained, casting a fond look in his direction, "is spending a few days in town, seeing the sights."

A matching sofa was drawn up at right angles to the fireplace facing its fellow, a low table set between them. A fire still flickered and glowed upon the hearth as yesterday, throwing its roseate blessing over the scene. And Mr. DeLacey occupied the same armchair as the previous day. As Saranne hesitantly entered the room, the old lady patted the sofa beside her with a heavily beringed hand.

"Come and sit here, child," she ordered in her high, shrill old voice. "Tell me what you have been doing this morning? Where did that young scallywag of a grandson of mine take you to dine?"

"Oh, we went to Barnes, Nev—I mean Captain Arundale and I," Saranne began, then paused in acute confusion when she realized how she had been caught off guard.

She stopped dead then, blushing at this untoward slip of the tongue, which, she saw to her utter vexation, had not escaped the attention of the attorney, Mr. DeLacey, watching her like a hawk—and who no doubt, she thought bitterly, did not let it evade his notice nor fail to grasp its meaning, if nobody else in the room did!

"And did you like it, down by the river?" Mrs. Arundale pursued the topic relentlessly, avid for news, with all the curiosity of the aged.

"Oh, yes, ma'am!" Saranne nodded eagerly, clasping her hands. "It was beautiful there on the river's banks, so cool, so green. You see," she added shyly, hesitantly, all her heart in her voice, "I have never been so far out of London before. At least, to the west."

Mr. DeLacey laughed shortly, hardly, his expression one of sardonic disbelief.

"Come, Miss Markham—are we to understand that you have never been to Barnes before? Or seen the Thames at its best, 'ere this?" he drawled incredulously, offensively. "I find that very hard to believe, you know, especially as we have been told that you are a Londoner born and bred." He ended cuttingly, so softly that she was hard put to catch his last words: "Or am I mistaken in that, too?"

She flushed scarlet. Nettled by what she deemed his studied insolence, she cried warmly, forgetting her place, everything, "It is quite true, sir, I swear it! I have never been out of London before, except to school in Epsom, at The Limes!" She stopped abruptly, immediately sobered. Oh, *why* had she mentioned The Limes? A short awkward silence fell upon the group around the fireplace.

"Indeed?" DeLacey drawled at last, watching her narrowly.

"Ahem!" Giles Fairley broke the ice at last. Striving to pour oil upon troubled waters, he licked his lips, glancing about him nervously, then turned to his betrothed. "It sounds most interesting, don't you think, Clara, this inn on the riverside?" Giles suggested in a pleading voice. "Why don't we drive out there, you and I, tomorrow morning—if Neville will lend me his gig?"

"Oh, yes, Giles—I do agree," Clara assented eagerly in her pleasant voice, gazing ardently at him as if he had just enunciated the most wonderful idea in the world. "How clever of you to think of it. And of course Neville will lend you his carriage, won't you, Neville?"

"Of course, sister mine," Neville replied lazily, caressing his mustache. "Any time."

And so the incident passed. But Saranne herself did not forget. It had been a passing storm, an inexplicable clash between herself and Mr. DeLacey, but one that might blow up at any minute in the future, alas. And it could destroy her—he was too strong, in too formidable a position for her to dislodge him in any way.

A slightly scornful look upon his darkly handsome face now, it was as if he washed his hands of the whole affair for the time being— until his client, Mrs. Arundale, came to her senses and saw this girl, Miss Markham, in the same light that he did.

Saranne had untied her bonnet strings by then, at Mrs. Arundale's invitation, and laid it aside on the nearest chair, in company with her dove-gray gloves and reticule, of which Neville relieved her, remembering his manners only too well now. Mrs. Dawson presently brought in tea, placing the tray laden with its priceless Georgian silver and delicate china down upon the low table.

Clara poured, deputizing as hostess for her grandmother. The talk drifted easily, naturally, from Barnes to other beauty spots in and around the metropolis. And from that, by a subtle step, to Drury Lane and other famous London places of entertainment, and the Theater Royal there. Old Mrs. Arundale's eyes twinkled as she surveyed her young companions.

"Why don't you children get up a party to see the play at Old Drury?" she asked slyly. "You could go on to supper at Vauxhall afterwards. I am sure the presence of such stalwarts as Giles and Neville will be enough to protect you two girls!" She then turned imperiously to her grandson. "Will you get the tickets, Neville?"

"Very well, Grandmamma," Neville agreed meekly, balancing a frail teacup upon his knee, to Saranne's inner alarm. "It shall be as you wish. And we can sup, as you say, at Ranelagh or Vauxhall Gardens after."

After a half bantering, half bickering display of brother and sisterly argument between Clara and Neville, a discussion in which Giles and she, as mere outsiders, diplomatically took no part, the two younger Arundales came up with a sort of compromise. Neville picked up the daily newspaper and reading through the theatrical advertisements came to the conclusion that they should—"take Grandmamma's advice and see the play at Drury Lane." He added: "And I see that there is a Harlequinade to follow—"

"Oh, I love clowns!" Clara exclaimed.

And so it was settled, just like that. Clara's innocent remark did serve, however, to relieve much of the tension still hovering in the air, aftermath of Saranne's spat just now with Mr. DeLacey, and all stemming from that silent figure in the corner, old Mrs. Arundale's legal adviser.

Clara, kind and considerate as ever, peace loving and thoughtful of others at all times, as Saranne was to discover in the days to come, here broke into the conversation again. Addressing herself tactfully to Mr. DeLacey:

"How about you, Jerome?" she asked gently. "Won't you join us?"

"What! And play gooseberry to you and Giles?" he teased her in mock dismay. Saranne could not help noticing a momentary softening of his dark eyes as they rested briefly upon his client's granddaughter. He shook his head. "No, thank you, Clara," he said gently. "It was kind of you to ask me, my dear. But—well, I rather think I will dine with your grandmother that evening, play backgammon with her afterwards. That suit you, Isobel?" he addressed the old lady whimsically.

She bridled. "Perfectly. Except that you always cheat at backgammon and win!" she retorted dryly. Nonetheless she was pleased, Saranne could see that.

"I will let you win just this once, then," he said soothingly in the same light, intimate tone Mrs. Arundale had herself used.

Yet his face darkened anew, became over-shadowed once more by that sullenly disapproving look of displeasure as his eye rested briefly on the slender figure upon the sofa at his client's side. His lip curled, as if he could not help it, even if he had so desired, as he continued cuttingly, "Especially as your—er—companion will be out enjoying herself, while you wait here—alone!"

Oh, it was all said so banteringly, jokingly, that no one could take offense, she thought wearily. But she knew better—that he had meant every word, tipped with venom as they were and directed at herself alone, that they were intended to hurt, pierce her to the quick.

There was little doubt about it, she thought resentfully—he was never going to let her forget the events of her unfortunate past. Nor that she was nothing but a paid hireling in the Arundale household. If Neville and his sister seemed able to accept her graciously at their own level, it was obvious that Mr. Jerome DeLacey did not.

Soon after, Captain Arundale excused himself on the plea of pressing duties and withdrew. The sunlight poured in through the three tall windows, but the room lost some of its light and grace after he had left. He kissed his grandmother on both of her overpowdered pink old cheeks and went, taking Giles with him.

This was after a short whispered conversation with Clara, during which her fiancé made hurried arrangements to take her out to supper that night at a respectable hostelry in the city that he knew. His London-born aunt, whom

Clara was yet to meet, would act as chaperone, Giles said, and Clara agreed with alacrity, dimpling with excitement.

After a short while, Mr. DeLacey also left, following the example set by the two younger men. He was staying in Chambers, as Saranne learned they were called, rooms in London with a legal friend, a fellow attorney. For Saranne, ignoring DeLacey, the room seemed strangely empty with Neville's going.

"Come along, Saranne," Clara cried gaily, jumping to her feet as Mrs. Dawson entered the room to clear away the tea things. Clara seized the other girl's hand. "I will show you to your—I mean *our* room, as we will be sharing it for the next few days while Grandmamma is still in town. Isn't that right, Grandmamma?"

"Quite correct, child," the old lady agreed calmly. "And don't you two girls keep me awake o' nights, giggling and talking about your beaux, mind!" she warned severely.

"No, Grandmamma," Clara promised demurely.

She took Saranne's arm and led the latter from the room. Clara steered her through one of the doors leading off the lobby into the room beyond, which proved to be a bedroom. Saranne's feet sank into a carpet like thick pink moss, with matching rose-colored drapes at the windows. The panes were further obscured by snowy muslin curtains that gave a glimpse of the quiet London square below. A small stone balcony lay above the green trees growing there.

Mrs. Dawson had preceded them, and was

filling a minute portion of one of the closets with the contents of Saranne's two trunks, taking out the few garments they contained, shaking them and fitting them over hangers taken from Clara's store. The underwear she folded and put away in a chest of drawers.

Janet Dawson announced somewhat unnecessarily, smiling broadly: "I've unpacked your things, Miss Markham. Laid out your nightgown upon that bed over by the door. Miss Clara's is the one nearest the windows."

"Thank you," Saranne murmured gratefully.

As Janet beamed and withdrew, Saranne was conscious of the contrast between her cheap cotton nightdress and the silken rose coverlet of the bed. One corner of the quilt had been dutifully turned down by Mrs. Dawson, but it served only to accentuate the peasant-like quality of her nightgown, she thought.

Her cheap dressing-gown was thrown over the back of a chair and her slippers placed beneath it. It all looked so cosy, normal, that it ought to have reminded her of home. Yet the dismal fact remained that it didn't.

"My things all seem wrong, somehow, out of place in these surroundings," she thought miserably.

Clara had gone to her own section of the closets, taking out a gown and holding it at arm's length while she examined it critically, her fair head held to one side. She frowned, squinting at the gown in question as if its choice were a matter of life and death.

"Oh, dear, I can't quite make up my mind

what to wear," Neville's sister wailed in dismay. She held the blue gown up against her and glanced at her reflection in the mirror. "Which would you choose, Saranne?" she cried. "This one, which suits me so well, or the green Giles likes to see me in?"

"Oh, I would pick the green by all means, if—if my fiancé liked me in it," Saranne retorted firmly. She gave it a due measure of consideration, thus directly appealed to, her brows knitted. "That is, if you don't prefer another color, Miss Arundale?" she suggested diplomatically.

"Oh, 'Clara', please?" Clara begged hastily. "'Miss Arundale' is too formal between friends, eh—as I hope we shall be?" She suddenly put the blue gown she was holding away in its closet again, closing the door decisively. "Well, that is settled, then!" Clara said more cheerfully. "The green it is, on your recommendation, Saranne." Clara paused, turning from the closets to face the other, her eyes kind. "By the way," she said casually, entirely without malice, "what are *you* going to wear for the theater party, my dear?"

What indeed? For the second time that day Saranne wished passionately that the floor might open and swallow her up. She did not possess anything that could be remotely described as suitable. She hung her red head in shame. Then something, she knew not what, prompted her to take the only course open to her. making a clean breast of the whole matter to Clara.

"I—I never realized that it was going to

be like this," Saranne blurted out at last. "Going to the Theater Royal at Drury Lane, meeting important people."

Clara laughed. Dabbing at her wet eyes with a handkerchief, through her mirth she told Saranne that she was not to worry. She, Clara, would lend her some clothes, until she bought her own. Chewing one fingertip thoughtfully now, all her interest alerted, Clara observed practically that the first thing to do, was to see which, out of the many gowns in her wardrobe, would fit Saranne.

"The *eau-de-Nil*, I think," Neville's sister murmured dreamily. "The pale green color of the waters of the Nile, with your vivid coloring, eh?"

With more than a hint of her grandmother's high-handed authority in her style, Clara ran over to the closets again, picking out a light, shimmering robe which she passed to the dazed Saranne all with the speed of lightning, it seemed.

"But—?" Saranne half drew back. "You are so tall, Clara," she demurred uncertainly.

Clara shrugged. "That can easily be got over," she cried flippantly. "Janet Dawson will see to shortening it to fit you," Clara continued calmly. "She is a rare hand with a needle."

And, as if to cut short any further objections from Saranne, Clara went off to the space behind a screen fitted up as a bathing cubicle. A metal hipbath was there, filled by Mrs. Dawson for her young mistress's use from the many cans of piping hot water brought up by a footman.

Left to her own devices for a while, Saranne carefully draped the green gown over the back of a chair. She also busied herself in laying out her own meager stock of toilet articles on one side of the dresser given to her. Looking enviously at all those expensive creams and lotions in exquisite flagons on Clara's portion, she took up one and was fingering it curiously when the former came out of her "bathroom" again.

Rubbing her still slightly wet brown hair with a big, fleecy towel—a towel so soft that it might have been a cloud of pink cottonwool, Saranne thought—Clara smiled as the former put the flagon down again, guiltily.

"Have a bath, if you like," Clara suggested carelessly. "There is plenty of hot water."

"Thank you, I will," Saranne said gratefully.

Now that she came to think of it, she reflected, a nice long soak in warm water was just what she needed to restore her lost morale, badly battered as it was through that encounter with Mr. DeLacey a short time ago. Time passed like a dream and when she emerged from the tub, refreshed and restored in body and mind, Clara was already dressed for going out to supper with her fiancé that night.

Wearing the green dress that Giles liked to see her in, Clara was seated before the dresser mirror putting the last finishing touches to her brown hair. She opened a drawer and from this lifted out a small leather case containing various modest items of jewelry. She chose a pair of earrings which she deftly clipped into her pink, shell-like lobes, a ring, a brooch, then turned round in her chair to smile at Saranne.

"How do I look?" Clara demanded anxiously.

"Really beautiful," Saranne said sincerely.

"Well, that is a relief!" Miss Arundale observed thankfully, not ill-pleased. She picked up her gloves, reticule and fan, and rose.

Saranne perforce had had to change back into her day dress after the bath. But she had left off the light shawl she had been wearing and contented herself with draping a simple white scarf about her slender shoulders, as a concession to evening. In the somewhat overpowering heat of Mrs. Arundale's rooms, she found that sufficient, anyway.

As the two girls crossed the lobby, there were upraised voices in the drawing room, a fresh, feminine voice that Saranne did not recognize. Clear as a bell, it mingled with the lower rumble of masculine tones, broken now and then by a high, rather empty sounding laugh, it was clearly that of a young rather than older woman. And so it proved when Clara and she stepped into the room beyond.

Mr. DeLacey was very much in evidence as usual. In contrast to his rather drab clothes of the day, he now wore a dark-blue coat of exceedingly fine cloth, a diamond pin glittering in the snowy folds of the lace cravat beneath that strong, determined chin. He was not alone. Seated by his side upon the sofa opposite old Mrs. Arundale's, was the most beautiful girl that Saranne had ever seen.

There was something almost "professional" about those striking good looks, she thought, a cool air of icy calculation. For a fleeting instant, Saranne wondered if Mr. DeLacey's companion were a famous actress, a celebrity of some kind. Who was she?

The newcomer had a complexion of translucent alabaster. Her enormous green eyes surveyed Saranne languidly, completely devoid of interest in another female, from under the twin crescents of her thin plucked brows. Her ash-blond hair was piled high on top of her head in the fashion of the day, one curl dangling coquettishly over her left shoulder. And Undine Seaham, when she moved, moved with the effortless ease and grace of the ballet dancer.

Willowy is the only way to describe it, Saranne thought forlornly. She sighed deeply.

Apparently even Mr. DeLacey could not take his eyes off her. Saranne felt grudgingly that Miss Seaham was of a kind to turn any man's head. Yet try as she might, Saranne could not like her.

Whyever not? she asked herself in some consternation. What is wrong with me that I cannot—or is it she? The uneasy thought intruded itself—was it because Undine Seaham was so obviously admired by Mr. DeLacey? Some of the mistrust, dread, she felt toward him rubbing off onto Miss Seaham in turn? She swallowed hard, trying to be honest with herself, but the idea would not go away.

"Undine, my dear," Mrs. Arundale interrupted Saranne's uneasy thoughts at this juncture, creating a welcome distraction, "allow me to introduce my new little companion, Miss Markham."

Miss Seaham was wearing a filmy creation of soft gray lace that evening. A material so diaphanous that it swirled round her like smoke when she stood up, setting off her tall slim figure to perfection. Wide bands of gold crossed her bodice in Grecian style, while thinner threads of the same metallic hue were cunningly woven into the hem of her wide skirts. Tiny golden slippers encased her high-arched little feet, feet which tapped irritably, betraying her utter boredom, as Mrs. Arundale introduced the two girls.

"I think we had better be going, Jerome, don't you?" Undine observed languidly, immediately turning away from Saranne.

He jumped to his feet obediently—more, with a flatteringly marked alacrity, gathering together Miss Seaham's fan, gloves and embroidered evening reticule. He picked up her stole, which she had carelessly thrown down upon a nearby chair, wrapping the sumptuous fur wrap in question about her shoulders. The statuesque beauty did, however, stoop and kiss old Mrs. Arundale upon a withered cheek before departing, remarking: "So nice to see you. And Mamma says she will call and pay her respects soon, before you leave for the Continent!"

With a gravely formal inclination of his dark head, a slight bow to Clara and her grandmother in turn, ignoring Saranne beyond a cool nod, the attorney escorted Undine Seaham out. It seemed that he was taking her to sup with him, her mother, whom they were to meet later, acting as chaperone. But the exotic, manifestly expensive perfume that Miss Seaham used lingered on the air of the room as a subtle reminder of its wearer long after she had gone.

Soon after, Giles Fairley, Clara's betrothed, arrived to take her out to supper in turn, the chaperone in their case being his London aunt, an accommodating lady. Clare departed, radiant with happiness, her hand upon his stalwart arm. Again, as before that afternoon, the room appeared strangely empty with their going. Mrs. Arundale glanced across at her young companion, her old eyes twinkling.

"So you and I are the only ones left behind, eh?" she said slyly. "We are going to have a nice, light supper, here by the fireside, for two. Then *you* are off to your bed and have a good night's sleep, my dear. You look fatigued."

"Yes, I am rather tired, ma'am," Saranne confessed truthfully. She could not help herself and yawned again, to Mrs. Arundale's satisfaction. "But I shall be all right in the morning," she added quickly.

"I don't doubt it," Clara and Neville's grandparent retorted dryly. "With the resilience of youth! But in the meanwhile, off to bed with you, directly after supper."

When Mrs. Dawson bustled in a few minutes later with a laden supper tray, which she placed down upon the low table by the fireside, Saranne found herself blinking again. Hardly able to keep her eyes open, she discovered that the tray contained a delicious omelette for each, crisp and hot and flavored with herbs, which, Mrs. Arundale revealed in the course of the meal, Janet Dawson had learned to cook when living abroad.

"You, too, must try your hand at French or Italian cooking," her employer said firmly and Saranne nodded, smiling at the notion.

It was all part of the exciting future now opening out before her. There was, further, a salad—green stuffs tossed in the Continental fashion in oil and vinegar, root vegetables, cucumber, with fresh fruit to follow as dessert. The coffee was the best she had ever tasted in her short life, a positive revelation she felt. Dreamily she said so, off guard, and Mrs. Arundale smiled wisely, but said nothing.

"Help yourself to some more cream in it, child," was all she said a moment later. "You look as if you need fattening up!"

After that, when Saranne could contain her yawns no longer, candles were brought and she was firmly packed off to bed by her employer. Truth to tell, Saranne was surprised at her own tiredness, her eyelids feeling like lead after an exciting day packed full of events.

She finally slid between the sheets of the bed next to Clara's empty one and blew out the candle upon the bedside table. She fell asleep then, despite her best efforts to keep awake for Clara's return. Soft red lips parted as she dreamed, one hand under her sleeping face upon the pillow. She did not hear Neville's sister come in quietly very much later.

On tiptoe and in her stockinged feet, carrying her evening slippers in her hand so as not to disturb her roommate, Clara undressed quickly, brushed her teeth and bathed her face, pouring water from an ewer into a china basin in the adjoining bath cubicle to do so. And making no more sound than was absolutely necessary, in performing these chores.

In the morning the two girls were awakened by Mrs. Dawson coming in with yet another tray, this one containing cups of hot, steaming chocolate, rich and creamy. Janet next went over to the tall windows of the room and swished back the rose-colored drapes with a vast rattling of brass curtain-rings, letting in the daylight.

"Morning, Janet—good morning, Saranne." Clara sat up in bed, yawning and stretching, looking very fetching in a pale heliotrope nightgown, a silken shawl of the same hue about her white shoulders. "I hope you slept well, Saranne?" Clara said, her brown hair tousled, her face pink and flushed from recent sleep.

"Don't let that chocolate get cold," Janet Dawson scolded at this point, practically. "Drink it up, both of you."

After the housekeeper had gone, the two girls sipped their morning chocolate, talking as easily, openly, as if they were friends of long standing. Clara was bubbling over with high good spirits, full of her evening with Giles.

"And what do you think—?" Clara raised her voice, pausing for effect. "Jerome DeLacey was there, too, at a table in an alcove not far from ours, with Undine Seaham! They were so wrapped up in one another, they didn't see us. But we saw them!"

"Oh." Saranne digested this in silence for a few moments, then: "Who is this Miss Seaham?" she asked with avid curiosity. "Member of your family or some connection of Mr. De-Lacey's?"

"Undine?" Clara echoed, puzzled. "No, she is the daughter of one of Mamma's oldest friends, an only child. Mrs. Seaham is the widow of an army officer, an ex-actress of the Theater Royal at Bath, as is Mamma. They live near us down in the country, in a little house—when they are not traipsing all over the land, doing the fashionable spas and other places, hunting for a suitable husband for Undine!"

"And have they found one yet—a rich match for Miss Seaham?" Saranne asked, smiling.

Clara giggled. "No," she said ruefully, shaking her brown head. With an abrupt change of mood, she said soberly: "I used to think once that Undine had a strong attachment to my brother, Neville, when we were children together. But that has all blown over now. Neville has no money of his own, none of us have, we are all dependent on Grandmamma. So that meant Neville was out, as far as a spouse for Undine is concerned."

"I see," Saranne said slowly. "But he will be rich one day, inherit your grandmother's estate?"

Clara shook her brown head.

"The Seahams, mother and daughter, cannot wait that long," Clara said cryptically.

Yet she found it in her heart to feel sorry for Undine Seaham now, after this distressing disclosure, Saranne thought earnestly. To feel that she understood her better, that almost professional beauty's absorption in her own charms. It was part of her stock-in-trade, no more, for which she had been trained, reared from babyhood up by a careful, managing mother.

Why, she is even worse off than I, Saranne thought in surprise. Poor Miss Seaham—at least I can earn my own crust, need not sell myself to the highest bidder in the marriage market!

They had breakfast in the drawing room that old Mrs. Arundale seemed to have turned into her living quarters for the nonce, the two girls at a small table before the open windows, overlooking the square outside, Clara's grandmother by the fire. Afterwards, the young footman who had brought the tray up took it away. And Clara went off to get ready for her drive out to Barnes with Giles, in her brother's loaned horse and gig.

With the withdrawal of Clara, Saranne felt at a loose end. But not for long. Wiping her lips firmly upon a white linen napkin heavily embroidered with her family's crest in one corner, Mrs. Arundale turned to her young companion with a firmly resolute air that was belied by the kindly smile upon her wise, tough old face.

"Well, young woman, and how do you feel this morning?" she began genially. "Ready to do a little work for me—writing a few letters, say, as a start? You will find quill-pens, ink, paper, in the highly-stocked drawers of that bureau over there."

Saranne went over to the beautiful antique in question, eyeing it with a little nod of appreciation that was not lost upon the old woman, who smiled in secret satisfaction. Saranne opened one of its smooth-running drawers as ordered, and took out writing materials, waiting expectantly with raised quill.

"Ready, my dear?" the old lady asked and Saranne nodded.

The communications of old Mrs. Arundale, as the minutes sped by, turned out to be no more arduous than a few letters to friends, acquainting them of the fact that she would be spending the winter on the Continent, possibly Italy, interposed with a series of notes carrying instructions to her household staff down at Bath.

There were, further, several very short to-the-point letters to her bankers and stock-brokers, ordering changes in her financial dealings. For an old lady, she seemed to have a remarkably keen commercial brain, Saranne thought. In the midst of this, Mrs. Dawson came in with a sheaf of papers in a folder that she had brought from the old lady's bedroom, on Mrs. Arundale's orders.

Without moving from her warm, comfortable position upon the sofa, Mrs. Arundale took these from Janet, and producing a pair of gold-rimmed spectacles from a case, clamped them firmly over her long, thin, aristocratic nose.

She remarked, peering over them at Saranne: "These will be your province in future, my dear. I shall expect you to know when and how to lay hands upon my papers at once, if needed. Is that understood?" And Mrs. Arundale gazed anxiously at her youthful secretary, pausing. Saranne laughed.

"Of course, Mrs. Arundale," she said soothingly, nodding coolly. "That was part of my duties at the Misses Patterson's school, helping them with their accounts."

"Thank goodness!" Mrs. Arundale looked relieved. "That is one weight off my mind at least, eh, Janet?"

"Yes, ma'am," the housekeeper agreed. "Especially," Janet Dawson continued simply, "when we are abroad and Mr. DeLacey isn't around to handle them for you."

Mr. DeLacey again! Saranne frowned, going hot under the collar of the demure gray gown she was wearing that morning. Always that hated name, she thought angrily, scowling. Was she always to hear it, she asked herself passionately, in the days, weeks, months to come in Mrs. Arundale's service? If she kept out of his way as much as was humanly possible, might she then escape his displeasure? Or would her mere presence be enough to add fuel to the flames of his active distrust of her? She sighed.

That evening, she never noticed how swiftly the time at the theater passed, with supper after, in Neville's company. It was such a wonderfully happy occasion, with the gallant captain near at hand, to dance attendance upon her, indulge her every whim, squiring her in a way that she had never experienced before. And it seemed that he liked her in her green gown, too, nodding approval as she emerged from the bedroom she shared with his sister.

Both girls paused in the drawing room for Mrs. Arundale to inspect them in their finery, Saranne still a little tongue-tied and hesitant, trying to hide herself behind Clara. For Mr. DeLacey was also there, and as ever he had that effect upon Saranne merely by his presence. But Clara would have none of it, half laughing, half seriously drawing Saranne forward, giving her a little push.

"Here you are, Grandmamma," Clara cried, thrusting Saranne upon their notice willy-nilly. "Will she do?"

Mrs. Arundale expressed her wholehearted approval of the picture her new young secretary-companion presented. Both girls breathed freely once more—Saranne had passed muster, then, under the gaze of those shrewd old eyes.

But Neville seized the opportunity to draw Saranne to one side, under cover of the distraction the arrival of his sister's fiancé, Giles, created. They found themselves momentarily alone in the window recess. Alone, that is, except for the near presence of Mr. DeLacey, who stood apart from the rest of the company, a short distance away.

"You look wonderful, my dear, in that green gown," Neville breathed ardently, softly, for her ear alone. Saranne was certain that the lawyer had overheard every word, was drawing his own sneering conclusions—making a note of it for future use, no doubt. "It brings out the color of your hair, too."

"I am glad you like it, Captain Arundale," she returned composedly, yet conscious of that silent listener in the background.

DeLacey's brow darkened, his eyes becoming hard and speculative as he glanced from one to the other of the pair by the window.

As sometimes happens in even the liveliest collection of people, an awkward pause fell. Mrs. Arundale was the first to create a diversion by motioning to her housekeeper, who glided to her side. Janet listened to the whispered instructions from her mistress, then went into the latter's bedroom, coming out again almost immediately with a flat leather case that she placed in Mrs. Arundale's hands.

"Come here, Saranne," Mrs. Arundale ordered, beckoning to her as she snapped open the clasp of the old-fashioned jewel case, for such it was.

Saranne obeyed wonderingly, as the old lady fumbled at the case with withered hands covered with rings like gem-encrusted claws. Hovering above the pieces of jewelry, the stones glittering upon their bed of red velvet, one hand emerged at last triumphantly flourishing her choice: A pair of elaborate, long drop earrings worked in fabulous gold filigree set with emeralds that shone with a dull green fire.

"Put these on, my dear," her employer ordered. As she held them out to the astonished girl, the old lady paused to look up at her. "Your ears are pierced, I take it?" she shot at Saranne, who nodded.

"Yes, ma'am," she agreed hurriedly. "My aunt had it done years ago—to improve my eyesight, she said."

"And old superstition, yes." And Mrs. Arundale nodded wisely. "Well, that's all right, then," she continued in a matter-of-fact voice. "Neville, help her to put them on, please?"

Neville was seemingly nothing loath to perform that small task, and as in a dream Saranne stood patiently while his willing fingers deftly slipped the jeweled rings into her ears. The short style of her hair this evening, molded close to her head, left her lobes exposed, which helped him in his work. The ease and adroitness with which he did it, so sure of himself, spoke volumes of his experience with such thing to anyone less innocent than she.

"They are yours, Saranne," Mrs. Arundale said gently, smiling her wise old smile. "And mind you take great care of them, for they belonged to *my* grandmother! And that is going back a bit!"

"I will, ma'am, indeed I will—and thank you exceedingly," Saranne said, awed and not a little touched at this generosity.

Her eyes were like stars as she joined the others, who were now moving in a bunch toward the door—Clara and Giles, with Neville. The earrings were worth a deal of money, but she had no means of knowing their real value. How could she? To Saranne they were but a pretty ornament given to her by Mrs. Arundale out of the goodness of the old lady's heart, to match the dress loaned her by Clara.

They passed out into the lobby beyond, Janet Dawson bringing up the rear to fasten the front door after them. Clara and Giles had already reached the doorstep outside and Neville and she were about to follow them, when Saranne suddenly halted with a smothered exclamation of vexation.

"Oh, fie, my evening bag—I've left it in the bedroom! No, don't stop, please, I will catch you up. I know just where it is, upon the dresser," she cried over her shoulder as she darted off, forestalling all offers to fetch it for her.

She was not used to wearing evening gowns and that was the whole crux of the matter, Saranne chided herself in disgust. As she reached the door of the room they had just left, in the deserted hallway, she noted that the door into it had been left slightly ajar. She heard raised, angry voices within and halted uncertainly with her hand still upon the doorknob, ready to step into the room beyond.

Mr. DeLacey sounded almost beside himself with rage.

"You had no right to give that minx of a Markham girl your jewels, Isobel, for they are not yours to give!" he stormed. "A scheming, redheaded little adventuress like that!"

"I shall do as I like with my own property," Mrs. Arundale began hotly, but he stopped her before she could go on.

"It is not your sole property, never has been," he corrected warmly. "It is Clara's if anyone's, or Neville's future wife when he finds one. Part of their inheritance, held only in trust for *them*."

"She is beginning to feel like a real granddaughter to me already, one of my own," Mrs. Arundale retorted stubbornly, with spirit, and her lawyer laughed. A grim laugh, without any mirth in it.

"Well, if you mean this young Markham woman," he said shortly, bluntly, "she isn't your kin, nor ever likely to be. Will you remember that, Isobel, the next time you want to be so—so generous? She is a mere employee, a hired companion, nothing more!"

Saranne's listless fingers dropped from the doorhandle. All thought of retrieving the missing evening-bag was abandoned forever now. She turned away, stumbled with bowed shoulders, feeling utterly lost, sick of heart. There was the frosty glint of unshed tears in the gray eyes now, instead of the misty happiness, the radiant gladness of a few short moments ago, as she joined the others and they walked down the steps of the house in Nightingale Square.

A few days later, driven through the narrow, rutted Kentish lanes by Winters, the old lady's coachman, to Dover, they embarked for the Continental mainland, the harbor of Ostend on the Belgian coast in particular, Mrs. Arundale, Janet Dawson and she. Winters, elderly, dour, and gruff as his name, had been in Mrs. Arundale's service since a lad, as stableboy.

It was cold on the packet-boat, distinctly chilly with a keen northeast wind blowing, whipping her cheeks, stinging them into a becoming pinkness beneath the gray bonnet with its edging of fur, setting the red curls dancing wildly. Janet and Mrs. Arundale had early on sought the shelter of the cabin below, set aside for lady passengers; winter had disappeared also, and Saranne was alone.

She looked down over the rail to see the gray waters of the English Channel curling and foaming in a frill like white lace under the ship's prow. Despite her earlier brave protestations, she could not believe, even now, that she was leaving the land of her birth behind her for the first time.

The grayness of the waters seemed to match her somber mood. Yet in next to no time at all, it seemed, they had landed on the opposite shore amidst scenes of the utmost confusion and bustle. They had taken refuge in an inn on the quayside there, to enjoy some rest and refreshment while Winters negotiated for fresh horses for the Arundale coach. Then on again, driving through the Belgian countryside to a hotel in Brussels, the capital, where they put up for the night.

Chapter
5

During the few days they lingered in Brussels, Mrs. Arundale, true to her own secret intention of treating Saranne like the kin she was not, showered the girl with all the new clothes imaginable.

When Saranne began in alarm, shocked: "Oh, but I couldn't accept, Mrs. Arundale," all the puritanical side of her upbringing rising to the surface at the very idea, the old lady cut her short, chuckling.

"You are, in a fashion, my responsibility now, child," she said firmly. "I owe it to you for insisting that you come here at such short notice! No time to go shopping properly, eh? Just regard it as my way of making amends," she suggested indulgently.

"But—" Saranne began again, then closed her lips and said no more as the old woman went on dreamily:

"Every woman born has an inbred love of playing with dolls, Saranne, dressing them up —don't you know that? I shall enjoy buying gowns for you, Saranne, much more than Clara, who is never happier than when playing at milkmaid, wearing a country gown!"

Mrs. Arundale made it her business to call upon the famous fashion houses in person, escorting her protégée there, in order to supervise the purchase of Saranne's brand-new outfit from chemise to pelisse, a short fur shoulder-cape for evening wear. To say nothing of shoes and bonnets and hose. Saranne duly noted the fact, digesting it, that her aged employer was greeted with the marked respect, consideration, given only to old and valued customers.

They threw up their hands in Gallic appreciation, chattering a welcome in rapid French.

"Brussels is so full, the season is brilliant at the moment," they said. "Madame could not have come at a better time! And this is Madame's so-charming granddaughter, Mees Arundale, is it not?"

And they threw up their hands again in real or simulated admiration, eyeing Saranne standing quietly in the background, slyly weighing all her good or bad points in the meantime, assessing her measurements, coloring, for future reference. Mrs. Arundale smiled blandly, a little wickedly. But she did not disillusion them.

"I want you to fit her out in the very best you have, eh?" she ordered. "And expense, of course, is no object, mind!" she added sharply, a hint of that haughty pride that was so much a part of her peeping out for an instant.

Outside, trees were in full bloom with the languor of midsummer, flowers everywhere in the market of the Town Square, horse-borne traffic clattering noisily over the *pavé*. In the green leafy shade, restful and inviting, people were sitting down at café tables upon the sidewalk. It was the *foreigness* of it all that was so enchanting, Saranne thought.

Inside the salon, her senses swam in heady delight amidst a plethora of color, materials, garments of all kinds—rich damasks and silk, heavy beautiful velvets. The staff evidently shared Mrs. Arundale's penchant for "doll dressing," for they fell upon Saranne as if she were a heaven-sent gift for them to try out their wares.

"Go ahead, then," Mrs. Arundale ordered sharply, seated upon a thin, spindle-legged gilt chair. She tapped the thickly carpeted floor imperiously with her amber-handled cane. "What are you waiting for?"

Mrs. Arundale said later: "It is also a matter of policy, my dear child. If you will remember," she continued crisply over supper a few nights later, "Mr. DeLacey, my lawyer, pointed out how important it was that you appear well dressed in my company? Myself, I don't care a fig for appearances, as you are no doubt aware. But society can be so very, very cruel, especially so-called polite society...."

Her old voice died away and she laughed. "We can't have you turning up at some grand soirée or ball dressed in burlap, now, can we?"

"No, I suppose not, ma'am," Saranne agreed sheepishly, smiling faintly in turn, and Mrs. Arundale nodded in satisfaction, sniffing.

"Splendid," she said. "Now we understand each other, eh?"

They drove out of Brussels eventually and took the road to the south through Europe by easy stages. The dour, rough-tongued Winters drove the Arundale coach with a pile of luggage on top, Mrs. Arundale, Janet and Saranne inside, jolted ummercifully on the bad country roads.

Saranne first saw Florence, that Italian City of Flowers, late one evening when the setting sun, tinting its banks with violet shadows, turned the Arno into a river of blood. And like many another traveler before her, she fell in love with the place at once. A love that grew with slow, close familiarity in the months which followed, getting to know it.

Mrs. Arundale rented a suite of rooms on one floor of an old, decaying palace. It had floors that were cool underfoot in summer, in the heat of the Italian day. The Contessa who owned it, and who was the last of her family, lived on the ground floor below them. She was one of Mrs. Arundale's oldest friends.

The palace stood on the river's banks, the heavy scent of the lime trees planted out front in the street drifting into the living quarters at all hours of the day and night. At the rear there was a small private courtyard of paved brick. An ancient acacia tree stood there, strongly rooted in the ground and rising to form a natural green shutter over Saranne's window. It was the haunt of innumerable Florentine sparrows, forever peeping inquisitively in at her.

"Why not?" Janet asked good-humoredly when Saranne mentioned this. "They are Italian sparrows, aren't they?" the housekeeper said slyly, laughing.

They had meals out there in the hottest weather, especially supper in the cool of the evening, under a luxuriant vine trained to form an arbor. The red candles in holders of terracotta, scarcely flickering in the still, humid air, unbroken silence all around them save for the sweet, drowsy tolling of church bells at rare intervals, made Saranne think of another such occasion.

"A penny for 'em, miss?" Mrs. Arundale broke in briskly upon her thoughts.

"I was thinking of that last evening I spent in the company of Miss Clara, her fiancé, and Captain Arundale," she confessed truthfully. "When we went to the theater at Drury Lane and on to sup at Vauxhall Pleasure Gardens afterwards."

Mrs. Arundale said "Umph!" to this, but enigmatically, nothing more. Life in Florence went on at a slow, dreamy pace, a soft timelessness that took no heed of the passing of the months. The living room, if "room" it could be called, was large and airy and there was a bedroom each for Mrs. Arundale, Janet and herself. The elderly coachman, Winters, lived out in quarters of his own.

There was a miniature kitchen for Janet off the dining room and a young Italian maid, Maria, to wait on them, who "went" with the apartment, always eagerly attentive and smiling. Saranne learned to exchange the books at the small English library most mornings, then take a leisurely walk along the riverbank or climb the heights above the town to look down upon the scene below. The old lady had been an inveterate reader in her youth.

"But my old eyes are not what they were," she confessed ruefully. "So you must be my eyes now, Saranne, read to me, please?"

So many of Mrs. Arundale's friends spoke Italian or French that it became necessary for Saranne to become proficient in both languages, in order to be able to converse with them with tolerable fluency, when her employer had guests, went shopping in the city on other occasions. Her kindly patroness arranged that the girl should have lessons with suitable tutors three times a week, in order to better equip herself.

Nor did it stop there. It was tacitly understood within Mrs. Arundale's wide circle of friends that Saranne was to be treated as a real kinswoman, the old lady's favorite granddaughter, next to Clara. Indeed, most of them were bemused as to in what exact relation she did stand to the Arundales. For the most part, they shrugged, accepting the situation.

Saranne, too, when she thought about it at all, with the resilience of youth, was puzzled in a mild degree by the old lady's great kindness to her, a stranger. She did not know that it was born of that nagging loneliness and fear of advanced age. A gap that Saranne alone could fill, the old lady shrewdly guessing that Clara had her own life, her own destiny to fulfill, unlike the drab future that seemed to stretch before *this* girl.

And there was another reason, too. With a rather wicked quirk to her old, worldly-wise lips, Mrs. Arundale recognized in Saranne her beauty, spirit, strength of will, a pale ghost of what she herself had been long ago. And such as the placid Clara never had or could be. So she continued to pamper, spoil, Saranne.

The Contessa had an adoptive "nephew," son of an old friend, a charming youth with dark, melting Latin eyes and impeccable manners, who became Saranne's devoted companion. He was a keen horseman. And one day Saranne returned to her bedroom to find, as a delightful surprise, a dark green velvet habit spread out upon her bed, a tall-crowned hat with an osprey feather curling ravishingly round its brim, and a pair of boots in the finest, softest kid, fitting her small feet like a glove.

"You are to have riding lessons, my dear," the old lady said in her most autocratic voice when Saranne came running to her, brimming over with excitement.

Thereafter she rode often with Lorenzo when Mrs. Arundale did not need her services. But time was running out for them all, although neither Janet or Saranne realized it yet. Mrs. Arundale was not well, a very old, physically frail lady despite her gallant attempts to keep death at bay. Despite her high-spirited, almost defiant contempt of encroaching age, the harsh, cruel facts of existence had to be faced at last.

There was little her doctors could do beyond minister to her failing heart with medicine and rest. The roses of fever burned in her withered cheeks now, under the layers of paint and powder, the rouge she still insisted be applied. Saranne and Janet, with the little Italian maid Maria, who was genuinely concerned, took turns as devoted attendants at their ailing employer's bedside.

Saranne had grown to love the old lady in the many months they had spent in each other's company. "You have been very good to me, ma'am," she said on one occasion, when Mrs. Arundale, rallying a little, would have attempted to thank her for her ministrations, patting the girl's hand feebly. "You spoil us all— and this is the only way in which I can begin to thank you!"

When she was well enough, Mrs. Arundale decided to return home to England. "Home" in this instance, as Janet explained to Saranne in an aside, meant the old lady's country place near Bath, The Grange, and not the London house in Nightingale Square as Saranne might have imagined.

Now almost as experienced at dealing with such matters as Janet herself, Saranne gave orders to Winters to get ready the coach for a return journey. She had a premonition, which clutched at her heart like a vice, that never again would she see Florence, that there would be no more expeditions with Mrs. Arundale out to the sunbaked Tuscan landscape, to visit the old lady's friends in their country estates around Florence.

Janet quite openly, thankfully, left all such arrangements as had to be made, to her younger compatriot now. It was Saranne who paid off the weeping Maria, adding, on Mrs. Arundale's orders, a generous sum of money to tide the Italian girl over until the apartment was leased once more to new tenants. It was now all shut up, the furniture draped with dust sheets, with the disconsolate Maria drifting like an unhappy ghost from room to room, and the key handed over to the caretaker.

Then Winters drove them by even easier stages than before back to Brussels and the same hotel they had stayed at eighteen months ago, when they first landed on the Continental mainland. It to Saranne seemed more as though a century had passed. Janet and she, and even Winters, prepared to cross the English Channel with some trepidation now, for old Mrs. Arundale had become very fragile indeed. To exchange the eternal sunshine and warmth of Italy for the soft gray skies and everlastingly falling rain of England.

This time, they did not linger in the Belgian capital a moment longer than was necessary to allow a breathing spell, a brief rest for Mrs. Arundale. On the morning of the second day after their arrival, they set off again toward the coast in the coach driven by Winters. And this time Saranne, cool and collected, even blasé to the point of indifference, was completely in charge of herself by then.

The hustle and bustle at the fishing port of Ostend, the babble of foreign tongues all around her—French and Flemish—by some alchemy of traveling experience was no longer a novelty.

Her sole problem now, she felt, was to get Mrs. Arundale safely on board with the help of Janet, comfortably installed in the stuffy cabin below for a choppy journey across the English Channel. Their employer dozed peacefully most of the time, setting the housekeeper and herself free for a brief walk around the deck. Once she asked Janet, as they paced side by side, without however any undue show of curiosity: "What is it like, Janet, this house we are going to, Mrs. Arundale's home?"

"The Grange? Oh, it is very beautiful down there, miss, the countryside around it is very lovely, indeed." Janet laughed apologetically. "But, then, I am prejudiced, I suppose, as I was born in those parts!" She added softly: "I am sure you will like it, miss."

"Will I?" Saranne asked herself, dreamily.

Would she be as enthusiastic as Janet hoped about the Arundale estate and the West Country in general? She was doubtful now, after the Arabella Crale letdown, the fiasco of that young lady's invitation to Bath. She did not know, had no means of knowing, she thought ruefully, smiling a little to herself. In the depths of her heart, mind, she felt so uncertain, she mused.

But with Janet's meager information she had perforce to remain contented for the time being. As she had never been that far out of London up to now, into Somerset county, she found she was looking forward to the experience with something like impatience. It held all the lure of the unknown.

The West Country, its people themselves, save for the few she had met and liked, were as a closed book to her, she thought. And then her heart seemed to stop, before going on again, beating uncomfortably fast. Her color rose with indignation as a sharp reminder came flooding into her brain again, filling her whole being with dire forebodings. Mr. Jerome De-Lacey, her employer's attorney!

She had almost forgotten the Arundale lawyer, she had persuaded herself, succeeded in putting him right out of her mind more or less permanently, during those long, happy months spent in Florence. Now it all came back to her, causing her distress. She shivered, thrusting the memory of the dark-haired, dark-eyed lawyer back into the dim recesses of some corner of her mind again, refusing to dwell upon the thought of him, spoiling as he did all her dreams of a bright, happy future. He is not worth considering, she thought hotly, contemptuously. Utterly beneath contempt!

She had come a long, long way, she told herself scornfully, since last she had seen Mr. DeLacey! Much water had passed under the bridges of her life between then and now, many things happened to change her outlook.

I am no longer a child, she reflected soberly. Or one whose eyes are still blinded by ignorance of a cruel, hard world!

But her spirits rose, all decorum flung to the winds, bubbling over with a delight that she could not hide, at the sight of Neville Arundale again.

As soon as his grandmother arrived at the house in Nightingale Square, where they would rest before going to The Grange, he called to pay his respects. He was in uniform, having, as he told them with a lazy twinkle in his eye, slipped out of barracks for a few hours in order to greet them all. He looked as incredibly handsome as ever standing there in the drawing room, the sun shining in through the windows falling upon his golden hair. As his bright blue eyes met Saranne's gray ones, he smiled. And her heart melted.

"Miss Markham!" he greeted her warmly, easily. He bent low over her hand. "I am so glad to see you again," he murmured softly, meaningfully.

It was intoxicating. All the old, unforgettable charm that she remembered so well was creating havoc in her heart.

Just to see him again, the sunshine creating a dazzling light about his fair head, his blue eyes apparently so earnest, interested, was enough to revive all her past original feelings for him. It was difficult for her to believe that nearly two years had passed since she last saw him.

And then, she did not know how it happened or what had brought it about, the unbelievable happened. She found herself in Neville's arms, held tightly there, her heart pressed close to his the while he showered

149

fiercely ardent kisses upon her bewildered, up-turned face. She shivered for a moment, her first instinct to recoil, then surrendered herself to the warm spell of his embrace. Raising shy, tremulous lips to his—

"Oh, Neville!" she breathed naively at last, lifting an adoring face to his slightly cynical, more hardened one. "I did not know, dream that you could ever love me?"

Her tone was awed, still in a daze of half disbelieving happiness. His gaze narrowed, became calculating as he gazed down at her, her red hair a living flame in the candlelight.

She did not know, how could she in her ignorance of life, that to him she was but a passing female opportunity to be seized and exploited according to the manner of his kind? To Saranne, he was Prince Charming, the answer to every girl's dream. Neville and she now shared a sweet, secret intimacy that was like a shield, no safer, surer antidote to the memory of her employer's odious lawyer, Mr. Jerome DeLacey.

To her, it all had the slightly unreal feeling of a dream, fuzzy at the edges. Something that had happened in another world, a different sphere of living altogether, as if they, Mrs. Arundale, Janet and she had never been away in Florence at all. To the enchanted girl, completely under his sway, starlight in her eyes blinding her to reality, it was as if she and Neville were exactly at the point where they had met.

He dined with them that night, Mrs. Arundale retiring early on the plea that she was tired. Also, that she needed to get as much rest as possible for the journey down to the West Country on the morrow. Saranne wore a gown of deep, sea-green velvet which set off her superb red hair to perfection, brought out the misty grayness of her eyes. Also, in honor of Neville, the emerald drop earrings his grandmother had given her, and which had aroused so much bitter antagonism on the part of DeLacey. But it does not matter now, she thought happily. His anger or disapproval!

Nothing in the world mattered now, save to be here, with Neville smiling at her across the soft candlelight of the dining table. Having him at her side almost, basking in the rising admiration she sensed in him, with no thought of the morrow that must inexorably come. She was completely, wholly content for this state of things to go on forever!

It was a state of euphoria that lasted right through to the following day. Amidst all the fuss of reloading the coach with luggage, all the brouhaha of departure, some of Mrs. Arundale's friends and neighbors in the square turned out to bid her a temporary farewell. They were a well-dressed, well-mannered lot of people, obviously amply endowed with this world's goods and Saranne was impressed despite herself.

At the very last, an elderly, distinguished-looking gentleman who looked like a retired judge, thrust his head into the coach in order to chat for a few minutes, pay his respects to Mrs. Arundale before going off to his club for the day. He raised his tall, stovepipe hat with old-fashioned courtesy to Saranne, as introductions were made.

"Are you a good horsewoman, a tolerable rider, Miss Markham?" he asked Saranne suddenly, after a few exchanges of polite conversation. He smiled. "Not much else to do in the country, heh? Like the West Country, do you?"

It was her turn to smile ruefully. "I am afraid I have not had much experience of it up to now, Sir Hector," she confessed.

He snorted. "Then you must get young Arundale to take you out, show you the moors, on horseback, young lady," he said earnestly. "The next time he is down that way for a point-to-point, heh?"

And the old gentleman, shaking his head, went off, leaving Saranne wondering what a point-to-point *was*, when it was at home? It was all so easy, effortless, she thought, glowing inwardly. It was hard to believe, at first, that it was all merely part of their tradition of good manners and nothing more. Surface politeness, a polished charm that was as a second skin to them and meant little.

She leaned her red head back against the blue-and-gold plush of the carriage seat and closed her eyes, giving herself up to pleasant thoughts of Neville once more. Presently she nodded without being conscious of doing so, lulled by the musical refrain of the hurrying wheels bowling over the country roads. She slept, following the example of Mrs. Arundale and Janet in their respective corners of the coach.

It was evening of the second day before they finally entered the environs of Bath, that famed watering place. But the dour Winters did not stop there, driving on through the falling dusk. They turned in between the tall stone gate-pillars of The Grange a short time later. The massive wrought-iron gates were opened by a lodge-keeper and clanged to behind them.

"We are home, Saranne," Mrs. Arundale murmured drowsily, rousing herself.

At least Mrs. Arundale and Janet were, she corrected in her own mind. For herself, she was not so sure that The Grange meant that word to her. The Grange itself, at the end of a long, winding, tree-lined drive, proved to be a large white mansion, rather stark looking, bare. A series of tall windows, like narrowed lids, seemed to watch all newcomers with suspicious eyes, pursed lips.

Set in a sheltered fold of the moors, down below, glittered the waters of a large dark-brown lake fed by hidden springs and shining in sinister fashion. This was her first glimpse of Neville's ancestral home, The Grange, and Saranne's soul thrilled at the sight of it, not wholly on his account. It was an impressive rather than appealing house, betraying wealth and the careful use of it in every inch of its well-kept gardens and grounds.

The conifers which hemmed it in looked positively scissored, so regular were they, flowers in the beds almost mathematical in their orderly, severe array. And acres of grass, stretching on every hand as far as the eye could see, sloping down to the banks of the lake, were mowed into the likeness of a smooth green baize-cloth.

As the coach slid to a halt, Mrs. Arundale sat for a moment almost motionless, staring impassively up at the pile of stone and masonry she called "home." Then she sighed, while the rest of the little party waited respectfully, attendant on her every wish, a long-drawn-out sigh, expressive of vast relief, as the front of The Grange suddenly sprang into life, with lights in every front window.

The front door was flung open, and abruptly it seemed as if a crowd of people appeared on the top step out of nowhere. Janet and the coachman helped their mistress out of the vehicle and half led, half supported her up the flight of steps to join the group of persons standing above.

Saranne recognized Neville's sister, Clara, in a riding habit of dark-blue cloth that suited her fair coloring well, obviously not having had time to change before her grandmother's arrival. Clara's betrothed, Giles Fairley, was at her side, as well as, beyond him, a slim fair-haired woman, no longer young. A man, evidently by his livery a major domo, lingered in the background, and she saw that it was Starn, the Arundale butler from Nightingale Square. And yes, someone else was there, too. Holding himself very erect, tall, his dark eyes hooded as he surveyed the scene before him coolly, Mr. Jerome DeLacey.

The woman at Giles's side moved first,

breaking the ice. She advanced toward the little party mounting the steps and seemed to take over from Janet and Winters, placing one arm around the old lady's shoulder in proprietory fashion and kissing her. Just one kiss—no more—a quick, brief peck upon the withered cheeks.

"Hullo, Grandmamma," she said in a high, clear, carrying tone, as if she were addressing a hidden audience. "So nice to see you home once more!" Mrs. Arundale Junior, for such Saranne rightly guessed her to be, went on, greeting her mother-in-law: "Did you have a pleasant journey down, my dear?"

"As pleasant as could be expected," Mrs. Arundale retorted dryly, with a brief flash of her old fire. "But you are right, Amanda—I am glad to be home at long last, I confess!"

They passed into the house, a close-knit family group, Janet and Winters, the latter carrying a traveling rug over his arm that his mistress had just testily discarded, respectfully bringing up the rear a few paces behind. Saranne was still standing by the open coach door, down upon the sweep of gravel drive in front of the house. Sensitive, she did not seek to thrust herself forward, push herself to the front in any way, in what might be termed the gathering of the Arundales after a long absence.

In any case, she had something else to do first, one final task to perform for her employer before she, too, joined the others inside the house. She reached into the rear of the coach's interior to retrieve the old lady's leather jewel-case, which had been left in Saranne's care earlier with the strict injunction, half in jest, half in earnest: "Guard it with your life, child, and don't let it out of your sight!" A mock severity that was belied by the sly smile which lurked behind Mrs. Arundale's fine old eyes. On the surface, Saranne took this order as a joke, yet with an underlying seriousness. So now she took precautions accordingly, keeping it on the seat beside her or upon her knee during the long, tiring journey down from London to Bath. Its safety had delayed her, getting out of the coach last while the rest alighted first.

Saranne turned then, shutting the coach door and, case in hand, prepared to mount the steps in turn. Then she started, glancing up in momentary dismay, taken aback and off her guard, confused as she caught sight of the figure of the Arundale attorney standing at the top of the stairs, staring down at her somber-ly, impassively. His dark glance searched her face and, as his eyes met hers, he seemed as surprised as she.

But only for a moment and for a different reason. He, however, unlike Saranne, seemed in full control of himself an instant later. His cool, heavy-lidded gaze flitted down over her slight form hesitating there, took in the trim gown she wore—made in Italy with deceptive sim-plicity, in dark green silk—the matching vel-vet cloak she wore, the hood drawn up over her red hair.

The hood slipped back now, as she stared up at him, wide-eyed with apprehension. He noted that even her hairstyle was different, had been changed in some way. It was longer, softer, curling in delicate tendrils about her small, sensitive face in a more feminine, less childish way. His lips unconsciously pursed in a silent whistle of disbelief, wonder, staring down at her somberly.

Gone was the shy, gauche young wench of a few short months ago. Where was the girl who had so raised his ire? And then he thought of Captain Neville Arundale and his brow clouded over, frowning. For this girl was no longer to be regarded as a mere paid employee of the gallant captain's grandmother. And he feared for her safety, virtue at the hands of that brave officer.

He even persuaded himself now that the detested autumn flame of her hair had more bronze-gold than red in it, his eye lingering upon her downcast head. The ugly duckling of yesterday, the fledgling with bedraggled feathers, had turned into a very beautiful, desirable swan, indeed.

Old Mrs. Arundale lay dying in her bed in the big house near Bath. She knew that she was dying, yet she did not care, prepared to meet the end with a calm fortitude built upon faith. Her face was composed, serene, like an ancient mask carved out of ivory, against the paleness of her silken pillow.

One thin old hand lay out on the counterpane beneath the shade of the vast Elizabethan four-poster bed, its chintz-draped top lost in shadows near the high ceiling. Through the open window she could see the light, scudding clouds drifting over the distant hills and moors like sky schooners, borne upon the fitful breezes. They fluttered the drapes at the windows, too.

Mrs. Arundale was calm, at peace because she was facing death now and not fearing it, feeling very old and tired, like a child falling asleep. She had lived a good life, had had a long innings, as he who had been her husband might have said, she thought drowsily, smiling a little. She was going to join the loved ones she had lost, the son who died when Amanda and he had been married for such a tragically short time—

"Clara and Neville were two mere babes then," she mused dreamily, quite small children, playing about their grandmother's knee. Memories—and Mrs. Arundale smiled again, lost in a bemused reverie, a daydream without pain or sorrow now. Was that all life consisted of, memories dredged up from the past? No, she refused to believe that—life was for the young, for living! There must surely be more to the state of existence she was now leaving than that!

She dozed again, vaguely conscious of a figure, Janet or someone very like her, hovering in the background, busying itself at the foot of the bed. Mrs. Arundale awoke a few minutes later, struggling up on one elbow through the mists of her comfortable fantasies, striving to pierce the fog all around her, make herself heard, her presence felt.

"Janet?" she called weakly. "Is that you?

Where is my other granddaughter?". she pleaded, seeking reassurance. "Saranne—why is she not here?" she continued querulously, distress in her old voice now, a troubled look in the faded eyes.

Janet hastened to soothe her. "I sent her out for a short walk a little while ago. Poor young lady, she needs some sunlight and fresh air." She did not add that Saranne and Clara had been up half the night, taking turn and turn-about to sit with the dying woman.

"Then send her to me, directly she gets back," Janet's employer ordered weakly, falling back on her pillows with her eyes closed. Janet stood gazing at her for a few seconds longer, then shook her head.

"Poor lady," she said softly, half to herself. "Other granddaughter, indeed! She must be wandering in her mind!"

Next day, Mrs. Arundale roused herself sufficiently to order Janet to send for her attorney, Mr. DeLacey, whose more modest estate adjoined The Grange. He came at once, riding over post-haste, for he felt, knew, that it was a summons which could not be disregarded at this late hour. There was not time, he thought soberly. Anticipating the worst, he was immediately taken upstairs and shown into his client's bedroom by Janet, who had been hovering in the hall below, awaiting his arrival.

Saranne, returning from what seemed to have become her daily routine now—a brisk walk through the springing green heather of the surrounding moors—saw his horse tethered in front of the mansion. Her heart sank, recognizing it.

He remained in the house, up in her room in close conclave with Mrs. Arundale, for some considerable time. As Janet, working in the small dressing room next door, could testify, hearing raised voices: the deep, masculine one of Mr. DeLacey's and the weaker one of her mistress.

Janet was, as she confided to Saranne later, much worried. For there had never, to her knowledge, been a real trace of friction between Mrs. Arundale and her legal adviser, up to now. Sadly, the elderly housekeeper confessed that she felt her small, enclosed world was falling apart.

"Crumbling into tiny pieces, miss, like a cracked pot," she said gloomily.

The first faint, hairline cracks were beginning to appear in Saranne's world, too, she told herself somberly, appearing upon the skyline like an ominous warning. Janet sighed, recognizing, like the paid companion, the end of an era at The Grange. Soon after, Janet heard the door of Mrs. Arundale's room open then close, and footsteps dying away along the landing outside.

"Janet, will you come to me at once, please?" It was her employer's voice, calling feebly, and the housekeeper hastened to obey.

There were few secrets between Janet and her mistress, for they had been together for a very long time by now. Mrs. Arundale trusted Janet, not without cause, had implicit faith in her old retainer's strong commonsense and loy-

160

alty. And Janet did not let her down now, when she needed her most. Mr. DeLacey had just left in a towering rage, Mrs. Arundale said with a faint trace of satisfaction, his brow black as the proverbial thundercloud!

"But, why, ma'am—in heaven's name, why?" Janet asked her in some bewilderment, privileged to speak her mind on this occasion.

"Because I dismissed him summarily, out of hand," her mistress said tartly, with just a particle of her old fire.

"Why, ma'am?" Janet persisted quietly, her face grave. She looked shocked, staring aghast at her employer. Mrs. Arundale's old head stirred restlessly upon the pillow.

"He refused to grant a dearest wish of mine," she said in weak indignation. "Can you imagine that? I wanted to change my will, Janet," she went on wearily, with an effort. "I asked him to draw up a new one, with some alterations I intended making—and he refused! He wouldn't do it, attempted to argue me out of it—"

"Oh, dear!" said Janet.

"So I told him to go," Mrs. Arundale continued. "And now," she ordered, with a brief return to her old autocratic fire, "you can send for Mr. Blair to come to me, Janet!"

Mr. Blair was another attorney, Janet knew, who lived within driving distance of The Grange and practised in Bath, like Mr. DeLacey. He was only too pleased to receive the rich plum of a summons to The Grange and draw up a fresh will for the wealthy Mrs. Arundale.

Saranne, having returned from her walk,

was resting in the great hall of the house before going upstairs to dress for the evening. When Mr. DeLacey stormed out of his client's bedroom above, some slight noise that he made in so doing, irritation making him careless, caused her to look up from where she stood by the fire, warming herself in the glow from the pile of logs there, slowly drawing her gloves from her chilled hands after her walk over the moors. Their eyes met as he came swiftly down the staircase toward her. For all the world like a hawk, an eagle—or a vulture, she thought, fascinated, seeing his swift, gliding flight down the stairs.

Then she started, looking at him more closely. She knew then what he reminded her of, something that had been nagging at the back of her brain ever since she had first seen him, coloring her opinion of him. That dark, proud head held so high, upright in self-respect, fierce pride carried to a fault, the keenness of his dark blue eye, so penetrating and sharp, seeing all, understanding all without effort, seemingly.

He appeared to be spiritually soaring away on his pinions of power, up and out of view, out of the reach of lesser, more ordinary mortals. Tirelessly hovering above the abyss of life, unfaltering, he had that "look of eagles" she had read about, many moons ago, in her browsings. She gave a little nod of her head, without being conscious of doing so. Yes, she thought, he is just like an eagle, wild, fearless!

And as cruel? She felt nervous at her discovery, so bizarre, unconventional. And, as their eyes met now, she could see that he was almost beside himself with suppressed anger, rage. So much so that he gave the impression of scarcely seeing her slender form by the fireside, beneath the massive Arundale coat-of-arms carved into the mantlepiece. She was dwarfed, cast into shadow by its height, standing there.

But he saw her at last, it was obvious, reaching the bottommost stair and pausing. He halted there for an instant that seemed like an eternity to the waiting girl, staring at her as if he had seen a ghost. All the bottled-up frustration, the sense of helplessness in regard to this—this interloper, that he had felt over the past two years, ever since she had first swum into his vortex, rose searingly to the surface now.

All his worst fears, darkest forebodings, had proved true, as he knew they would! His warnings to old Mrs. Arundale had all fallen upon barren ground or else had been ignored, wilfully. Now they were likely to come home to roost, a bitter fulfillment to Mrs. Arundale and her unfortunate heirs. He choked for a moment over his next words, flinging them at her bitingly, cuttingly, with all the menace of which he was capable: "Congratulations, Miss Markham, on the influence you appear to have gained over my client. It is nothing short of remarkable and you must let me into your secret some time."

"What—what do you mean, sir?" She stared

at him wide-eyed with shock, consternation, the color draining from her face, leaving it white.

"Oh, come now!" He laughed, his very tone an ugly sound, the expression upon his dark face as though an icicle ran up and down Saranne's spine. She shivered, she could not help it, and his expression changed, became harder as she winced. "Don't pretend you misunderstand me," he said curtly, "please don't play the innocent with me, miss!" He said over his shoulder as he strode away, almost hissing it: "You will hear more of this, Miss Markham!"

And with that dark threat he was gone. She stood there, staring at the place where he had been, long after he had walked swiftly out the front door, slamming that heavy piece of wood behind him. She did not even begin to understand what he meant by his furious outburst. She finally shook her red head in perplexity, going slowly upstairs to change, seeking the temporary haven of her beautiful room upon the same landing as Mrs. Arundale's own.

Mrs. Arundale died that night, quite peacefully, in her sleep. Janet made the discovery when taking up her mistress's early morning cup of chocolate. She took one look at that still, placid face upon the pillow, the eyes closed and all the lines miraculously smoothed out into a smiling gentleness, and raised the alarm.

It seemed odd to Saranne, not quite right or respectful somehow, that the old lady's daughter-in-law, Amanda, was suddenly "Mrs.

Arundale" instead of the "Mrs. Amanda" she had always been. It was brought home to the entire household now, including Saranne, that Amanda was in sole charge henceforth, at the head of things in every way.

The change is so swift, so thoughtless, from one to another, Saranne thought regretfully, sorrowfully, mourning her old friend and benefactor.

Yet this was amended in time to "Young Mrs. Arundale," people taking to its usage naturally, without thought, as more befitting. Amanda Arundale had been an actress in her younger days. She had left the stage early, after a fairly successful if not spectacular career, in order to marry Graham Arundale, the old lady's sole issue, a dedicated farmer, lover of country life, if Amanda were not.

After barely a decade of marriage he had been thrown on the hunting field, his horse rolling upon him, and so died, leaving Amanda to raise Clara and Neville alone.

A thin, nervous woman who seemed all bones rather than solid flesh, Amanda Arundale gave strong hints of having been extremely beautiful in her youth. Now, however, the full bloom of her loveliness was over and she clung fiercely to the last vestiges of that past. Tinting her hair, she avidly pursued beauty treatments of all kinds in an effort to restore her lost looks.

Saranne gazed at her wonderingly. Those looks, it was an open secret to everyone, had been passed on to her son, missing Clara altogether, who, Saranne was sturdily convinced, must have taken after her dead father.

I know what it means to be the odd-man-out in a gathering! Saranne thought. So I can sympathize with Clara in contrast to her more glamorous brother and mother!

No wonder, Saranne mused darkly, that Clara was only too anxious to marry her Giles and escape with him into the obscurity of married life.

For the next few days The Grange was the scene of much feverish activity as arrangements for the funeral were made. Neville came down to Bath at once, after a message had been got through to him in town from his mother and sister. And although Saranne was glad to see him again, overjoyed at his presence in their midst once more, Neville on his part was distrait, almost distant with her. She had to be content with less of his notice than she had hoped.

It was as if he said, with an indifferent shrug, "The prize apple is still hanging upon the tree, ready and willing, ripe for the picking when I stretch out my hand." They did not see much of each other at all, for his mother had no hesitation in calling upon Saranne to help in dealing with the clerical side of the proceedings. Saranne was kept busy answering and writing letters, sending out notices of the death, invitations to attend the funeral to all and sundry who mattered in Amanda's scheme of social things.

The late Mrs. Arundale was to be buried

in the churchyard of the ancient little church where she had attended services on Sundays. It was a bright spring day when she was finally laid to rest, yet with more than a hint of rain, even snow in the wind, like unshed tears. Some spring days are only like winter's face wearing a smile, Saranne thought sadly.

She stood back from the graveside itself and a little to the rear of the Arundale family, who were grouped around the pile of newly up-turned clay. The surpliced clergyman, Amanda and her children, Clara's fiancé, Giles Fairley —and Mr. Jerome DeLacey, who was now Amanda's legal adviser. There was one comparative stranger—DeLacey's fellow lawyer, Mr. Blair.

The churchyard was only a short distance from The Grange and most folk, from the estate and household especially, simply walked there, Saranne included. It was only those who came from far afield, the guests, old friends and neighbors of the deceased, paying their last respects to Isobel Arundale, who turned up in carriages, and incidentally swamped the little village at its gates with their vehicles, standing there in waiting.

Young Mrs. Arundale was in smart, very new and expensive mourning, a fur cloak about her shoulders against the keen breeze that was blowing on the morning of the funeral. As she presently removed one of her gloves, the better to dab affectedly at her wet eyes with a minute scrap of lace-edged handkerchief, the diamonds in the many rings she wore shone and sparkled in the thin sunlight. Saranne's heart contracted for a moment in a spasm of pain, sorrow, recognizing them. It did not take Amanda long to claim her inheritance, she thought bitterly. Those rings are unmistakably Mrs. Arundale's.

As they entered the churchyard in a small, tight bunch, with Neville and Mr. DeLacey walking a little ahead of the others in their role of supporters to the grieving Amanda, Saranne hesitated, hanging back. And when the service began, she was convinced that she had no right to be there at all, intruding upon their mourning—the old lady's nearest and dearest, plus her attorneys.

She quietly withdrew from the circle around the graveside and joined a smaller group of people a little way off, standing in respectful silence, mostly estate servants and indoor staff of The Grange, including Janet. Janet moved up as Saranne approached, recognizing her.

"Stand here, miss, beside me," Janet whispered with a welcoming gesture, making room.

So Saranne saw her friend and benefactress, the woman who had been so good to her, laid to rest on that cold spring day. It was, she reflected with a heavy sigh, like the closing of yet another chapter in her life—whither next? Where did she go from here, she asked herself sorrowfully? She stole a forlorn look at Neville, standing very straight, looking incredibly handsome as ever, between his mother and sister.

And Neville, she reminded herself sternly, was now heir to The Grange estate, the Arundale wealth. Would that fact make any difference to *them*—the dawning, wonderful understanding that seemed to be growing up between Neville and herself—she wondered naively. The fact that Neville was now a very rich man might conceivably alter things. She did not know.

They drove back the short distance to The Grange, each busy with her or his own private thoughts. The housekeeper, Janet, had made arrangements beforehand for the funeral repast, light refreshments being served in the great hall, with coffee, wine for those who stayed to partake of it. The guests all left soon after and the rest filed into the dining room, at Mr. Blair's rather than Mr. DeLacey's request, to hear the reading of Mrs. Arundale's mysterious new will.

Chairs had been placed in a semicircle around the wall at the far end of the room and here such tenants, estate workers, and indoor servants who were beneficiaries took their places in due course, shuffling respectfully in, ushered by the butler. They left, too, as quietly and orderly, when their part of the will reading was over.

Again Saranne hesitated on the threshold of the room, wondering if she were needed merely in her capacity as secretary, to take notes. If, indeed, she were included in the invitation to enter at all?

How soon will Amanda want me to leave after this? ran her worried reflections. Perhaps, under the circumstances, I had better go and pack, to be ready for any eventuality.

It was a sharp surprise for Saranne, therefore, taking her aback, when Mr. Blair, the lawyer who had apparently superseded Mr. DeLacey in the late Mrs. Arundale's affairs, laid his hand upon the girl's arm just as she was about to mount the stairs, to go to her own room.

"One moment, please, Miss Markham?" he said meaningfully in his dry, precise legal voice. "*You* must be present in the dining room, too, if you don't mind?"

"I?" she echoed, startled. Taken unawares, she blurted out: "Why me?"

"You will see," the elderly attorney returned suavely, evasively. "And now, if you will come this way, please?" He added, relenting as he saw the utter bewilderment in her face, yet not relaxing his grip upon her forearm for an instant: "You, of all persons, must be there!"

Mystified, Saranne followed him obediently to the room in question, in the wake of the others. As she did so, she became fully aware of that other lawyer present there, Mr. DeLacey. She shivered a little, hanging back.

Darkly taciturn as ever, he was watching her intently from across the length of the room, his face grim. Nor did his expression alter, become less dour or soften as his glance met hers once more, Saranne's one of bewilderment. It became even sterner than before if that were at all possible, she thought despairingly as she took her place with the others around the shining mahogany table, its deep reddish lights reflecting a high polish. Arms folded impassively in a favorite posture, Jerome DeLacey waited without speaking, leaving the center of the stage, all the limelight as it were, to his fellow attorney, Mr. Blair.

And again, as Saranne would have instinctively gone to the row of chairs at the far end of the room against the wall, provided for those of lesser import, Mr. Blair stopped her. He motioned instead to one of a pair of carved chairs with arms, placed at each end of the long table and facing him. He was standing directly under one of the three tall windows there, the light falling over his shoulder onto a sheaf of papers he held in his hand.

"There, please, Miss Markham," he said evenly. "Will you sit at the head of the table, please?"

She obeyed as in a dream, utterly at a loss. Deep in their own thoughts, perhaps calculations, none of the other people present appeared to note the lawyer's gesture or read any significance into it, save one: Jerome DeLacey, his face bitter. His glance had not left hers since she first had entered and taken her place at the top of the table as Mr. Blair directed. Now the older lawyer cleared his throat and began to read from the papers he held in his hand, old Mrs. Arundale's last will and testament.

Saranne did not really listen closely for the first few minutes, busy with her own thoughts, unhappy ones. Scarcely heeding what Mr. Blair was saying, she was too engrossed by her own churned-up emotions, and uncomfortably aware of Mr. DeLacey's scrutiny, his withering gaze bent in her direction.

The recent date of the will seemed to surprise many of those in the room. Ill news, it appeared, had not traveled fast enough, in this case at least. For the first part, it merely consisted of a repetition of Isobel Arundale's bequests to servants and dependents. Estate workers of long standing, her cook and butler, Winter the coachman—none had been forgotten. The list droned on. Janet was provided for with a comfortable annuity that would keep her in comfort for the rest of her life. The lesser legatees left the room then, at a signal from Mr. Blair. They filed out in orderly fashion, leaving only the Arundale family present now, Giles Fairley, the two lawyers, and Saranne herself. Mr. Blair paused.

"And now we come to the main body of the will, ladies and gentlemen," he said.

Chapter
6

There was a stirring of activity then, a quickening of attention as all faces turned hopefully, expectantly, toward the blandly inscrutable one of Mr. Blair. A sigh ran round the table again, a sound like the dry rustling of leaves in the winter wind, a half-stifled collective gasp.

Saranne felt, almost scornfully, that she herself was detached, remote from it all, so why was she here? What had she, Saranne Markham, to do with the reading of her late employer's will? And yet Mr. Blair had insisted that she be present. It was all extremely puzzling. Boring, too, into the bargain! she mused, feeling exasperated.

It had nothing whatever to do with her,

she thought passionately. Now Clara and Neville's names were being mentioned, that of their mother— "To my daughter-in-law, Amanda, and my two grandchildren, Clara and Neville, I leave the sum of ten thousand pounds each. Having provided generously for them during my lifetime, I consider these sums will cover all their expectations now. The bulk of my estate therefore, including The Grange and all its contents, and the house in Nightingale Square, I leave to my dear adopted granddaughter in all but name, Saranne Markham—"

Saranne closed her eyes in shock, the color draining from her lips, her face, leaving them white and bloodless. So overpowering, intense, was her emotion that she gripped the edge of the table without realizing fully what she was doing, her fingers digging into the polished wood. She opened her eyes at last, after a long, long pause of stricken silence on the part of all present, to stare wildly about her at all those hard, accusing faces, the eyes turned in her direction like those of puppets pulled by strings.

There was stupefaction, stunned surprise, even stark, naked hatred in each pair of eyes turned upon her, save Clara's and to a lesser extent Giles's, who showed only bewilderment. Saranne's glance sped round the table, taking in the assembled Arundales—the two lawyers classed as belonging to that clan, too, for the nonce, she thought incoherently.

Only Mr. Blair and Clara, out of all the persons there, seemed to have kept cool. The mouth of Amanda Arundale had fallen open, her thin, clawlike hands poised motionlessly in midair as she raised a lorgnette to peer at this presumptuous upstart. Her face looked positively old, haggard, as she stared in frozen horror at the girl at the head of the table.

Saranne's glance shifted hurriedly from his mother, fled to Neville's, miserably, silently imploring his help, understanding. But none was forthcoming from that quarter. His face was implacable, hostile, his blue eyes openly inimical, dangerously so, glaring at her with unashamed hatred. Saranne made a gesture of despair. It is utterly mad, she thought, too fantastic for words—is all this really happening to me?

She felt, in a sort of light-hearted delirium, that they would all rise to their feet in a moment, descend upon her luckless red head like a crowd of angry birds, pecking her to death. As in a dream, a nightmare, she heard, without really distinguishing the words, Mr. Blair's voice going on. Stricken and silent at the table's head, she strove to break the evil spell which bound her.

She, Saranne Markham, heiress, actually the new owner of The Grange, its lovely furnishings, the house in Nightingale Square. Inheritor of a fortune beyond her wildest dreams. No, it could not, must not be—and she gave herself a little shake, shivering, trying to regain her hold upon sanity and terra firma again. The whole notion is wickedness, wholly, criminally wrong—and I want none of it! she thought passionately.

And yet it seemed that she had been misled after all, that she still had one friend left in all those frosty faces staring at her, an ally in this, the enemy's camp. As her gaze traveled round the table for the last time, despairingly, her eyes met those of Clara.

Only Clara's eyes were not accusing, like those others'. They were deeply troubled, but there was no animosity in the glance she bent upon Saranne, twisting a handkerchief to shreds in her slim, sunburnt hands. Clara's eyes seemed to say "I'm really sorry, Saranne, that this had to happen. Really I am," and Saranne gave a tiny nod, relaxing a little.

"It's not your fault, Clara," she said aloud, quietly. "I am the one to blame, if any."

Suddenly Saranne stood up—indeed, they all did now, the assembly breaking up in hopeless confusion, anger. She pushed her chair away and stood her ground, facing her accusers, adversaries, with a courage she did not feel. It was all surface, an empty show. With a clarity of vision which cut her to the heart, she knew them all for what they were now, her enemies, never friends.

All the illusions, all the false dreams she had woven about them—Neville above all—were never to be resurrected again. She was mentally free but emotionally scarred, like a mountainside that had been burned of its gorse and heather, bare to the healing, cleansing rain, the sunlight.

Young Mrs. Arundale spoke at last, breaking the spell, addressing herself bluntly to Jerome DeLacey: "Did you know of this—this monstrous will, Jerome? This terrible injustice to me and my children?"

"Yes." He nodded coolly. "And advised your mother-in-law not to change her original one, Amanda! That is why she dismissed me as her attorney, in favor of Mr. Blair here."

"But what are we going to do?" Amanda almost wailed, raising distracted eyes to his.

"Do?" He laughed grimly, a laugh singularly devoid of any humor, so menacing, harsh, did it sound, Saranne thought. Her flesh crept, she could not help it. "We will fight it, never fear, Amanda!" he cried. "Take it through every court in the land—yes, right up to the very highest, if need be!"

Saranne thought she detected in Mr. De-Lacey's eyes a gleam of triumph lightly veiled. It was for all the world as if he were saying to the room, crowing with delight: "Don't say I didn't say so, tell you all what this girl was like. You disregarded my warning—and now you can see for yourselves!"

She turned to him at last, her own gray eyes brimming over, misty with the unshed tears of her utter misery. Her small, proud head with its shimmering coronet of red hair held high, she cried scornfully:

"There is no need to go to that trouble, sir! No need at all." She tried hard to keep the feelings of despair, fear, and dislike of this man that were uppermost in her heart at that moment out of her voice as she went on: "I will sign all the necessary papers, all that you wish me to—"

"What do you mean?" It was his turn to

start, staring at her from between narrowed lids with a sudden new, alert interest.

"Do all that is wanted to revoke that will," she said wearily, in a low, muffled tone. "I renounce every part of it, here and now—if that will satisfy you? I want no part of it, Mrs. Arundale's houses, furniture, fortune, nothing!"

And she ran from the room precipitately, somehow fumbling for and finding the handle of the door blindly, and stumbled through. She made her way up, how she scarcely knew, climbing the stairs and hurrying along the corridor above, to the temporary safe haven of her bedroom.

Once there, she took off her shoes, the habits and training of a lifetime under Miss Hanley and Aunt Bertha still holding good, strong in their influence even then. Carefully turning down the blue satin counterpane—matching the window drapes—she flung herself down at full length upon the bed, where she lay staring up at the ceiling in a prefect abyss of absolute dejection, misery.

Her head was going round in a whirl, an orgy of self-accusation, wretchedness, going over and over in her mind the happenings of the morning just past, writhing in an agony of shame, regret for her own imagined part in it, blaming herself in some way. Her heart felt heavy within her breast—with guilt, perhaps? she asked herself earnestly.

A vast, deep pool of unhappiness engulfed her, a lake of despondency in which she was drowning. Fate, destiny, call it what you will, she thought, had taken yet another unexpected, startling turn for the worse in her affairs.

And then the natural normal release of tension set in and the tears came. Racking sobs shook her slender frame and she cried as she had never cried before. Her whole being was given up to such a storm of helpless weeping as she thought would never stop. Yet once this tempest of tears was over, she came out of it feeling stronger, calmer, and better able to face up to things.

She could see the situation in better perspective now, Saranne thought sadly, her eyes no longer clouded by passion or emotion that she could not control. She was more grateful than she could express in words, she mused, touched beyond anything that old Mrs. Arundale should have thought fit, made such a wonderful gesture as naming her, Saranne, sole legatee of her main fortune. Or at least, named me in her will, she thought, dabbing at her eyes. She caught her breath with a gasp that was half a sob, shaking her head regretfully. "But oh, how I wish she had not!" she mourned aloud, sorrowfully.

She had made the only possible decision in renouncing that legacy, but it had distilled a poison that set her at variance with all of them, excepting Clara and Giles, as long as she remained under the roof of The Grange, long after the original reason for it had evaporated.

Janet presently brought up some supper on a tray. A concerned Janet put the laden dishes down upon a small table in the window bay, drawing up a chair before it. Saranne stared at it in consternation.

"Oh, but I couldn't touch a thing, honestly, Janet," she pleaded. "I'm not hungry—"

"Yes, you are, a healthy young woman like you," Janet retorted coolly, whisking the cover off the main dish. "Look—I've brought up some cold fowl, with a nice bowl of soup to start," she coaxed, guiding the unresisting Saranne toward the window and pushing her firmly into the chair there. "And a pot of hot coffee to follow, eh?"

"Yes." The girl smiled wanly. "It certainly looks tempting," she admitted feebly, weakening. "Thank you, Janet."

"Yes, I thought you'd change your mind when you saw it!" Janet said, chuckling. "So suppose you get started on it, then?" she suggested with strong common sense.

So Saranne made a pretense of eating, giving in meekly to Janet's kind thoughtfulness, and felt the better for it, oddly enough, as Janet said she would. Life must go on, Saranne reflected, when Janet had departed. The heavens might fall upon one's luckless red head, a chasm open yawningly beneath one's unsuspecting feet, but the wheels of ordinary, everyday existence must be kept turning at all costs.

She kept to her room for the rest of that fateful day, and as the afternoon wore on Janet came up once more with some tea and sandwiches. Saranne drank the tea gratefully, but left the food untouched. She went to bed early that night and soon forgot her present troubles in fitful sleep, uneasy, full of bad dreams. Not before, however, gazing out over the sleeping parkland outside her bedroom windows, the drapes undrawn, she made the discovery that she was quite fatigued after all. Which is perhaps hardly surprising, she mused, considering all that I have gone through during the last twenty-four hours!

She thought of that attorney, Mr. DeLacey, and her face darkened anew, pausing as she languidly drew a brush through her shining red hair. Staring blankly into the mirror before her, she did not really see her own reflection in the glass, seeing instead the features of DeLacey as they had been earlier that day, contorted by fury as he had confronted her across the table in the dining room below, his eyes dark and smoldering, boding ill.

Despite her extreme tiredness, or perhaps because of it, Saranne spent a wretched night after all.

Saranne went down to breakfast next morning after a short inward battle with herself, looking and feeling white-faced, peaked. She hoped that she did not look as washed-out and pale as she felt, she thought grimly. She pinched her cheeks to bring back a moiety of their normal color, in vain it seemed, and squaring her shoulders resolutely grasped the doorhandle and marched into the room beyond.

Young Mrs. Arundale did not breakfast in the ordinary way, keeping rigidly to whatever diet fad she was pursuing at the moment, so that Saranne was not at all surprised to find that her hostess was not there. But if Amanda were not to be seen, her son and daughter, Clara and Neville, were very much in evidence and already started on their meal.

Saranne greeted them both with some uncertainty, in a low, nervous voice, wondering what sort of reception she might expect—from Neville most of all. And to forestall any unpleasantness, she went immediately after that to the sideboard at the far end of the room and began to help herself mechanically, without really noticing what she was doing, to the array of edibles there. She absently picked up a plate, lifted the covers off the silver dishes.

But it was the coffee she craved the most, she thought feverishly, pouring out a cup for herself. Clara greeted her pleasantly enough, as if nothing had happened at all to change her attitude of warm friendliness toward her late grandmother's companion. As indeed nothing had, in Clara's opinion!

But Neville was a different kettle of fish altogether. It was his behavior that was to hurt her most, as, Saranne told herself sorrowfully, she had known in her heart of hearts it would be. Far from being cool and distant, his attitude toward her could only be described as arctic now, she reflected bitterly. He barely glanced up as she entered, nodding coldly in response to her timid "Good morning."

Muttering something that might be construed as an answer of sorts, if one listened hard enough, she mused sadly, he returned to his newspaper at once, burying his face behind its folds. She sighed. It was, she reflected dismally, bowing her head to the inevitable at last, as if a thick steel door, a door without a handle, had clanged shut between them. Never to be opened again, at least on *his* side. She had been firmly shut out of his life for good now.

Oh, Neville, how could you? she asked herself over and over again, bewildered. How can you do this to me?

She excused herself soon after breakfast and escaped up to her room to start packing. She had been too upset yesterday to do so. She surmised that she would be required to remain on at The Grange for at least a few more days, in order to sign the papers resigning her legacy, that they must now be preparing in the various legal offices in Bath.

But in the meantime, she mused philosophically, shrugging, I will gather my things together, preparatory to leaving. That way, I will be ready for an immediate departure from The Grange when required.

And then a fresh idea struck her, making her pause. Would Young Mrs. Arundale want her to leave so soon after all? Might she not need Saranne to work out her days there, after giving her notice of dismissal? She did not know, had no means of even guessing at that lady's plans for the near future. Amanda was now head of the little domestic empire formerly ruled over by her late mother-in-law, and her word was law.

Saranne felt at a loss then, all at sea, wondering what to do. She snapped to the lock on the last of her trunks, leaving out only those few bare necessities she was likely to need. In the midst of it all, Janet looked in, asking if there were anything she could do to help? Eyeing the trunks, all ready to be carried down to the hall now and out to a waiting carriage, if and when Amanda gave the word, Janet nodded approvingly.

"That's right, miss, best to be prepared," she said. "I shall be doing the same myself, any minute now. There's nothing to keep me here, with Madam gone, so I plan to spend a few weeks with my brother and his wife, on the other side of the county, while I look around. He has a small farm there." Janet paused, looking straight at Saranne now. "What are you aiming to do, miss?" she asked innocently.

"I don't know," Saranne confessed slowly, shrugging. "But I expect to go, Janet, like you, at any minute!"

She wanted to be off now, away from The Grange forever, to make a clean break of it as Janet was doing, show a clean pair of heels and shake the dust of Somerset and the West Country, all that it stood for, off them forever more.

There were no ties now, either of sentiment or devotion, that could bind her, Saranne, to any of the Arundales save Clara, or even The Grange itself. She went downstairs presently and knocked with a mixture of trepidation and boldness upon the door of Amanda's private sitting room. Young Mrs. Arundale bade her enter in a loud, clear voice, if slightly shrill and on edge, calling—"Come in."

Amanda had taken old Mrs. Arundale's small sitting room for her own now, as a subtle touch of authority and to remind the world that she, Amanda, was in full charge of all. Besides, it suited her, she liked it, she told everyone simply. It was one of the many changes effected that Saranne, for one, could not fail to note and digest.

As she obeyed, walking into the familiar room at Amanda's summons, Saranne half expected to find Clara and Neville's parent stretched out languidly upon the chaise longue there. Instead, surprisingly, Amanda was seated on a hard, businesslike chair before the writing desk in the window, placed strategically there for the light to fall upon it at a correct angle.

Amanda was sorting through a positive mound of papers, letters, bills, invoices of all kinds, piled high on the table before her. She looked harassed to a degree and the further litter overflowing into the wastepaper basket by her side told its own tale. Saranne felt it in her heart to be sorry for her.

Young Mrs. Arundale looked up as the girl entered the room, swiveling round in her chair. Her face, under the mask of skilfully applied make-up, looked positively haggard, her brow furrowed with worry beneath the elaborately arranged, tinted golden hair so like Neville's own. Amanda's brow cleared as she recognized her visitor, hope dawning in her light blue eyes as a thought struck her.

"Oh, it's you, Miss Markham," she exclaimed. Amanda fixed her gold-rimmed reading glasses more firmly on the bridge of a thin, aristocratic nose. "What can I do for you?"

"It is about my leaving The Grange, ma'am," Saranne began hesitantly. She screwed up her courage after a slight hesitation, shifting from one foot to the other, awkwardly. "I have already packed, Mrs. Arundale—when would you like me to leave?"

"Why?" Amanda stared at her wide-eyed in what seemed like genuine surprise. "Are you in a hurry to go, then?" she asked smoothly, silkily. "You have another post to go to, is that it?"

"Oh, no, ma'am—it's not like that at all," poor Saranne protested hastily, flushing. She shook her red head, again feeling unsure of herself, her ground. Amanda had adroitly turned the tables on her, it seemed, by some alchemy of young Mrs. Arundale's own. Saranne sighed. "But don't you think I ought to go, Mrs. Arundale?" she almost pleaded. She shrugged then. "I suppose it all depends on those papers in connection with the will," she said wearily. "The ones I must sign?"

"I'll send a messenger to Mr. DeLacey or Mr. Blair for you, if you like, asking them to hurry it along," Amanda suggested blandly, helpfully, reaching out a thin, heavily be-ringed hand to the bell-pull of crimson silk at her side. She withdrew her clawlike hand a moment later, however, without tugging at the cord, staring at Saranne thoughtfully. Amanda cleared her throat. "Miss Markham—" she began formally, then stopped.

"Yes, ma'am?"

"Will you—how would you like to stay on here for a while, as *my* secretary?" Amanda asked diplomatically. She waved a hand over the hopeless mass of papers before her. "As you see, I am nearly swamped by all this—and Neville is no help! I need someone to aid me in sorting it all out. Besides—" Amanda paused, gazing at Saranne suspiciously, enigmatically. "I expect you know more of my late mother-in-law's affairs than I do!" she cried bitterly. "And there is another thing—Clara's marriage with Giles Fairley can be brought forward now. I shall need help with that, too."

"Oh, I am so happy for them both!" Saranne exclaimed involuntarily.

Amanda looked doubtful. "Umph—well, yes," she murmured vaguely. She returned doggedly to her original purpose, harping on it. "Will you take the post, Miss Markham, even on a monthly basis rather than quarterly, as before? I will raise your salary, of course, if that is necessary?" Amanda added almost coaxingly.

Saranne hesitated, doubtful. She had no real ties to bind her to the Arundales or The Grange—but then, she reminded herself gravely, she had no bonds, roots, *anywhere*. She was alone in the world now, with the death of old Mrs. Arundale, really on her own and at a loss. And she was not sure how she liked the prospect.

Yet it also solved the problem of whether or not she should accept Amanda's proposition. Even if the post offered were only a temporary one, after all she had nowhere else to go now. Aloud, she said quietly:

"I shall be very happy to help you out, ma'am. But the salary I already receive is quite adequate for my needs. In fact, it is very generous—I do not want any more." She finished simply: "When would you like me to start?"

"Oh, if you could only begin now!" Amanda cried with heartfelt relief, flinging down the quill pen with which she had been writing. She rose from her chair, smoothing down the full skirts of her lilac-colored silk gown of half-mourning. She gestured toward the welter of bills and other correspondence before her. "It is all yours!" she said with a grimace of repugnance.

A splinter of frost penetrated into Saranne's heart then, a tiny sliver of winter itself, like an icicle. It was to linger there for many a long day in the weeks, months, to come, rankling, as the full realization of the difference in her circumstances *then* and now came home to her.

And so Saranne slipped into her place at the desk. And into a new phase of living, in more ways than one, making the transition from companion to Amanda's general helper, without fuss or bother. Neville returned to town a day or two later, having urgent business there. Saranne heard via Janet that he had gone to officially resign his army commission in order to run the affairs of The Grange, which was now his.

Nor did she see much of Clara or her mother after that, either. Both were bent upon a positively feverish round of shopping for Clara's trousseau, mostly in Bath, but there were also expeditions up to the shops in London. The old schoolroom that had been Clara and Neville's when they were young was now turned into an office for Saranne.

A bleak room facing north, it overlooked the stables at the rear of the house and was rather plainly furnished with an ink-stained old table and a chair. The fireplace was too small and only lukewarm heating emanated from it in winter. In one corner was a big closet containing an ample supply of writing materials, pens, paper, all the stationery she might need in her work as Amanda's amanuensis.

Amanda had effected changes in the girl's status in the house, too, in one fell swoop as it were, removing Saranne from her former sheltered existence as unofficial favorite of old Mrs. Arundale, into that of mere paid menial. She evicted Saranne from the luxurious bedroom she had hitherto enjoyed, on the plea that it was needed for visitors.

"We shall need all the rooms we can get to sleep all the guests arriving for Clara's wedding," Amanda explained with sweet firmness, dripping honey. "Family connections who simply must be accommodated, you know?" There was a steely purpose in Amanda's voice as she continued: "Janet's old room is quite nice, I believe. I am sure you will like it!"

Janet's room was through a door at the end of the landing containing old Mrs. Arundale's bedroom, a door marked "Private. Staff Quarters." Saranne's new room was sandwiched between cook's and the butler, Starn's, in the floor given over to "upper servants." Janet had now departed to her brother's farm and the start of a new life, as she had promised.

The room was narrow, as were all the others in the block, a mere cubicle, but Janet had made it as comfortable as possible. There was a cheap, pretty cotton counterpane upon the single bed, matching drapes at the one window. It overlooked a spur of the moors, all green and brown now. But when the heather came out, it would be a-shimmer with glorious purple color, she mused.

She loved that view of the moors. As time went on, she clung to it as if it were a lifeline. It greeted her first thing in the morning when she opened her eyes, and was the last thing she beheld before she drew the drapes shut at night. In the chill of her environment now, it was like a warm friendly hand stretched out to hers. There was a thin rug upon the bare boards of the floor, but that was all. I suppose it could be made comfortable, she mused thankfully, her spirits rising again. If not elegant!

She unpacked her trunks once more, putting their contents away in the small closet beside the window, the one chest of drawers, old and rickety. The few books, treasures in the way of trinkets and ornaments she had salvaged from her life with the Soames in London, she laid out upon the mantleshelf, the broad windowsill.

The fact that she and Clara were away from home so often in those days, shopping for her daughter's nuptials, gave Amanda just the excuse she needed to further encroach upon Saranne's freedom of movement.

"Why don't you have your meals on a tray, up here in your office?" Amanda suggested. "Much better than eating by yourself in the dining room!"

"Of course, Mrs. Arundale—anything you wish," Saranne agreed heavily, with an inward sigh.

"Besides," Amanda wound up practically, her brilliant, artificial smile deceiving nobody, least of all Saranne, "it will make it easier for the servants that way."

A few days after she had moved into Janet's old room, Saranne was called downstairs to Amanda's sitting room, where she found the two lawyers, Mr. Blair and DeLacey waiting for her, a happily beaming Amanda in the background. It was DeLacey who took out a penknife, trimmed and handed a new quill pen to her. Saranne took it coldly, distastefully, keeping an icy distance.

She signed the array of documents laid out upon the table before her without a word. She bent her shining red head low over them and when it was finished, silently handed his pen back to Jerome DeLacey without speaking. There was a new, thoughtful expression on his lean lawyer's face as he took it from her gently, a strange look in the dark blue eyes.

But she noticed nothing of this, anxious now only to get it all over and done with, for good. It was out of her hands and she wanted to thrust the whole sorry business out of her mind forever, never to be dredged up again. She gave them all a stiff little curtsy and walked from the room, her red head held proudly high.

She felt her attitude toward the Arundale attorney changing, becoming harder now. No longer the raw, inexperienced girl of a few short summers ago, her eyes full of dangerous, precious dreams, she saw him now with a clearer vision altogether, from a different angle—and scorned what she saw.

She made a silent vow then to herself, to keep out of his way in future, for the few short weeks longer she would remain at The Grange. As far as it was in her power to do so, she would avoid him like the plague, she vowed! I will give him no further excuse to cross my path, she thought firmly.

But plans, she discovered, oft went awry, however carefully made. Within the orbit of his marked distrust, dislike, of her, the outlines were becoming blurred, losing their distinct outlines. And the sands of his prejudice against Saranne Markham were running out for Jerome DeLacey, too, had he only known it.

Having learned to ride in Italy, she borrowed a mount now from Clara, a quiet mare called Brownie. Clara jumped at the offer of having it exercised other than by a groom and agreed eagerly, too busy herself to ride Brownie every day now. The breathtakingly lovely landscape around The Grange was simply crying out to be explored and this was Saranne's opportunity. Clad in her green velvet habit, which brought out the misty grayness of her eyes, alight with anticipation, she clasped the reins in her gloved hands staring down at Clara.

"I think I'd better get in some practice first, don't you?" she hazarded.

She walked the mare down the drive in the bright spring sunshine, out of sight of The Grange and its many windows, like inquisitive eyes, spying upon her. Rounding a bend in that dim, sheltered tunnel of trees at last, she cantered away. Although sadly out of practice, she persevered, her slight awkwardness in the saddle soon wearing off. In an hour or two she found herself picking it up where she had left off, in Italy.

Thereafter she was no longer tied to the immediate environs of The Grange itself, the grounds, but happily mobile now, free to go where she wished, without question. On Brownie she took off like a bird in flight, in any direction she chose, under the wide blue skies, over the moors. She had ample free time, for her post with young Mrs. Arundale was not an onerous one.

On one of these afternoons, when she had taken a book from the saddlebag upon Brownie's back, she sat with her spine comfortably against a boulder, a moorland stream gurgling and purling at her side, plunging down from the hills. The silence, peace, up there was golden, its balm sinking into her sore spirit, healing and cleansing, emptying her mind of all its ragbag of troubles.

Presently she laid her book down upon her knees, while the mare grazed quietly nearby, when a shadow fell across the page. So engrossed was she with her own thoughts that she had not heard him approach silently over the springy turf. She looked up, startled, to find the dark eyes of Mr. DeLacey gazing down at her quizzically. Instinctively she shut the volume to with a snap and scrambled to her feet, vexed with herself for thus being caught off her guard.

"Enjoying the freedom of the moors?" he asked her ironically. "You are welcome to, as far as I am concerned," he went on with a slight bow. "These are my lands, you know?"

It was the worst possible thing he could have said under the circumstances, as he realized later to his acute dismay. Involuntarily she recoiled from him, towering above her in the heather, taking a few steps backward as her face clouded over. No, she was aware of no such thing, she told herself forlornly! That any part of the moor belonged to him. The moor was a solitary place, miles from anywhere, free to all—or so she had thought.

Certainly the last thing she had expected was to find her privacy, peace, invaded by, above all people, Mr. Jerome DeLacey. She bit her lip, straightening up to face him, her chin raised at a mutinous angle, challengingly.

"I imagined these moorlands were wild, free, belonged to nobody!" she cried.

He cut her short, almost with amusement, coolly. "They mostly are," he assented calmly. "But some are what is termed 'enclosed' and they have owners. I am one of them." He

paused expectantly and Saranne sighed inwardly.

She reflected dismally that she never
seemed able to come off best in any encounter
with Mr. DeLacey! He was dressed casually in
rough country clothes that day, a fowling gun
under his arm, a sporting dog, an Irish retriev-
er whose ruddy coat shone like copper-beech
leaves in the sun as it squatted a short distance away, tongue hanging out like a slice of
pink ham.

With an air of defeat she turned away,
prepared to mount Brownie. Automatically he
stepped forward to assist her, laying down the
gun, and as mechanically she accepted that
service, placing one slender foot in its riding
boot of soft Viennese leather into his cupped
palms. She was half lifted, half helped into the
saddle, gathered the reins in her hands, and
rode away without a backward glance.

Her head, in the plumed hat, was bent
low against the slightly blowing spring breeze,
fresh and chill, the gray eyes misted now,
bright with unshed tears. Her cup of unhappiness was full to overflowing, she thought incoherently, guiding the mare home while
scarcely knowing what she was doing. Tears
Jerome DeLacey did not see—how could he, in
his ignorance?

She left him in undisputed possession of
his moor, Saranne reflected indignantly, the
mare's hoofbeats dying away as horse and rider
vanished from his sight. And he—was he proud
of his victory, he asked himself truthfully, now

that his petty hour of triumph had again come and gone? He did not know, was not sure of any of his feelings, emotions, now, tramping the ling underfoot as he went, his dark eyes brooding, concerned. If only she had said something, behaved differently, he reflected angrily, watching that slim figure in the green habit ride away.

She was getting under his defenses, disturbing his peace of mind in a way that he did not like. For Saranne, her unpleasant encounter with him upon the moor just now strengthened her resolve never, if possible, to cross paths with him again. In future, she determined, she would take pains not to set foot upon his land, but keep to the verges of the moors, which could not be said to belong to anybody but the king!

Yet on one further occasion Jerome DeLacey drove by in a light, fast, sporting carriage. His hands firmly upon the reins, he went swiftly by without stopping. But he had seen that slight figure down below, sitting reading in a dip of the ground, sheltering just off the road from the wind, the crisp breezes which blew there at all times, up on the moors. His brow knitted, as he passed on his way in an oddly disturbed frame of mind. Moved by he knew not what impulse of remorse, regret for the past, he drew rein then upon the crest of the hill above, staring down at the object of his thoughts, dwarfed by distance.

Saranne, engrossed in her book, had not noticed the carriage on the bluff above. And by the time she had become conscious of it, turning her head to gaze after it with only indifferent interest, it was gone, too far away in its own cloud of summer dust for her to recognize its occupant.

He had experienced a wholly irrational desire to break his journey and go down to where she was, beg her to forget their differences, the many angry words he had used toward her and forgive him, to use any part of the moor, *his* moor, as she wished. He curbed that impulse, as he had curbed so many others in his life, clamping down on it as a disgraceful sign of weakness, and drove on. Yet his heart was strangely heavy, cheerless, as he did so.

Clara was married that autumn, a very pretty wedding as it turned out, to her beloved Giles Fairley. There were boy pages in mock court dress, knee breeches, filmy white lace ruffles at neck and wrists, miniature bridesmaids to accompany them. Neville came down from London to give his sister away. He had a land agent now, spending most of his own time at the gaming tables in Bath or town.

Saranne plunged more feverishly than ever into work after that, to take her mind off other, more important things, clearing up the last vestiges of correspondence connected with the marriage, posting off the tiny boxes of white iced cake festooned with silver horseshoes, Cupids, favors of all kinds, settling bills and drawing up checks on Amanda's account.

She awoke one morning in her narrow bed, just before the bridal pair returned to their new farmhouse from a honeymoon in Brighton, to the dismal certainty that there was nothing more for her to do now. And then fate or young Mrs. Arundale, or both, struck out of the blue once more to save her. Amanda had a large share of the innocent vanity which seems a predominant trait in the make-up of the artist.

"It has long been my intention to write my memoirs, Miss Markham," she announced. She added, half proudly, half shyly: "I was on the stage, you know, before I met Mr. Arundale and married him."

"Yes—your daughter told me," Saranne said.

"Did she? I thought you could write it all down for me, copy it in your best copperplate hand, to send it to a publisher," Amanda went on. "I have all the notes for it somewhere!"

Saranne smiled. "Very well, Mrs. Arundale," she said.

And so she went to work again. Mrs. Seaham had accompanied her daughter to Clara's wedding—Undine was one of the maids of honor—and Saranne thus met that lady for the first time. She was not impressed, judging her to be a vain, purseproud social climber of the worst kind, who looked down on those she considered her inferiors while assiduously cultivating the company of her "betters."

Mother and daughter stayed on for a few days longer at The Grange after Clara's wedding, as guests of young Mrs. Arundale. Their own modest villa was shut up for the nonce—"Not worthwhile bringing our staff down from town," Mrs. Seaham said airily, to any who would listen.

As an old friend of the attorney from "way back when," as she let it be known, Mrs. Seaham spent most of her time trailing after Mr. DeLacey, whenever he put in an appearance at The Grange, while Undine occupied herself with Neville during the short time he was there before going back to London. For some reason that she could not fathom, Saranne took an instant dislike to Mrs. Seaham. Which is foolish of me, I know, she told herself ruefully, for our paths are hardly likely to cross!

Nonetheless, those nebulous fears, doubts, remained, unspoken questions taking root in her mind. But, as time went on, she forgot Mrs. Seaham and her daughter, driven out of her thoughts by pressure of work, laboriously copying down by hand with a quill pen young Mrs. Arundale's famous memoirs. Nor did she see Mr. Jerome DeLacey again for some time, for which small mercy she was duly thankful.

Except for one unfortunate occasion when Amanda came to a point in her projected volume when she struck a snag. Dictating to Saranne, she needed to write, she said, a chapter dealing with the old County families like the Arundales, into which she had married.

"I know—or care, so little about the subject," she admitted to Saranne, who was busy scribbling, her pen scratching. "But I suppose Mr. DeLacey would know—he's our archivist of the district, interested in such things, ancient history of the neighborhood and the like. It is a hobby of his."

"Indeed, ma'am?" She was shaken out of

her normal diplomatic neutrality where the memoirs were concerned, at the mention of the hated name.

Amanda nodded and pulled the heavy crimson cord of the bellpull in order to summon a servant. A maid came and young Mrs. Arundale instructed her to have a groom saddle a horse and ride over to Lacey Place, the attorney's home, with a message, asking his help. The result of this correspondence by proxy, as it were, was seen a few days later, when Amanda informed her assistant that they would be going to tea with Mr. DeLacey on the morrow's afternoon.

"To pick his brains for my book," Amanda announced with glee. "Don't forget to take pens and papers with you, therefore," her employer continued, "to take notes!"

Saranne felt trapped, but she also realized that there was no way out of this impasse, at least for her. Aware that she was in no position to demur, to evade yet another critical encounter with the Arundale attorney, she duly thrust writing materials into a bag as ordered by Amanda and prepared to accompany that lady over to Lacey Place. They were driven in the carriage by Winters, the aged coachman, whom Amanda had retained in her service.

They were shown by Mr. DeLacey's pleasant faced elderly housekeeper into a room which Saranne rightly presumed to be the library. A huge fire of logs burned and crackled upon the open stone hearth, sending out a warm welcome. Ripples of golden light, reflections of the flames, danced upon the oaken paneling of the walls, the seemingly endless tiers of books, in rich scarlet and gilt bindings. The firelight shone, further, upon the solid silver tea set laid out upon a tray, with plates of wafer-thin sandwiches, freshly made hot scones and tiny, feather-light cakes.

The housekeeper bustled in at this moment with tea and hot water, as Amanda pulled off her gloves languidly, preparatory to pouring, playing hostess for Mr. DeLacey. At one end of the long refectory table there, a number of books had been laid out, with slips of paper protruding from their pages.

"I have hunted out these volumes for you," DeLacey said quietly, following the direction of Saranne's enquiring glance at them. "You will find all you need there." He paused, gazing enigmatically at that red head under the dove-gray bonnet, turned away from him now. Then he laughed, lightly. "But I am afraid they are only a random sample of the books on my shelves," he cried. "I need someone to catalogue them for me!"

Saranne did not reply, beyond composedly getting out the pencil and notebook she had brought with her, starting to write, taking down notes. And so the incident passed, not referred to by either again during the rest of the visit.

Autumn drifted into winter and the leaves on the solitary tree outside the ex-schoolroom window began to fall, leaving it bare and shivering. It became colder, grayer out of doors, with more than a hint of coming snow upon the wind. She could not ride anymore with a degree of comfort, even in a heavy cloak, and so was confined more or less to the house.

By mid-December the book was nearly finished. Young Mrs. Arundale in a state of twittering expectation, excitement, as Saranne transcribed the last few pages of the manuscript, so that the latter had little leisure, even if she had wanted to, to note the air of feverish gaiety about The Grange as Christmas drew near.

A radiant Clara and her new husband, back from their honeymoon, were staying at The Grange, as their own home was not quite ready. The Seahams, mother and daughter, were also there. And the master, Neville, was coming down from town as soon as he could tear himself away. There were also almost daily visitors, young folk from neighboring estates, coming over in carriages or upon horseback to congratulate Mr. and Mrs. Fairley. It is going to be quite a lively house party, Saranne mused wistfully, looking on from the sidelines.

Great branches of fir were chopped from the trees upon the estate; vast quantities of ivy and other greenstuff dragged by the Arundale foresters into the house. Clara, Undine Seaham and the female household staff became exceedingly busy, festooning the dark-green sprays and trailers up the banister rail of the staircase and along the paneled walls, turning the grand entrance hall into a bower.

When it was all finished, laughing and joking amidst much teasing of the female maids by their male counterparts, the mistletoe was hung up, in huge bunches. They threw colored paper streamers over it at the last, oranges and apples, nuts on strings that glowed cosily in the soft light when the candles were lit. At the foot of the stairs stood a large tub, securely ensconced in its massive brown wooden foundations, in which were laid the gaily wrapped parcels, packages, the presents to be exchanged between the family and their friends.

It was all very cheerful at The Grange on that snowy December night. Or so Jerome De-Lacey thought, having ridden over early and entered the house amidst a general chorus of welcome. A huge fire of logs was burning upon the stone hearth, every chandelier in the place was alight, casting their assembled brilliance down upon the company below. Clustering around the fireplace, sharing its warmth, all the ladies present bloomed like so many flowers, he mused, surveying them with approval. Jewels in their hair, upon slender arms and wrists, about white throats, flashed muted fire.

Above all, the ivy and holly wreaths, twining the stairs, dominated the scene. Gazing up into all that greenery, the loaded branches, as Clara and Undine Seaham put the finishing touches to it, he smiled quizzically. Undine, pouting, archly pointed out the salient features of their handiwork, asking prettily for praise.

"Worked like Trojans all the afternoon, didn't we, Clara?" she pleaded, greedy for approbation.

"I'm sure you did—and it does you credit, my dear," he said soothingly.

At this point Mrs. Seaham broke loose from

the crowd around the fireside and made for the attorney with a determined air, well aware of how handsome he looked in the stark severity of his evening wear, the white ruffles at neck and wrists setting off his dark eyes and hair. The best looking man in the room, Mrs. Seaham mused complacently. And what a catch, too, matrimonially speaking!

Bar one, of course, her prospective son-in-law, Neville Arundale. But Mr. DeLacey seemed distrait, absent-minded, this evening, his mind upon other things. His replies to Mrs. Seaham's bright, vapid, determinedly coy chatter were monosyllables for the most part, as if his mind, his real self were miles away, up in her lonely office with Amanda Arundale's amanuensis, Saranne Markham, perhaps.

He glanced hurriedly around the great hall as he entered, as if he were searching for something—or someone. His face fell as he saw that she was not there, his expression thenceforth becoming crestfallen, glum. Yet he aroused himself sufficiently enough when Amanda, an old friend, appealed for his help in acting unofficially as master of ceremonies, to get the party going. Neville, whose chore as host this really was, was otherwise engaged at the moment, dancing attendance upon Undine Seaham.

DeLacey shook off his mood of despondency and agreed, appealing for volunteers. Nor was the significance of his swift glance around the hall, as he entered, lost upon Mrs. Seaham. Nor the distant, unflattering answers he gave to her wittiest sallies. Her brilliance was manifestly lost upon him, she thought indignantly. His mind, his reflections, to say nothing of his dark, searching glance were obviously elsewhere.

Searching for *what?* she demanded of herself, feverishly. Mrs. Seaham frowned, pouting like her daughter just now. Indeed, the likeness was remarkable, he thought. . . . She resolved to make one last effort to gain his attention, make him rise to her bait at last. Unable to contain herself or her chagrin any longer, she began archly: "I wonder where dear Amanda's little maid-of-all-work, her so-called secretary, Miss Markham, can have hidden herself?" she observed sweetly, dripping a mixture of honey and pure vinegar.

He started, vexed at her reading his thoughts. "How should I know?" he retorted gruffly, shrugging. He added, pointedly: "I am not her keeper—she may have gone home for the holiday."

"Is that your solution?" she cooed, and shot him a surprisingly sharp look. "Your explanation for her absence?"

He shrugged again, saying no with such a chill lack of further interest in his level tones, that even the thick-skinned Mrs. Seaham hurriedly decided to change the subject for the nonce—or else drop it altogether! Warned by his look of cold finality, she accepted defeat at last, but with a very bad grace. If only for the time being— But I will tackle him again on the topic, at some future date, she promised herself darkly.

Or else "pump" her friend and former colleague at the Theater Royal in Bath, Amanda Arundale, on the curious behavior of Jerome DeLacey in relation to Amanda's little chit of a companion. After a cold collation in the dining room on this Christmas Night, to spare the servants, the company played old-fashioned parlor games around the fire in the great hall, games that many had not indulged in since their childhood.

One of these was "Consequences," wherein each player wrote down a line of prose or poetry and handed the folded paper on to his next-at-hand to add his or her line, the whole being read out at the end amid much hilarity. Naturally, this needed pencils and papers, so pockets and vanity-bags were hastily turned out. In vain.

Then Amanda remembered the stationery closet up in the old schoolroom, where her secretary normally had her office. As the intensity of the games increased and there was a feverish hunt on for the necessary pencils, some paper having been found, Amanda, as the hostess, began to look harassed, her enthusiasm waning. She turned impulsively to her son.

"Neville, will you go up to the schoolroom and get some pencils?" she wheedled.

But Neville was otherwise engaged and seemed reluctant to obey his parent. Rather slowly, therefore, he began to disentangle his long legs from the melée of young people sitting around the fire and started to rise. Yet it was obvious that if he wanted to leave the group, it would mean that a number of people would be disturbed, especially the ladies in their elaborate long evening dresses. So it was Jerome DeLacey who went upstairs.

On such small pivots do earth-shaking events hang. . . . Despite his comparatively sedentary work, the attorney was far more athletic than Saranne, for one, would have given him credit. Besides, he kept himself in good shape by horse riding, walking whenever he could spare the time in his very busy professional life. He took the thickly carpeted stairs two at a time now, skimming over them.

He knew the geography of The Grange by heart, having been familiar with it since childhood. Knew exactly, too, where the young Arundales' old schoolroom lay. He had no difficulty in finding its whereabouts immediately, turning left and going straight to it directly he reached the wide landing at the top of the staircase, overlooking the hall below with its seasonal decorations.

DeLacey reached the door of the old schoolroom with no thought in his mind save to get the pencils and return to the hall below with no further delay. He seized the doorknob and turning it, stepped into the room beyond, only to stop in consternation the next instant, however.

"Miss Markham!" he exclaimed in utter confusion, surprise. He stared at her in a kind of shock, the brass doorhandle still gripped in his fingers.

Saranne, in turn, was almost as startled as he, staring at him. She dropped the book she was reading, sitting huddled over the miserable fire. A woolen shawl was about her slim shoulders in a vain attempt to foil the truly ferocious drafts that played about her red head in that old house and would not be located. Furthermore, the room was poorly lit and in that dim light looked more uninviting than ever, more so in contrast to the brightness of the hall he had just left.

They stared at each other in something like mutual shock for perhaps half a minute more. Then he acted, more in command of himself than Saranne, even completely taken aback as he was at the encounter. He stepped farther inside the bleak room then, closing the door behind him as he did so, as if conscious of the extra chill in the air he was letting in by his mere presence.

"Good evening," he said quietly. His ever-alert eye fell upon a tray at the end of the table, with the remains of a frugal meal upon it. He blurted out the question, sounding futile, foolish, even in his own ears: "So you have had your Christmas supper?"

"Yes, thank you, sir," she replied tonelessly.

Her voice was flat, as devoid of expression as her face, pale and downcast, as she looked at him standing there. But she did not move or rise from her chair by the fireside—indeed, she thought drearily, there was nothing to get up for, no reason why she should rise at this, his intrusion upon her privacy. Aloud she said coldly, from between stiff lips that scarcely seemed to move:

"Is there anything I can do for you, sir?"

"Pencils," he retorted briefly, with equal stiffness. He went on slowly, thoughtfully, not taking his dark eyes off her face, as if mesmerized by what he saw there: "Yes, that is it—some pencils, please?"

"Pencils?" she echoed in surprise.

"Yes." He nodded coolly. "For a silly parlor game the company is playing below. You did not go home for the holidays, then?" he shot at her suddenly, going off sharply at a tangent. She shook her red head slightly.

"No," she said icily, but did not vouchsafe any further information. She rose then and laid down her book. Placing it on the table face down, she went to the closet in the corner of the room. With her hand upon the door, she asked quietly: "How many pencils do you want, sir?"

"A number—more than a dozen, at least," he said.

Still without glancing at him or, indeed, giving any hint that she noticed his presence there at all, she reached up and opened the closet, took from one of its well-stocked shelves an unopened box of pencils. She held this in her hand for a moment, as if weighing something, then asked distantly, in a blank tone:

"Do you wish to have them sharpened, sir?"

"Yes, I suppose they must be—can you arrange it for me?"

"Very well, sir," she said composedly. She added pointedly: "It will take some little time to do, sir—please don't wait. I will bring them down to you when done."

Chapter
7

Strangely enough, it seemed that this was what Mr. DeLacey did require, was quite agreeable to the suggestion. His eyes narrowed as he watched her, as if in the grip of a sudden idea, one that had abruptly occurred to him out of the blue. As indeed one had. He would let her carry the sharpened pencils down to the hall, he planned exultantly, then by a stroke of sheer, unashamed cunning prevail upon Amanda to invite the girl into joining the company there!

It was a shame, a disgrace, he thought self-righteously, that she was up here, shut away from all that gaiety and light below! He murmured a preoccupied word of thanks and withdrew then, intent only on his plan and its successful conclusion. She did not reply or look up as he le t, her shining red head bent low over the pearl-handled penknife she had taken from a drawer in the schoolroom table.

Jerome DeLacey went downstairs once more, thoughtfully this time and more slowly than he had mounted them a short time ago. He found that during his absence the company had shelved by mutual consent its wish for parlor games and was now engaged in desultory conversation among themselves. Yet Amanda glanced at him sharply as he reached the bottom stair.

"Ah, there you are, Jerome—you have been a time!" she exclaimed suspiciously. "The pencils—did you get them?"

"No." He shook his dark head absently. "Miss Markham was there—she will bring them down in a minute. They needed sharpening," he explained.

He decided that his tackling of Amanda could wait until Saranne herself appeared in person in their midst. Therefore he waited, biding his time, until some movement, the flutter of a skirt perhaps, drew his attention to the rear of the hall, where a green baize-lined door gave onto the servants quarters. Saranne was coming through that door now, but she did not approach furher. With a slight gesture toward his, DeLacey's, direction, she gave the packet she carried to the nearest guest, a young man.

Why did she not use the main staircase? DeLa ey marveled. He frowned, for then he knew. The wedge, it appeared, had been only too firmly driven between Saranne Markham and the Arundales and their guests. A wedge partly of his own making and for which he himself must take most of the blame, he reflected with an inward groan. A line of division for which he, and to a lesser degree Amanda, were responsible. They had succeeded finally, beyond their wildest dreams, in putting "the Markham girl" in her place. At this point in his reflections, his heart heavy, he glanced up at the minstrels' gallery above.

The glimmer of a pale face caught his eye, a slender figure crouched in the shadows beyond the railings there, staring longingly down at the happy scene below. Then he acted swiftly for the second time that night, on his own volition, leaving his hostess and fellow guests and racing up the stairs. And, as she saw him coming, Saranne started to her feet in dismay.

And so they confronted each other once more, in the gloom at the top of the grand staircase. Staring frozenly at him as if he were a ghost, some spectral visitor from another world, she was wide-eyed, on the defensive at once. This time, however, she did not tarry. Her whole instinct lay in flight, to get away from his dangerous proximity as soon as possible.

And so she moved, darting past him before he could thrust out a hand to detain her. Running soundlessly along the thickly carpeted landing and through the door marked "Private," out of his reach. He did not hear any bolt shot nor the key turned in its lock, but there was no need for that, he knew. She was as effectively cut off from him, separated from him and his kind as if an iron shutter had clanged to in his face between them, in the servants' block of the house.

He faced the truth then, in that bitter moment of anguish, self-realization. Knew that, beyond the bounds of all reason, expediency, he loved her, that nameless little nobody, wanted her with every fiber of his strong being, longed for her—now, when it was too late. By his own conduct toward her in the past he had alienated her from him forever—yet had he? Was there still a tiny glimmer of hope?

He did not know, yet he felt a surge of pain, a fierce pang of remorse, regret, going through him, his heart as low as his spirits. He raised a hand to rap upon the door panel, then let it drop again hopelessly, despairingly, to his side. What was the use?

"Oh, Saranne, my little love," he whispered to the empty corridor, in a voice that was almost a groan, so charged with emotion was it, a longing that he could not control. "I love you, my darling, I realize that now, when it is too late!"

The echo of an old poem came back to him:

Look in my face, my name is Might-
    Have-Been,
I am also called No More, Too Late,
    Farewell,
Unto thine ear I hold the Dead Sea
    shell,
Cast up thy Life's foam-fretted feet
    between . . .

There was no reply from beyond that closed door, no sign that she heard him, nor did he expect one. Saranne had gone straight to her room and lay weeping, face downward on the narrow bed, her burning cheeks pressed into the damp pillow. She was worn out with the events of the evening just past, all her nerves distraught and on edge. And so, crying softly, she dropped off to sleep at last, to dream, not of Neville Arundale, but of Mr. De-Lacey like an avenging Nemesis, pursuing her.

The Christmas vacation merged into the New Year and one day, in the weeks which followed, young Mrs. Arundale was able to announce gleefully that her memoirs had reached their end. The book was finished, all neatly copied down in Saranne's best handwriting, bound and ready to be sent to the London publishers. Saranne herself took it to the village posting-box, to be collected by the stagecoach which carried His Majesty's Mails, and so brought to town.

Returning from a brisk walk on this errand, as she flung back the hood from her red curls and unfastened her cloak in the hall Saranne thought it a good and opportune moment to reopen the question of her future at the Grange again. Amanda seemed scarcely to listen, in a twitter of excitement.

"Oh, but you can't leave me yet, Miss Markham!" she exclaimed in alarm when Saranne broached the subject. She frowned. "I can't, won't allow it! Who is going to help me with the proofreading and so on, when the book is accepted? Write to my friends and acquaintances, telling them to buy a copy? No, I need you."

Saranne felt a curious mixture of relief and exasperation at the news that she was to stay on at The Grange for a further period of time. She had undoubtedly grown attached to the West Country in the short while she had been there, she thought, learned to love it. She would be sorry to say goodbye to it all. She did not look forward with any enthusiasm to the idea of searching for another post just yet.

Mr. DeLacey came to tea, closeted in her drawing room with Amanda a few days after that. And the outcome was oddly bizarre from Saranne's viewpoint, at least, filling her with a gloomy sense of foreboding, rather than bliss, when the suggestion he had made was broken to her gently that evening by her employer. It was a scheme that, while sensible enough on the surface, had pitfalls, hidden menacing quicksands that appalled Saranne.

"There is nothing at all for you to do here at present, Miss Markham," Amanda said sweetly. "So, until the book is ready, I have agreed to lend your services to my attorney, Mr. DeLacey, to help in cataloguing his extensive library."

Saranne gasped. It was a plan that distressed her beyond words, yet she also reminded herself grimly that she was powerless to resist if she desired to keep her present post. And she was fair-minded enough to see the logic of it. The issue was brutally clear. She could bow her head to the inevitable and agree, or refuse and be out of a job. It was as simple as that.

She chose the former solution. Saranne sighed, reflecting that there was no way out of this impasse save the one she had chosen. Swallowing her pride, resentment, with an effort, she said meekly to Amanda:

"Very well, Mrs. Arundale, I will do as you—and Mr. DeLacey wish. When would you like me to begin?"

"As soon as possible, please," Amanda said briskly, relieved that the girl was going to be "sensible" about it after all, raise no objections. "How about tomorrow morning, if you like?" she suggested eagerly, reaching out a thin, clawlike hand to the crimson-cord bellpull. "I will send to Mr. DeLacey, tell him you are coming."

"If you please, ma'am," Saranne said wearily, nodding. No sense in stalling any longer, she thought sadly, with a shrug of resignation.

On the following morning she gathered together all the impedimenta she might need for her new situation, and entering the Arundale's second-class carriage, kept for such expeditions as this, was driven over to Lacey Place. It was a short, easy ride between the two homes, and if she had not been so depressed, feeling like a criminal going to her doom, Saranne might have enjoyed it.

As it was, she reached DeLacey's house in record time. To her surprise the man himself was waiting for her, early as it was, standing bareheaded upon the topmost of the three stone steps which led up to his front door. His carriage was waiting upon the gravel a short distance away and she noticed that he was wearing dark, city clothes.

He greeted her gravely, politely, and she replied with a marked stiffness, overcome by her usual tongue-tied diffidence in his presence. He wasted no further time, but led the way into the house without another word and into the library off the hall that she knew from her previous visit. A cheerful fire had been lit there on his orders to welcome her, and he then showed Saranne a few simple plans he had formulated for listing the books there.

"Adding a brief description to each," he said and laughed wryly, laughter in which she did not join. "It is only the tip of the iceberg, I'm afraid," he went on apologetically, ruefully, with a grin. "You won't be able to do much more than skim the surface of things, Miss Markham, in the time available." He paused, stroking his chin thoughtfully. "Has Mrs. Arundale heard anything of her volume of memoirs yet?"

"Not yet," Saranne said evasively.

"Ah, well," he murmured absently, staring down at her. Amanda and her affairs seemed markedly remote from his thoughts just then, despite his query. Finally he shrugged, reluctantly turning to leave. "Please don't attempt to touch any of the books on the higher shelves," he said earnestly. "Leave them—I don't want you falling off stepladders when there is nobody here to catch you," he finished genially, but Saranne's expression did not change.

"No, sir," she said woodenly. He hesitated then, looking at her thoughtfully before he spoke.

"Now, as to meals—?" he continued quietly, refusing to be put off by her chilly tone or discouraged. "Unfortunately I must go into Bath today, on legal business, to my office. But when I am at home—well, then I shall expect you to dine, have meals with me in my dining room."

"Oh, but I couldn't!" she began hastily in alarm, choking. "I always take my food alone, on a tray, at The Grange," she said quickly.

He smiled slightly. "I am aware of that," he retorted cryptically. His expression, as he looked at her, was an enigmatic one. "But there are no trays here," he went on pleasantly. "You must dine on your own today, but tomorrow I look forward to sharing a meal with you!"

And then he was gone, with that parting shot that sounded remarkably like an order. He was intolerable, she thought angrily, high-handed to a degree. Her ire rose, but before she could open her mouth to protest, however weakly, he was no longer there to listen, having scored his point. He had left, leaving her to work on in peace.

Surprisingly, considering all the events that had brought her there, she found it quite a change from the schoolroom at The Grange, far more comfortable, working in his library for Mr. DeLacey. She worked on busily and happily until the middle of the morning, when his housekeeper, whom she had already met, brought in a cup of hot chocolate. She beamed approval at the new young librarian, although it was also obvious that she was puzzled why, exactly, Saranne was there at all.

"Getting on all right, miss?" she asked in friendly fashion and Saranne smiled.

"Yes, thank you," she said.

The housekeeper nodded. "Well, drink up your posset, then," she said kindly. "Dinner is at twelve o'clock noon, in the dining room across the hall."

It felt strange, after the housekeeper had gone out again, to be sitting there in Mr. De-Lacey's house, drinking his chocolate, figuratively breaking bread with him even though he was absent, having the midday meal presently in solitary grandeur, eating his food. Tea was brought into the library in the early afternoon and after that she closed her notebooks, wiped her quill pens tidily with the penwipers provided, and prepared to go home, the Arundale carriage now having arrived for her again.

She left all her writing paraphernalia behind, as it seemed foolish to tote it all back and forth between the two households. But next morning, when she arrived at Lacey Place, she found a pile of notebooks, freshly cut quill pens, all that she might need in her work. A brief note in a strange handwriting that she rightly took to be his was propped up against it:

"This will save you from the chore of

bringing your own materials over. Jerome De-
Lacey."

And so life fell into a new pattern for Saranne. She successfully overcame the first ordeal
of a meal under his roof alone with Mr. De-
Lacey, a painful effort on her part. Just the two
of them at the long, polished table in his dining room, when he was at home and not in his
Bath office.

He had perfect manners when he chose and
he so chose now, seeking to put her at ease,
undo the harm done in the past. On the surface, at least, she seemed to respond, whatever
hidden tensions and emotions seethed beneath.
She was quietly aloof, remote, having learned
her lesson only too well, she thought bitterly!
Scarcely replying beyond a word or two to his
remarks.

Yet gradually, almost without her knowing
what was happening, he set himself out to
wear down all her poor defenses, win her con-
fidence once more, treating her gently, kindly,
with a consideration she would have never
imagined possible. She blossomed in turn, under this treatment, like a flower opening its
petals to the sun.

He showed a side of his nature now, a
facet of personality, his character, that she had
never even guessed at before. And slowly, so
imperceptibly that she scarcely knew it was
happening, she timidly learned first to like,
then trust him at last, the past forgotten. He
kindled a warmth in her heart toward him
which, although she did not realize it yet,

deepened in the end into true love. She looked forward now to the days when he stayed home.

And then one morning, soon after she arrived in the library and was spreading out her writing materials upon the table, he firmly gathered them all up in a pile again, sweeping them together.

"No work today, Miss Markham," he said with a slight smile, staring down at her almost boyishly, his keen, dark eyes unusually soft for him. "We are going shopping into Bath, you and I. That is, if you will accompany me? I find it necessary to buy a piece of jewelry for a young lady and would like your advice."

"Mine, Mr. DeLacey?" She looked up at him, startled. Then, as he nodded coolly, gathered up her reticule, gloves, the cloak that she had just taken off, preparatory to meekly obeying him.

Her mind was a jumble of excitement and despondency: pleasure at the thought of going into Bath with him, spending the morning there, disappointment and some other emotion that she could not fathom, a pain in her heart that was like a dagger, as her thoughts instantly flew to Undine Seaham. But Miss Seaham was in London, surely, doing the "season" with her mother, she reminded herself hopefully.

And no doubt seeing a great deal of Neville Arundale into the bargain! she thought scornfully.

It was a subdued Saranne who pulled up the hood of her dark-blue cloak again, hiding the red hair. It was a bright morning nonetheless and her spirits rose accordingly as she stepped into Mr. DeLacey's carriage, driving into Bath with him along the country lanes, narrow and winding and full of mud.

Bath, the city itself, enchanted her, with its hot pools dating back two thousand years to Roman times, the soft, grayish-yellow sandstone of its old, graceful houses. She gazed about her with vivid interest as they presently drove into its environs, her gray eyes alert and sparkling, so that he glanced down at her sideways, quietly smiling to himself, amused at her enthusiasm.

An inveterate sightseer ever since her days in Florence, she showed her pleasure at all the tourist sights, treasures and relics of the remote past placed on view. Good-humoredly, he indulged her every whim, acting as patient escort and guide all through the morning. Afterwards they dined at an ancient hostelry where it seemed Mr. DeLacey was an old and favored customer and greeted as such.

And where, also, it seemed that only the "best people" went, for seated at the next table in an alcove were the two people who had been foremost in Saranne's mind all that day: Mrs. and Miss Seaham. So it appeared she had been wrong, Saranne mused, in thinking they were in London, in close proximity to Neville Arundale. They were down here in Bath—and near Jerome DeLacey instead.

Her heart seemed to miss a beat at the thought. He was exchanging greetings with both mother and daughter now, easily, agreeably, but also without any undue warmth, threading his way past their table without stopping in his stride, a confused and unhappy Saranne in his wake. Both the Seahams gave her a long, cool stare as she passed, and an even colder, shorter nod of acknowledgement of her presence, but no more. It went no further than that for the time being.

"A small table for two, in the window preferably?" he asked the deferential elderly waiter.

They were given the table he asked for, in a corner overlooking the river below, the busy scene outside the bow-fronted window for Saranne's benefit. After the meal, which she enjoyed despite all her fresh forebodings about the Seahams, Undine came over and announced in a high, girlish voice, pointedly ignoring his companion:

"So sorry, but I simply must fly, Jerome! I have an appointment with my hairdresser, such a temperamental little man, he's coming at two of the clock to dress my hair, I must be home—I daren't keep him waiting!" She paused, changed her tone. "Shall we be seeing you soon, Jerome?" she asked almost casually.

"We are bound to meet somewhere, in Bath!" he countered lightly.

Undine, looking well pleased with herself for some unknown reason, went off then, scarf flying, again ignoring Saranne completely. Her mother was nowhere to be seen at that moment, having apparently gone off to the powder room of the inn. Saranne herself, his firm, guiding hand upon her elbow, stepped outside into the thin, wintry sunshine of the street and so they made their way to a jeweler's shop in the main thoroughfare. Yet oddly enough, Mrs. Seaham turned up again here, too—almost as if she had been following us, Saranne thought irritably.

Saranne was sitting upon a gilded chair beside the counter inside the shop by then, Jerome DeLacey by her side, both examining the tray of jeweled bracelets the assistant had laid out upon the glass-topped counter for their choice, when she happened to glance toward the shop window. Mrs. Seaham was outside, peering in through the bottleglass panes at the scene inside. She started back as she saw Saranne's enquiring gaze upon her, then deciding to put a bold face upon it, entered.

"So we meet again, eh?" Mrs. Seaham said with an attempt at gaiety, her eyes snakelike, glittering like the stones in one of the jeweler's bracelets.

Oddly enough, Saranne could have sworn in a court of law that Undine's mother seemed *triumphant*, rather than putting any other construction on it, at the sight of the tray of bracelets, nodding to herself in satisfaction. It was certainly very puzzling, Saranne mused in the background. Mrs. Seaham's small, beady eyes never left the jewelry, as if she would imprint its image upon her mental retina forever. But Mr. DeLacey was equal to the occasion, as she might have known, Saranne thought ruefully! He got rid of Mrs. Seaham somehow, suavely, then turned to Saranne, his face inscrutable.

"Choose one you would like," he urged

her with a forceful intensity, in a low voice. "As if you were choosing for yourself, Saranne!"

And it was at this moment that enlightenment burst like a glorious bombshell of certainty in Saranne's mind, filling her with joy, unbelievable happiness. Not only in his use of her given name for the first time, although that was wonderful enough, she mused delightedly. It might have been a kind of telepathy or perhaps just mere wishful thinking, but she was as certain as she had ever been convinced of anything in her life 'ere this, that he meant to buy the bracelet for herself!

Saranne glowed secretly, her eyes like twin stars at this discovery. She had never felt this way about Neville, deeply infatuated with him as she had been in the past. No, nor with George Bellemy, Arabella's George. This was something new, untried, that had never happened to her before. And her spirits rose accordingly to new heights, until they were in danger of hitting the ceiling! She dimpled, playing for time, savoring her delicious notion, asking demurely:

"What color are her eyes, this young lady? That is always a good indication, you know!"

"Eh? Whose eyes?" He looked baffled for a moment, staring down at her, his expression vague in the extreme. The next instant, however, he recovered himself, straightening up. "Oh, the young lady's? Blue-green, Saranne, something like your own," he said softly then.

"I somehow thought they might be," she said teasingly, with a smile.

She shyly indicated a particular bracelet with her gloved finger, a slender, exquisite trifle in worked gold set with diamonds and sapphires in a design of blue forget-me-nots, that marsh-loving flower.

"That one?" he asked tenderly. She nodded her red head.

"Yes, that is the one I prefer," she agreed simply.

It was not just the bracelet, lovely enough as that piece of the jeweler's art was, Saranne mused dreamily. It was the care, thoughtfulness, which lay behind the prospective gift that touched her heart, beating fast, high with love, gratitude, toward him now. It was the promise implicit in the present, in her rosy-tinted dreams, which held her. She watched as the clerk picked up the bracelet from its velvet bed amidst its fellows, laid it on one side as he looked around for a special box to put it in.

It was only when Jerome DeLacey was reaching into the inside pocket of his coat, to extract a little bag of gold coins, that Saranne awoke from her daydream at last. Sensitively, she hastily arose and wandered away from the vicinity of the counter, out of earshot, where Jeome DeLacey was now in earnest conversation with the clerk. She pretended to examine some Georgian silver in a display case while he paid for his purchase. He rejoined her at last, however, and Saranne—she could not help herself—looked at his hands in pleasurable expectation.

To her disappointment, they were empty. Then she remembered seeing him thrust something into an outside pocket as he came toward her and relaxed, her heart beating normally once more. It was manifest that if the bracelet, as she was quite sure in her own mind now, were for herself as she surmised, then it was obvious that he had decided upon a fitter, more opportune occasion in the future to give it to her! She was in no hurry, anyway, she thought, hugging her delicious secret to her breast. He will no doubt give it to me when he is ready, she mused impishly. As a big surprise!

But time went by and still Jerome DeLacey made no move to hand over the jeweled bracelet to her. Then the reaction set in and doubts, fears, began to creep into her sorely troubled mind. Could she have made a huge error, been mistaken in his motive for asking her aid in choosing the bracelet? Her spirits, from being mountain high, plunged right down to zero again.

Amanda Arundale's book of memoirs were accepted by a publisher in due course and would be brought out in the coming summer. She would be needed now, Amanda said, to help in the proofreading. Saranne's days as Jerome DeLacey's librarian, sorting out his books, were numbered, it seemed. And so she broke the news to him, secretly in sorrow, one morning when she arrived in the Arundale carriage at Lacey Place.

"Yes." He nodded calmly, apparently without regret or surprise, accepting the news coolly. "We both knew it could not go on forever, did we not, Saranne?" he said quietly. He smiled down at her. "All good things must come to an end at last, eh?"

So that was it, they were back where they started from, the barrier between them again —or so she imagined, in her ignorance. She faltered as her dreams faded away, died, turning from him that he might not see the gray eyes frosted with the tears of lost hope. Her happiness all quenched, like a flame that had cold water thrown over it. And it is all my own fault, alas, she thought forlornly. Oh, fool that I have been, to take him at his face value, after all that has passed between us in other days!

It would seem that she had been mistaken in his supposed reformation, tried to read more into his kindness than was really there. His change of heart did not exist, except in her fancy. Nothing had changed, nothing at all, and she had been a trusting fool to believe that it had, against her better judgment. Now she was being punished for it.

A day or two later she was dining at midday with Mr. DeLacey, perhaps for the last time, she reflected mournfully. It was one of the last meals she was likely to share with him à deux, for Amanda definitely wanted her back at The Grange at the end of that week. Saranne was in the midst of clearing up one or two things in the attorney's library before she left him for good.

"Mrs. Arundale wants me back now," she had told him earlier, quite calmly, even casually, as if it did not matter in the least to her.

For pride would not allow her to betray

her real feelings, confess how wretched she felt, to him of all people. How hurt she had been at his hands once again, wounded and humiliated in her secret dreams, hopes—this man, around whom she had woven such golden visions, in the few short weeks they had been together. Weeks glowing with an unspoken promise—was it all false, then, a mere figment of her heated imagination?

All that was gone now, she mused unhappily, crumbling a bread roll to pieces in her nervous fingers. For it seemed that he was still carrying a torch in his heart for the beautiful, the perfidious Undine Seaham, and further, had not a second glance to spare for one so humdrum, so ordinary, as her lowly self.

It was at this crucial moment, as Mr. De-Lacey was about to sit down to dine, that his housekeeper announced—"Two ladies, sir"—and ushered into their presence the very persons she had been thinking about, the Seahams, mother and daughter.

Each lady wore an identical royal-blue velvet riding habit, the long plumes in their high-crowned hats drooping coquettishly over one shoulder, to the right in the case of a virgin of marriageable age who was seeking a husband, like Undine, and to the left if a wife, as the strange protocol of the day demanded. Mrs. Seaham, in her tight jacket, looked big, over-busty, but Undine was slim and lissome as a boy. Mrs. Seaham apologized fulsomely: "Unwarranted intrusion, Jerome!" while taking the chair he wearily offered her with remarkable celerity—as if she feared he might change his mind.

She rarely took her sharp, inquisitive little eyes off Saranne all the time they were there, as if her carefully plucked and shaped eyebrows were curved into a silent, permanent interrogation mark. And yet, once again Saranne forced herself into a purely negative, passive role as a mere onlooker, the thankless place of second-best, stifling her own feelings, emotions, for the time being. As I am used to doing, she thought forlornly.

She became all that she had ever been before the incident of the bracelet, a humble menial, no more, in their eyes. He may or may not have been deceived by all this, the studied lightness of manner, impersonal to a degree, that she put on for the benefit of his visitors now. There were moments, off her guard, when Saranne found his dark eyes fixed upon her, a curious questioning, appealing expression in their depths, as if he were about to ask her something.

Undine, looking radiant in her velvet habit, elegant and completely at her ease in these surroundings, smiled at DeLacey and explained prettily that her mount had developed a sudden lameness in one of its legs and was out on the driveway now, being attended to by one of his grooms, aided by one of the Seahams'.

"As we were not far from Lacey Place, yours was the nearest house, Jerome, we decided to throw ourselves on your mercy, ask for help! We were on our way over to The Grange, to dine with Mrs. Arundale and her family," Undine finished.

"I'll look at your horse myself presently," he promised, looking none too pleased, Saranne thought. "Meanwhile you must dine here, of course. I will send a messenger over to Amanda to tell her what has happened."

"Or perhaps you could drive us over yourself, in your phaeton?" Undine suggested hopefully.

He shook his dark head. "Sorry, no—it is out of action, that is why I am home myself today. But I will send you in my carriage, if you will accept the loan of it after dinner. Your groom can take the horses home, then."

And with that, Mrs. Seaham had to remain content for the time being. Not for the first time, Saranne mused, during the rest of the meal that followed, did she know what it felt like to be the "gooseberry" at the feast, the fly in the ointment! A skeleton in the background of things, as far as Undine and her parent were concerned, she was sure.

By every means within their power mother and daughter succeeded during dinner in making Saranne feel the odd man—or woman—out. When it came to an end, had reached the stage when the housekeeper came in with coffee cups, she was glad to escape to the haven of the library again, where she was promptly joined by the elder of the two ladies, Mrs. Seaham. It was a dull, lowering day with more than a hint of coming snow upon the sharp wind. The candles had been lit in the book-lined room with its paneled walls, throwing a soft light over everything.

"Mr. DeLacey is out looking at my daughter's mount at the moment," Mrs. Seaham's explanation ran sweetly, to Saranne's disinterest. "So I thought I would wander in and chat to you, Miss—er—Markham, to while away the time, eh?" She laughed in an artificial manner, tittering. "I expect he will be out there for ages, as Miss Undine is with him—young people being young people, as they say!" And she laughed again, meaningfully. Her eyes as she spoke, indeed ever since she had first entered the room, were glued to Saranne's hands, her wrists, poised above the writing pad before her.

"Is there anything you wish to say to me, ma'am?" Saranne asked quietly, pausing.

Mrs. Seaham exclaimed aloud, then, ignoring that question. "Oh, I see you are not wearing it, after all," the unwelcome visitor cried in pretended astonishment.

Saranne started, but quickly recovered her poise. "Wearing what, ma'am?" she riposted dangerously.

"Why, the bracelet, of course—come, don't be coy with me, my dear! The one I saw you choosing with Mr. DeLacey in the jeweler's, that day in Bath."

"Oh, that bracelet." Saranne hedged again, wondering how best to foil this grossly inquisitive woman with her foxy eyes, how best to lull her vile suspicions. Aloud, she said slowly: "Yes, I helped Mr. DeLacey choose it, certainly. But," she admitted at last, reluctantly, "it wasn't for me, Mrs. Seaham. You are mistaken—it was meant for someone else!"

"I know that," Mrs. Seaham retorted unexpectedly, nodding, and incidentally taking all the wind out of Saranne's sails, metaphorically speaking. To her surprise, Mrs. Seaham added calmly: "It was for my daughter, Miss Seaham—or didn't you know?"

"Oh!" Saranne went red then white, gulping. "Did—did she like it, ma'am?" she asked after a long, long pause to cover her consternation, dejection, for want of something better to say. Her worst fears were realized now.

"No, I'm afraid not!" Mrs. Seaham laughed once more, simpering. "I will let you into a little secret, Miss Markham—she turned it down! You see, she is expecting to announce her betrothal to Captain Arundale at any day now. So it would not do, would hardly be wise, to accept a valuable present from one gentleman, while engaged to another, now."

"N-no, I suppose not," Saranne managed to stammer from between dry lips.

Mrs. Seaham glanced at her curiously, as she went on: "I imagined Mr. DeLacey might be buying a gift for Miss Undine that day," she admitted. "That is why I followed you into the shop. Call it a mother's natural curiosity in her daughter's interests, if you like—and he had strong hopes of my little girl, you know!" Mrs. Seaham laughed for the last time, a harsh, dry sound without any warmth in it, like the crackling of twigs under a pot. "So—forgive me, my dear, that is why I thought *you* would be

233

wearing it, that he had passed it on to you instead. After all, it can be of small value to him now, once Undine refused it."

Saranne passed a nervous tongue over her lips.

"But—but why should Mr. DeLacey give it to me?" she asked faintly, almost pleadingly, her face white.

"Oh, I don't know." And Mrs. Seaham shrugged in the tight jacket of her habit, as if the question were only of academic importance. "To sort of—er—repay you for working here, perhaps?" she suggested vaguely.

And then, having broken her phial of poison under the girl's nose, let the lethal vapors free, Mrs. Seaham smiled triumphantly and left the library, going in search of her daughter. Long after she had gone, Saranne sat motionless before the writing table, her sleek red head bent low, her hands lying listless and idle, while the noxious dose sank into her brain, the tissues of her being slowly dying by inches.

After a time she arose and quietly began to gather together all her writing materials for the last time, piling them in a little heap upon the table, for they were really Jerome DeLacey's property, not hers. She was dry-eyed, beyond tears, for all her heart was crying with a bitter, inward weeping.

She put on her heavy cloak, which she normally kept in a closet in the library, handy for going home every day. Busy with her own wretched thoughts, she did not hear his carriage start up outside the windows and drive away with the Seahams. Nor his entrance as he came noiselessly into the room soon after that, as she was fastening the clasp at her throat. He started as he saw her standing there, already dressed for going out, the hood drawn over the shining red curls.

"Why, Saranne!" He halted in amazement, taking in the fact that she was about to leave, the pile of writing things neatly stacked away for the night. "Leaving so soon?"

"I—I have a very bad headache coming on, sir!" She uttered the white lie desperately, in a toneless voice, 'ere he could go on. Her face, under the shadow of the dark-blue hood, was colorless, deathly pale. "So if you don't mind, sir, I would like to leave now?"

He frowned, his glance involuntarily going to the timepiece in the corner of the room, a massive grandfather clock, its hands crossed upon the ancient brass dial of its face standing at half-past two. Then he shrugged, nodding slightly, his own face clearing. The Arundale carriage always came for her each day at around half-past three, but today, perhaps, it was coming a trifle early in view of the lowering skies, boding snow.

"I am sorry to hear you feel unwell," he said with what seemed like genuine concern in his tone—only she knew better! His dark eyes looked thoroughly mystified as he gazed at her searchingly. A false concern, consideration, knowing what she knew now, Saranne thought scornfully! She stiffened, facing him accusingly, with a hostile air that did not escape his puz-

235

zled notice, as he went on smilingly: "A headache, my dear—or just the aftermath of those two ladies who have now left?"

How can he? she asked herself indignantly. Speaking of Undine and her mother like that, as if they meant nothing to him!

But Jerome DeLacey was speaking again:

"I would drive you home to The Grange myself," he said regretfully. "But as you know my phaeton is out of action. And the Seahams have borrowed the carriage. However, before you go, Saranne, there is something I want to give you—"

His expression changed then, became softer, less judicial, less stern, in a transformation that made his whole personality seem different somehow, more pleasing. Gone now was that brooding "look of eagles" she had noticed about him that day in the hall of The Grange just before old Mrs. Arundale died. And which she had applied to him, in her own mind, ever since.

He dipped his hand—oh, so casually, she thought—into the pocket of the coat he was wearing that day, taking out a small, flat leather case. Her heart contracted in a spasm of pain, turning over in anguish as she recognized it. It went on again in an uneven gallop after that, threatening to choke her.

A pleasant, innocent grin still faintly wreathing his dark face, he held the case out to her. "Here, my dear—catch!" he said jocularly. "It's yours—you chose it, remember?"

Yes, she remembered only too well, Saranne thought hotly, resentfully, all her worst

236

fears, suspicions, of him now well to the fore, about to be fulfilled. Ignorant of all the emotions the sight of the case aroused within her breast, he continued to hold it out toward her as she made no motion to take it from his outstretched hand. He narrowed his eyes as she raised a mute, reproachful face to his at last, the gray eyes on the verge of tears as she met his glance bravely.

"How dare you?" she flared, gasping. She flinched away from him, shrinking from taking the case from his extended grasp as if it, and he, were tainted, forbidden, evil.

"Why, Saranne, what is wrong?" he cried then, in dismay. "Why are you looking at me like that?" he demanded sternly. It was his turn to register doubt, uncertainty, now, his gaze going from the case to her white, agonized face, and back again. He frowned. "Look—it is only the bracelet you chose yourself in Bath," he reminded her quietly.

He sprung the catch of the jeweler's case with a flick of his strong fingers, revealing the ornament within. At once so lovely and so utterly wrong, it winked back at Saranne from its bed of white velvet, like a glittering, dangerous little snake. And, as she still made no move to take it, he seized her hand gently, closed her unresisting cold fingers around the offending case.

"Oh, no!" It was a hoarse, strangled cry that was torn from her then, her voice dropping to a whisper. She came to life as her fingers touched the case, almost as if galvanized by the feel of it. She dropped it upon the table beside her, near the clutter of writing materials, as if it had suddenly grown red hot, burned her flesh. "Yes, I remember it, Mr. DeLacey!" she cried stonily, raising scornful gray eyes to his dark blue ones. "As if I could ever forget it! Yes, indeed, you asked me to choose one for you—to give to another—Miss Seaham!" He started as she went on in a chill, frozen little voice that she scarcely recognized as her own: "And now that she has refused to take it, you think you can pass it on to me? A second-hand gift at best, for a paid hireling who has outlived her usefulness to you!"

She turned then, blindly groping for and finding her gloves, reticule, scarf, seized them and ran out of the room. Out of his house and, she hoped through her stifled sobs, out of Mr. DeLacey's life forever. He was too stunned, shocked even, to make any move to stop her in her headlong flight from his presence. Shaken to the very core of his being by this outburst, he could only stand as if rooted to the spot, staring at the place where she had been.

In front of his house was a circular gravel sweep which emerged from the drive, went round a bed of stiff, formal flowers in the middle, and thus down the entrance avenue to the gates again. He heard the sounds of the Arundale carriage approaching, the noise of the horses and jingle of their harness as the coachman cracked his whip. It paused for a scarcely perceptible moment to pick up Saranne from the steps, then moved on again, rumbling off down the drive out of carshot.

But a tragic mistake had been made, of

which Jerome DeLacey did not become aware until it was too late. After Mrs. Seaham had taken a fulsome leave of him and stepped into the borrowed carriage to join her daughter who was already seated in it, they had barely made the perimeter of the central flowerbed to reach the drive proper when Undine shouted a peremptory "Stop!" to the coachman.

It seemed that she had hidden in a pocket of the voluminous skirts of her blue velvet habit, a purloined apple from the dining table for her ailing horse. She now demanded to be set down near the DeLacey stables to comfort the animal with this.

"Really, what a tiresome child you are!" her mother exclaimed with some vexation. "Well, don't be long about it," she ordered testily. Ever her motto in life to be gracious to inferiors when it cost nothing, she smiled archly at the coachman aloft on his box, muffled to the ears in a livery greatcoat and woolen muffler. "I'm sure Grimes doesn't want to keep the horses standing about in this wind, do you, my man?"

Grimes said that he did not and Undine, ignoring her parent completely, walked away with her lithe, graceful stride, more like a youth than a girl in its easy freedom, to the DeLacey stables. She was gone for some considerable time, disobeying her Mama's strict injunctions to the contrary.

Like many of his calling, a lifelong professional coachman, Grimes was inured to spending long hours perched upon his driving seat in all kinds of weather. Even muffled, as he was now, up to his eyebrows in a long woolen scarf twisted around his neck and covering his mouth and chin, to say nothing of his great-coat, he began to grow restless. He could still feel the cold wind, penetrating like a knife. And, more important from Grimes's viewpoint, so did the horses, patiently awaiting Undine's return.

At last the coachman could stand it no longer. As Mrs. Seaham poked an exasperated head out of the carriage window for perhaps the third or fourth time, Grimes acted. Gathering together the leather reins in his gnarled, gloved hands, he brought the thongs smartly down upon the back of the nearest horse and made clicking encouraging sounds between his teeth, sounds meant to awaken it to life.

The horses responded and the carriage jerked forward, Grimes driving it at little more than walking pace around the sweep of gravel drive in front of the house. It was its wheels crunching upon the gravel that DeLacey heard, making the unfortunate error of taking it for The Grange equipage coming to collect Saranne. Mercifully, as Grimes approached his starting point again, Undine chose this moment to reappear from the stables, greeted by a tirade, a scolding from her irate mother that she bore with the stoicism of long experience. Hampered by the long velvet skirts of her riding habit, Miss Seaham then clambered into the carriage, which rumbled off into the night.

Jerome DeLacey stood without moving, in

frozen uncertainty, for some minutes after Saranne had fled his presence so angrily. She left him standing beside the long library table, very tall, very quiet, still as a statue carved out of wood rather than a living man. He seemed deep in thought, puzzled rather than infuriated, as she had been. Then he squared his shoulders proudly, not easily given over to be the prey of emotions, his expression calm rather than showing any regret, disturbance. Finally he picked up the offending piece of jewelry from where Saranne had flung it down and, replacing it in its case, put that in turn in his pocket.

Confound those Seahams! he thought, his brow growing dark under the even darker hair as his speculations uncannily flew to the only possible explanation of Saranne's behavior. It *must* be Mrs. Seaham or her empty-headed, silly daughter, Undine. Laura Seaham or the beautiful, feather-brained Undine, a dutiful copy of her scheming, cunning parent, must have plotted together and told a pack of lies to Saranne, turning her against him. Either that or I'm a Dutchman, he mused grimly.

Why or how they had managed it he could not tell, but they undoubtedly had succeeded, only too well! And his dear, foolish girl had been taken in by it. He shrugged then, determined to ride over to The Grange in the morning and make his peace with her, give any explanations that were necessary, that might be called for. If Saranne came back no more to Lacey Place—in the role of amanuensis, at any rate! And he smiled tenderly, lost in dreams.

He went over in leisurely fashion to an

armchair by the fireplace and sat down, drawing out and lighting a long, white, old-fashioned clay "churchwarden" pipe, much affected by fashionable men of the period. It gave him some comfort, puffing on it, soothing his ruffled nerves. He was so preoccupied by it that he did not this time hear the approach of yet another vehicle to the house, the crunch of its heavy wheels upon the gravel outside, which in any case was now fast becoming cushioned with snow.

He had scarcely lit and puffed out the first bowlfuls of tobacco from his pipe, when his housekeeper put in an uneasy appearance in the doorway, glancing about the library in some surprise. He gazed at her mildly, one eyebrow raised slightly.

"Yes, Mrs. Saltire, what is it?"

"The young lady, sir, Miss Markham? Is she not here?" He shook his dark head, smiling.

"She left a short while ago, in The Grange carriage, when it came for her. Why?"

"Oh, sir!" The housekeeper looked more than uneasy now, scared. She shook her head firmly. "No, sir, that was not the Arundale carriage you heard—it was our own, with Grimes driving. Miss Seaham wanted to take a last look at her lamed horse, so while she was in the stables he drove the carriage round the drive in front of the house, so *our* horses would come to no harm, sir, taking chill."

It was then as if all his plans, his hopes for the future rose up like a pack of cards and fell down around his head in confusion, despair. He started to his feet, mechanically laying his pipe down upon the mantlepiece, staring at Mrs. Saltire in consternation. But the housekeeper stood her ground stolidly. And in the silence, unbroken save for the sound of their breathing, he distinctly heard the soft hiss and flutter of the driven snow outside, dashing wetly against the windowpanes.

It was obvious what had happened, he reflected with an inward groan. Saranne could not wait for The Grange coach to come for her, but highly incensed had rushed from his house to set out and walk to meet it halfway. Or at the worst, walking the whole distance between the Arundale place and his own. He set his mouth in straight, grim lines.

Driving between the two estates was merely a journey of short duration in that age, when distance was measured by horses' hooves. But walking it on a dark winter's night, perhaps in a coming blizzard, without even the aid of a carried lantern, was a different matter altogether. He followed his housekeeper out into the hall, the front door open to reveal Winters, the surly Grange coachman sitting aloft upon his driver's seat outside, the whirling snowflakes about him, settling upon his shoulders, confirming DeLacey's worst fears.

"No, sir," Winters replied stolidly to the attorney's quick questions. "I saw no young woman on the way over." He added, almost with satisfaction, as if he were congenitally glad to be the bearer of bad tidings: "But then, I could've missed her quite easily in the twilight, sir, coming down fast, now, it is!"

Stating the obvious, DeLacey thought

testily. From the safety of the portico of the house, the attorney saw the snow coming down in sheets now, whitening the coachman's head and shoulders, falling thick and fast, whirling and dancing in a wild measure of its own in the arc of golden light cast forth from the open doorway behind him, fed by the carriage lamps throwing bright lozenges upon the ground. The horses pawed the gravel impatiently, not liking this waiting.

DeLacey frowned, his feelings a mixture of gloom and elation, relief. Saranne could not have got far in this blizzard, inexperienced as she was in rural ways. On a strange road and without even a lantern to guide her, she would be utterly at a loss as to which way to turn. He must go after her at once! Aloud, he gave swift orders to Winters to return to The Grange immediately and arrange a search party at that end if Saranne had not returned there by then. Meanwhile, he would raise the alarm locally himself.

He turned on his heel then and marched back into the house to order a search party of his own from among his tenants, the outside farm workers, and menservants. This was done in a remarkably short time, and thus mustered the little party set off into the night, with De-Lacey at its head, all well wrapped up against the cold and armed by stout sticks. A frail young woman could not have strayed far under these conditions, was their comforting conclusion. Or be expected to withstand them, for long, was his own pessimistic, grim thinking.

The Bath Road, from London to the West

Country, ran beside his estate for some distance, bordering it, confining it within an ancient, ivy-grown stone wall topped by tall elm trees, empty of all traffic at this time of night. For all that it was the King's Highway, it was barely the width of a single stagecoach for most of its length, no more, and beaten flat by the passage of such vehicles during the daytime.

"Spread out in a fan," he ordered, as they stood uncertainly in the light of the swinging lanterns. "One band of men on each side of the road—and shout at intervals, wave a light, so that you do not lose touch with one another. And the first man to find her gets a guinea!"

It was only when they heard answering shouts through the blackness of the night, saw flickering lanterns advancing toward them, that they realized at last that they had met up with the party from The Grange, that the chain of searching was complete, joined up, without anything—or anyone—to show for it. It had failed and the missing young woman had not been found. The band of searchers hastily arranged by an indignant Amanda was halfhearted at the best, resenting being kept from their warm beds, and all for the sake of a person of no importance, a paid companion.

"No better nor no worse than any one of us!" a groom grumbled indignantly, yawning.

But the dismal fact remained that The Grange party, too, reported a singular lack of success in finding the missing girl. With a gloom that matched DeLacey's own, yet for different reasons, they finally disbanded and each went his own way, after exchanging notes and observations. DeLacey turned on his heel and strode back toward Lacey Place alone, warning his disgruntled and weary men that they must snatch what sleep they could during the rest of the night that remained, in order to be ready at the first break of dawn to resume the search.

His heart was heavy, filled by forebodings of the direst kind as he walked swiftly through the falling snow. His tall figure seemed even taller than it really was, the lanterns casting a grotesque shadow like the Brocken before him. Although it was well past midnight by then, the front of the house was a blaze of lights. The housekeeper and her female staff below-stairs were still up, waiting to dispense hot drinks, refreshments, to master and his men, whenever they should return, minister sooth-ingly to the cold, wet, disappointed search party.

He slept fitfully for the rest of that night in an armchair in the library, ever and anon starting awake, fancying he had been called, a sleep, beside the dying fire, that was full of doleful dreams, nightmares. He finally awoke shivering, just as the dawn was breaking redly behind the bare, stripped trees of winter out-side. He rose and went over to the windows, flinging aside the wooden shutters of the near-est, a feature of Georgian life, unclamping the iron bar across it. He peered out.

The candles in their silver candlesticks in the room behind him had extinguished themselves sometime during the night and now stood in small untidy pools of melted wax. The scene which met his glance in the quiet parkland beyond the window was one of pure, unsullied serenity. The snow had stopped, the whiteness stretching for miles, lying inert, silent like a shroud, a winding-sheet over the land. And somewhere, he thought, for all he knew to the contrary, lay the body of the woman he loved. She must be dead, could not have survived the night. There was no sound save a shrill, piping breeze that had sprung up and was moaning about the corners of the house.

Presently he bathed, shaved, and changed his clothes, and refusing all offers of breakfast from Mrs. Saltire save a cup of hot coffee, hurriedly gulped down, gave orders for his horse to be saddled and brought round. He must go into Bath at once, although it might already be too late, and call out the militia to comb the countryside more thoroughly than they had the night before. He mounted and cantered swiftly away down the driveway of Lacey Place.

But Jerome DeLacey was not the only rider out so early on that coldly beautiful day, dark figures against the landscapes, upon the icy roads. As he almost reached the outskirts of Bath, lying sunning itself in the thin wintry sunlight, bathing the old sandstone buildings, houses, in a mellow glow, another horseman topped the rise from the town and rode toward DeLacey. As the other passed, something in the cut of the blue coat he wore with such an elegant air, his whole appearance struck a chord of familiarity, remembrance, in the lawyer's keen brain.

He drew rein to stare back at him over his shoulder, only to find that the other man had halted too, had turned in his saddle to stare at DeLacey in turn. Recognition smote the lawyer like a blow in the face as he saw those light-blue mocking eyes, beneath the brim of a rakishly tilted tall beaver hat with a shining buckle in it. The whole air of insolent bravado the other wore like a buttonhole was an affront to DeLacey, setting his teeth on edge. It was an old enemy, the notorious cardsharp, George Bellemy. The trickster and scoundrel who three years ago had married the banker's runaway heiress, Arabella Crale.

Chapter
8

It had seemed so easy to Saranne, the simplest thing in the world, indeed, the only possible solution at the time, to rush out of the library at Lacey Place, out of the house itself, carried along upon her fury as if desperation had lent wings to her heels. Through the lobby, running to the massive mahogany front door in her anger, barring the way out into the night. She fumbled blindly at the heavy iron bolts with numbed, icy hands, somehow managed to unfasten it at last and sped through, closing it behind her.

She stood on top of the flight of stone steps outside, pausing there, breathing hard. Dusk fell fairly early in those climes, in the wintertime, helped now by the darkness of an imminent fall of snow, blowing in off the desolate moors, blackening the sky with its sullen stormclouds, threateningly, as she came out upon the steps at Lacey Place, it was already nearly night. Certainly it seemed that there had been little time for any intermediate twilight in the moments that had elapsed since she fled the library and its hated inhabitant.

No! she corrected herself wildly, passionately, facing the truth at last, painful, hurtful as it was. That is the last thing I feel about Mr. DeLacey!

She had intended in her first rush of indignation at his high-handed treatment of the bracelet incident, brushing aside her feelings as if they were of no consequence at all, to speedily put as much distance between him and herself as was possible, yet scarcely knowing what she was doing, if truth be told. If she made her way along the Bath Road on foot, with any luck she would meet The Grange carriage, with Winters driving it, coming to fetch her.

It did not occur to her that she might miss it altogether in the dark—or it her—as she ran swiftly through the lobby, her feet scarcely seeming to touch the ground in her flight, skimming over the ancient Persian rugs scattered there in their soft, muted colors like stained glass in a church window. Yet she was forced to stop as she reached the open air by the sight of DeLacey's carriage carrying, as she well knew, the two people she least wanted to meet just then—the Seahams, mother and daughter.

She shrank instinctively back into the shadow of the portico, concealing herself behind one of the pillars.

The carriage was standing at the far end of the circular gravel sweep in front of the house, just where it turned off into the driveway proper. Even as she watched, wondering what it was doing there, frowning slightly, she saw Undine emerge in her long velvet skirts and stride off toward the DeLacey stables with a purposeful air. Soon after Grimes, the DeLacey coachman, began driving his equipage round the circular flowerbed in the middle, evidently to keep the horses exercised in the cold.

She shrank back farther in the gloom of the portico as it came abreast of her, hoping against hope that neither of the two occupants of the vehicle had seen her. Her luck held it seemed, for it passed within a few feet of her without any sign of recognition from it. Saranne breathed a silent sigh of relief. But, as she was only too soberly aware, this was only the start of her problems. Soon after, as she waited in a positive fever of impatience, she saw Undine coming from the stables. Miss Seaham clambered into the carriage once more and was driven away.

So far, so good, Saranne thought thankfully.

The coast was now clear as far as the Seahams were concerned. She stepped from behind the shelter of the portico pillar with the feeling of one from whose shoulders a burden had been lifted. It was now nearly completely dark as she half ran, half walked quickly down the tunnel of trees that closed in the drive, in the wake of DeLacey's carriage, which was fast vanishing into the distance.

She realized then, perhaps for the first time, how utterly alone she was, a small, human speck in the solitude all around her, with no other living being in sight, no sign of habitation, not even a friendly light to hold out its hand to her, beckoning to her in the dark—nothing. She was now, above all else, conscious of how cold she was, the buffeting of the wind spinning her almost off her feet like a top, aware of the hard gravel underfoot in her thin indoor shoes, which she had forgotten to change.

"It is a nightmare," she said aloud from between clenched teeth, as she battled her way through the encompassing darkness.

She felt the damp and wet seeping up through the thin soles of her slippers. The trees of the drive met overhead, plunging the way below into Stygian gloom. The bare skeletal branches tossed and complained, groaning in the blast. She drew the hood of her cloak more closely around her head, and held the edges of the cloak itself together with frozen fingers. As she neared the entrance gates, the first few flakes of icy snow began to fall.

They stung her already cold cheeks into wetness, so that she instinctively put up a hand to brush them away, only to find that they fell faster and more thickly now, increasing in pace and volume with every passing second. The big gates with their ornamental flourishes in wrought-iron were closed. The lodgekeeper had obviously refastened them after opening them to let the carriage through and had now gone into his small cottage again, shutting the door to lock out the night and all it contained, for good or ill.

There was, however, a narrow side gate for pedestrians and this she discovered to be unlocked. She slipped through like a snow-wraith and made her way in a few short steps to the highway which lay beyond, not clear in her own mind now as to where she was going, or indeed, what she was doing out on such a night. It was becoming difficult to see any distance ahead. A real sense of fear, seized her.

She battled on more by instinct than any sense of direction, without any conscious volition on her own part. All she knew, gritting her teeth, was that she must keep walking, that she dare not halt now in peril of being stopped forever. The snow did strange things to her eyes, her brain itself, so that presently she lost all sense of place and time and walked stiffly, like an automaton, trudging through the snow-drifts. She stumbled a little every now and then, her knees going weak beneath her.

Not only had she lost all sense of time and direction, it seemed that she had mislaid memory, too. It was hours, surely, since she had left the gates of Lacey Place behind her in the gloom. And although she had only covered a short distance in a brief while, it appeared to Saranne that she had been walking for days, even weeks now. At first she had the highway to guide her, a faintly darker ribbon in the blinding snow, to keep her faltering footsteps on that dubious path. But as the ever falling flakes thickened, began to settle, even that vague lifeline failed her in the end.

Once she nearly fell, brought to her knees and momentarily sinking almost up to her waist in a hidden snowdrift, the whiteness covering all, pitfalls and obstacle alike. She managed to extricate herself that time, struggling to her feet, but the escape had been a narrow one, she knew. Instinctively clawing her way free of the cloying, dangerous stuff, so soft and so treacherous. It could not last, this fantastic journey through the darkness of the snowstorm, and despairing, she knew it. An unknown, uncharted country of whose contours she was ignorant.

"Help!" she cried weakly, cupping her lips with chilled hands. "Please, somebody help me—?"

Nobody answered and her feeble cry was swept away on the wind, lost in the vastness of the moors. It was useless, she thought, despair enveloping her now like a cloak. Bedeviled by cold, fear, the darkness all around her, all grasp on reality seemed to leave her, and light-headed from fatigue, losing the unequal battle, she staggered, scarcely aware of what she was doing, toward a clump of trees beside the road a little way ahead. She had some dim idea in her mind of trying to reach their shelter.

Then agony, like a burning, searing flame shot through her as her foot twisted under her. A straying tree-root, a trailer of bramble, strong as a hawser in miniature, concealed under the snow, had caught at her shoe, tripping her. She screamed a cry of terror as she fell, losing consciousness for a second or two until the coldness of the snowdrift into which she had tumbled, wet against her cheek, revived her. Saranne sat up again, nursing her swollen ankle.

Already she could feel the throbbing distortion of its shape—it did not seem *right*, somehow, she thought, half deliriously. It almost seemed to swell in her hands as she tightly held the injured limb. She longed now, as she had never done before, for the lights of The Grange carriage to come at last into view. But there was no sign of it, only the grim night all about her, cutting her off.

She pushed the soaked tendrils of red hair out of her eyes. The hood of her cloak had fallen down in the tumble and the snow fell unchecked now about her head and shoulders, covering them with white. The sting of the cold revived her somewhat again, prevented her from going to sleep—which she longed to do, oddly enough, she thought drowsily, the cold fastening upon her limbs.

Yet aid was closer at hand than she imagined. As she crouched there despairingly, Saranne suddenly saw far off, approaching rapidly in the distance, the blessed glimmer of carriage-lamps.

Her first impression was that it must be the Arundale vehicle on its way to Lacey Place to fetch her. Relief, thanksgiving, flowed through her like a warm tide. The light of the lanterns on either side of the unseen carriage threw unsteady golden lozenges upon the snow, cutting a swath of hope through the darkness. She stirred herself then, lifting her head to listen.

"Help!" she called again, one hand fluttering toward the approaching vehicle. "Help, please—?"

She realized the foolishness of this almost before the words had left her lips, blown away upon the wind. Yet by some miracle that faint cry was heard, her feeble movement noticed by the driver of the carriage and his companion on the seat beside him, huddled in a cloak. Saranne caught a glimpse of fair hair beneath its hood. . . . But she had no very clear memory of what happened after that.

It was all an unhappy blur in her mind, a vague recollection of the carriage pulling up sharply, disclosing the outline of a phaeton meant for two, instead of the bulkier Arundale carriage she expected, looming out of the dark. She looked up through mingled tears of thankfulness and confusion as she felt herself being lifted, helped to her feet. Or rather, one foot, wincing a little and crying out as the injured one touched the ground, a stab of pain shooting through it.

Now I know that I am dreaming, that all this is not for real! she thought, lightheaded, gazing into the blank staring faces, like those of shocked, frightened children, of George and Arabella Bellemy! George Bellemy spoke at last, as Arabella gave an incredulous gasp:

"Saranne Saranne Markham, as I live! What in the world are you doing here?"

Then Arabella spoke, shattering Saranne's fixed illusion that they were not flesh and blood like herself, but phantoms born of the night who would dissipate into mist with the morning. As she winced again and would have stumbled standing there, Arabella cried, with a practicality which seemed far from the old Arabella she knew, Saranne thought delirously! "Oh, George, she's hurt—look, she's done something to her ankle."

And then, half carried, half helped by the two, she somehow found herself in the phaeton, her head resting upon her old schoolfellow's shoulder, Arabella's arm comfortingly about her waist, holding her upright between George and herself. George Bellemy had always been a good driver, she knew. And now, with a flick of the wrist, he awoke his horse to life and the phaeton bowled away through the night toward Bath, as fast as the snow and the darkness would allow.

Almost delirious by now, Saranne became aware of silly, unimportant things that yet looked large in her consciousness. Of the soft, warm feel, like a caress, of the sumptuous fur cloak Arabella wore, the diamond rings upon her fingers, which flashed in the glow of the carriage lights as she lifted a hand to adjust her fur hood. Of the skill George showed in handling the horse and vehicle under those appalling conditions of a nightmare journey down from the moorlands to the safety of Bath lying below.

Once she would have spoken, feeling that she owed them an explanation of sorts, strug-

gling to keep awake 'ere oblivion, a deep tiredness, overtook her, in the reaction. But Arabella laid a wilful, imperious finger against her
lips, with a light laugh.

"Not now, my dear—later," Arabella said
soothingly, almost like a mother talking to a
fretful child. She laughed again. "I expect it
will keep, eh?" Arabella said shrewdly.

Saranne told them later that night, when
she was somewhat revived, of all that had happened to her since they had last met at school
in The Limes at Epsom. By tacit consent the
unpleasantness that had occurred then was not
mentioned, and indeed never referred to again,
each party agreeing to pretend that it was now
forgotten.

"Is it only three years since?" Arabella
mused wonderingly, aloud. "It seems like a
lifetime!"

This was after a surgeon had been found
in the town who came and set Saranne's broken
ankle, bound it up with bandages and gave
Arabella a potion to dose the patient with that
night in a hot posset.

"We can all do with a posset," George said
genially, proceeding to make one of mulled
wine from a funnel thrust into the embers of
the dying fire in their living room. Saranne
touched but lightly on her brush with Jerome
DeLacey, hoping its significance would escape
them. She brushed it aside as if it were of little
importance.

Yet again, in her very artlessness, naive
to a degree compared to the more sophisticated

Arabella, Saranne told them far more than she knew. Once more meaningful glances were exchanged over her unsuspecting red head by that shrewdly worldly-wise pair—who were yet so trusting, oddly childlike in their regard for each other, giving little nods of comprehension behind her shining red hair in the candlelight.

They had a modest apartment over a small milliner's shop in a back street of an unfashionable part of town, where George also rented space for his ramshackle phaeton—which had seen better days—and the horse, in a livery stable nearby.

They were real children of the night, Saranne discovered to her amusement during the next few days of her stay under their roof, folk who only seemed to come alive after nightfall, untidy, relaxed during the daytime, like players waiting in the wings of some theater. After sundown they appeared to be fired by a positive demon of energy—like actors, she thought. Dependent upon patches and powder, greasepaint and costume to make them turn into real people!—and not puppets, worked by strings. She had learned something of the theater, the shadowy precariousness of life lived by such characters, during her months of helping to write Amanda's memoirs. She sighed. The furniture in their dilapidated dwelling was shabby, but they did not seem to notice it. She was put to bed, on that first night, in the only bedchamber the little apartment had, sharing it with Arabella, while George slept upon the sofa in the living room.

But as time went on and a further visit from the physician confirmed that the damaged ankle would need further rest for the bone to "knit" properly, Saranne was relegated to a tiny room off the kitchen, little more than a large closet really, where Arabella was wont to keep her extensive wardrobe. It contained a truckle bed, a rickety chair and table, and nothing more, but she took possession of it gladly, thanking Arabella.

She now had time to inspect her old schoolfellow and liked what she saw, nodding approval. Mrs. Bellemy had lost most of her puppyfat and marriage seemed to have improved her. She was now a very personable young woman, indeed, blooming with an indefinable inner grace that had been missing before. Beneath the bubbling, champagnelike effervescence of her personality there was a certain serenity which served but to enhance her charm a hundredfold, Saranne mused. She gaily informed the semi-invalid, when Saranne was still confined to the sofa in the living room, held captive:

"When George is in funds, has a winning streak at the gaming tables, I want for nothing, my dear! He gives me anything a woman could desire—furs, jewels, fine gowns!"

"And when he isn't lucky, Arabella—what then, eh?" Saranne asked quietly.

Arabella was silent, evasive, frowning. And Saranne's heart ached for her old friend—indeed, for both of them.

"We live literally from hand to mouth," Arabella confessed sadly at last. "And more often than not my precious possessions have to go into pawn until times change and George can redeem them for me again! Why, even at this moment George owes a truly enormous bill for fodder for his horse in the local stables . . ."

As Arabella's voice died away, Saranne could not help wondering, her gaze going around the cheap lodging, if this were one of their "best" periods, what must an inferior one be like? On the first morning after her arrival in their home, Saranne awoke with an overwhelming sense of loss and lay for a few minutes while she gathered together her scattered thoughts in the unfamiliar room. Her aching foot brought her back to reality again, as she remembered.

Her second urgent thought, once she had recollected the circumstances of being here—where she was and what had passed the night before—was to get word at once to Amanda at The Grange, tell her employer the whole story. Let young Mrs. Arundale know at the first possible opportunity what had happened overnight to her paid companion. Saranne struggled up on one elbow as Arabella came into the room, carrying a tray with a cup of hot chocolate upon it. Arabella had risen early, while Saranne was still sleeping.

"Tell Amanda Arundale where you are, that you are safe?" Arabella echoed with an unusual hardness as Saranne made her plea. Mrs. Bellemy dismissed the subject with a shrug of her well-rounded shoulders, pooh-poohing the idea. "Let 'em stew in their own juice, the Arundales, for a change!" she said briskly. "Do 'em good, wondering about you, Saranne! That is," Arabella added more thoughtfully, "if they are capable of worrying about anybody, or anything, but themselves!"

"Yes, but—?" Saranne refused to be drawn, reveal her true feelings, lying back wearily upon the pillows. "All the same, I would like Mrs. Arundale to know I am safe," she pleaded huskily, an anxious gleam in the gray eyes under the tumbled cloud of her red hair. "Please, Arabella—will you get word to them?"

"Oh, very well." Arabella sounded resentful. Yet she relented enough to promise the guest soothingly: "George shall ride over to The Grange after breakfast, if that will set your mind at rest."

"It will, Arabella, indeed it will," Saranne said gratefully.

And there the matter rested for the time being. George, too, showed no great enthusiasm for the task set before him, involving, as it did, a reunion with his wife's old friends and acquaintances who had, in his opinion, treated them both very badly. He said so aloud in no uncertain terms when Arabella first put the proposition to him while he lingered over his breakfast meats and the daily edition of the Bath *Times*.

But Arabella cooed at him, running her light, cool fingers through his fair hair, and in the end he agreed, though with very bad grace. She could understand his hesitation, Saranne thought, his reluctance to undertake the errand, seeing things now through their eyes. For

George and Arabella, as well as herself, had suffered from the local gentry.

George had his second-rate nag saddled and brought round by an ostler, then mounted and set forth for the Arundale place. It had ceased to snow and for that he was duly thankful, turning up the collar of his riding coat in the keen air. Despite himself, Bellemy's spirits, as mercurial as Arabella's own, began to rise with the exercise.

And it was as he breasted the top of one of the steeply rising streets out of the town that he was unexpectedly confronted by another solitary horseman like himself, out riding in the snowy slush the overnight blizzard had left upon the highway. They nodded briefly to each other in passing, with the common, everyday courtesy of the road which meant little, but was a mark of respect, impersonal as the white landscape itself.

And then George Bellemy let slip an exclamation of surprise, an oath, as he recognized the other in the same moment. There could not have been a greater contrast between the two men upon horseback if some painter had arranged the composition of it—one fair, the other so dark of hair and eye. But there it ended. And although Bellemy sat astride a most sorry specimen of horseflesh, he was dressed in the height of London fashion.

The well-laundered white of his exquisitely, even fastidiously tied stock encircling his lean neck, showed up almost dazzlingly against the royal-blue of a well-cut coat, the silver buttons of which winked impudently in the clear, cold light of early morning. The brim of his tall beaver hat with its shining steel buckle was tilted with just the exact amount of bravado to incense the more soberly attired attorney, Jerome DeLacey. The fine black leather of Bellemy's boots was highly polished.

DeLacey, as befitted his profession, presented a far more somber appearance altogether in dark clothes, and his horse was of the finest compared to the other's. His hat was placed firmly and squarely upon his darkly handsome head in the most formidable and uncompromising fashion possible. So they eyed each other as they came face to face and halted, each in turn bristling with the mein of two sporting terriers meeting in the prize-ring.

Giving the effect of warily circling one another with invisible hackles raised, they seemed to be spoiling for a fight. Yet both being civilized men, each after his own fashion, they did nothing of the kind, nodding coolly and riding on, until Bellemy, several yards away, was struck by his sudden idea and reined in his horse, wheeling round, at the same instant that DeLacey did likewise.

They stared at each other in hostile mood, across the length of highway which separated them, then Arabella's husband touched his heels lightly to the thin ribs of his horse. He rode up to DeLacey, and with a cool relish that he was at no pains to conceal, George asked the lawyer if he would be seeing Mrs. Arundale soon. DeLacey countered with another question, curtly:

"Why?"

"If so," Bellemy went on, ignoring this, "would you have the courtesy to convey a message to her, a vital piece of information?"

"What message, what piece of information?" The lawyer's tone was sharp now, on edge with anxiety as he stared at the hated figure before him from beneath lowering brows. Unconsciously, his whole face twisted into a sneer now, he looked Bellemy up and down scathingly, as if he would imprint his image upon his brain forever. "What possible business could you have with Mrs. Arundale?" he demanded brusquely. Bellemy shrugged.

"Only to tell her that her companion, Miss Markham, is safe, is staying now with my wife and me in Bath. She has broken her ankle, which I fear will lay her up for some weeks to come. Will you tell Mrs. Arundale that, please?"

"Saranne is safe?" Relief, joy, flooded into the attorney's heart, his expression changing from tenseness to something almost like gentleness at this happy news. But it was only for a moment. The next instant it hardened again, swiftly, all his old haughty arrogance to the fore once more. "Take me to her," he ordered. "I must see her—"

Bellemy laughed cruelly.

"Hold hard, sir!" he cried mockingly. "Miss Markham has no wish to see *you*, she has told us so! So your visit would be in vain—she would not receive you."

And before the lawyer could answer, George bowed slightly from the waist in the saddle and rode away, turning back toward Bath. He could not have resisted that last gibe,

George reflected, to save his life! A chance to get back at DeLacey and his high-handed manner on behalf of his wife, himself, and Saranne. They were all in the same boat, having been victims of Jerome DeLacey, and his kind, in turn.

And DeLacey himself? His first instinct was to ride after the insolent cardsharp, challenge him, to seize him by the throat and beat the knowledge of Saranne's whereabouts out of her host. But wiser impulses held. He knew, then, in that searing moment of helplessness, what it was to taste defeat, bitter upon the tongue, for perhaps the premier time in his successful, indulged life.

His lips tightly compressed, he sat there, motionless upon his horse, staring after Bellemy with dry, burning eyes until the latter dropped out of his view over the skyline, descending into Bath lying below. DeLacey digested an unpalatable truth then, that there was nothing he could do to change events now. It no longer lay within his power to do so, to punish Arabella, George Bellemy, Saranne herself, for having had the temerity to "answer back" to the established order of things.

Nor did he imagine that Bellemy, having married his Arabella and thus figuratively cocked a snoot at society in general, was likely to be on his, DeLacey's, side in the matter of Saranne Markham. The lawyer smiled wryly— he doubted if Bellemy cared a fig for what, he thought! But whatever his opinion of the Bellemys, he knew that Saranne would be safe with them, well cared for, for the time being. His contacting her could wait. With a heavy heart he turned his horse toward The Grange to tell Amanda.

But whatever thoughts he—and Saranne —may have harbored about relieving Amanda Arundale's anxiety over the whereabouts, safety, of her companion, proved misguided. Hard upon the heels of DeLacey's visit came a humble little note from Saranne, revealing her address and explaining the predicament she was in with a broken ankle.

"Please forgive me," Saranne wrote, "for thus leaving you in the lurch without either companion or secretary, Mrs. Arundale. Believe me, it is because of causes beyond my control. . . ."

Amanda's reaction to this was not long forthcoming. In a sudden fit of pique, she tore up the note into tiny shreds, then ordered that Saranne's trunk be packed and delivered up to her at the Bellemy lodgings. It was accompanied by a short, curt note of Amanda's own, in which she coldly dismissed the girl out of hand and sent the balance of salary owing to her. Saranne shrugged, meekly accepting the fresh blow as she had accepted so many others in her short life.

She set herself to patiently await the mending of her broken bones, when she could begin, all over again, the heartbreaking task of finding another post. She was perforce marooned upon the sofa in the Bellemy living room, consuming her soul in what tranquility she could command, until such time as her injury was healed.

A few days after the receipt of Amanda's cruel letter, while Saranne was still smarting from it, Jerome DeLacey called in person, one morning when both Arabella and George were absent, one at his club, the other at her dressmaker. He sent up his visiting-card to Saranne by one of the giggling young apprentices of the milliner in the hat shop beneath.

"Please—I must see you, Saranne," he had scribbled underneath his name. Her heart turned over at the sight of it, contracted momentarily in a spasm of pain. But she resolutely hardened in her resolve never to see him again, and sent the card back via the same messenger. His letters, in which he professed utter mystery as to the "misunderstanding which seems to have come between us," remained unopened by Saranne, unanswered. He was at his wits' end. And then something entirely unforeseen happened which put a different complexion upon events, caused him to abruptly cease in his courtship of her.

In a small country city such as Bath, gossip and rumor-mongering were rife. The idle few who spent their winters there had very little else to do to pass the time.

So when an entirely new, sparkling tidbit of news fell upon their plates out of the blue, as it were, their dinners and soirées were enlivened by it at once. A governess, a mere paid companion or someone of that ilk, a nobody, had leaped suddenly into a blaze of publicity, prominence, by being left a nabob's ransom in the way of a fortune—

"Nay, the very riches of Croesus, so I'm told, ma'am—my hairdresser did!" one dowager said in awed, hushed tones to another.

The father of this nobody, one Mr. Paton, a thriving haberdasher from Cheapside in London, the first lady went on, had died and left the "gel" his entire fortune, consisting of a mansion in the metropolis, the Emporium itself, carriages and horses, a house by the sea at Brighton, and innumerable valuable stocks and shares, having nobody else to leave them to, his wife having predeceased him by a few months.

"The gel's *natural* father, I should say," the informant dropped her voice archly from behind the barricade of her ivory-handled fan, adroitly waved. "She is, unfortunately, not legitimate!"

"A love child? Ah!" And she was rewarded for this disclosure by a thoroughly ardent sigh of satisfaction from her vis-à-vis. Each then feverishly began adding up, in her own mind, the chances or otherwise of this rich plum's hand— the heiress—for her favorite son or nephew.

Mr. DeLacey scorned to appear one of the fortune hunters. And if she had spurned his attempt at reconciliation when she was poor, would she not do so now with greater vehemence?

Although she should have been the happiest person in the world at this juncture of her affairs, the dismal fact remained that Saranne was nothing of the kind. The reverse, rather, unhappy and confused. It was like the old, old

269

story of Cinderella or from rags to riches come to life, she mused sadly. Only for her there was no Prince Charming, no Fairy Godmother even to wave her wand and make all come right, change everything for the better in the twinkling of an eye, by magic. Only money.

Magic wands and Fairy Godmothers belonged to the realm of pure fantasy, not the living. There was only money and money was the key that unlocked all doors, opened every edifice however difficult, smoothed one's path through life. It changed scowls to smiles, harsh words to soft flattery, and brought in its wake not true love, but false-hearted suitors whom Saranne despised. She was sickened by it all.

Least of all did she hear again from Mr. DeLacey, who seemingly had dropped out of her life completely with the news of her inheritance. She did not know whether to be sorry or relieved at this turn of events, summoning all her pride to her aid. But as time went on and she lived in such a bemusing whirl of happenings, she had little leisure to let her thoughts slip back in his direction.

There were almost daily consultations now, over a period, with the firm of Bath lawyers her late father's London attorneys had appointed to take care of her affairs at that end. George Bellemy, surprisingly, turned out to be a tower of strength in those days. Partly because he realized that both girls, especially Arabella, whom it did not really concern at all, were in such a state of flustered excitement, their brains in a giddy spin, that it behooved him as a man to provide a steadying influence on them, an anchor upon reality.

"If I don't," he suggested slyly, "you will both sail away to Cloud-Cuckoo-Land without me, out of my reach forever!"

Arabella was bubbling over with high good spirits, as much on her friend's behalf as her own, rejoicing in Saranne's fortune. Saranne was slightly more subdued, as if she had other things on her mind. And despite their shocked protests, saying "no" at first, she insisted on settling a handsome sum of money on them in Arabella's name, so that George might not be tempted to gamble it away.

"Yes." Arabella nodded her rueful thanks. "George is the dearest, sweetest, best man in all the world," she agreed, "but he *will* gamble! You are wise, Saranne."

Saranne further bought a small, exquisite little jewel of a Georgian house for Arabella in a mildly fashionable part of the city, with all its furnishings. There was also a new carriage with the Bellemy crest upon its newly varnished panels, and a pair of brisk horses to go with it. Arabella shyly revealed a lifelong ambition then.

"Now I have an establishment of my own, plus an equipage," she said, "I would like to take on one or two girls of good family, open a sort of finishing school for them. Take them under my wing, you know, as a young married woman, and launch them in turn upon the sea of matrimony!"

"My!" And Saranne laughed, she could not

help it. But Arabella was quite serious. "A sort of marriage broker, eh?" Saranne suggested, sobering.

"Yes." Arabella nodded. "Just that."

She went on to point out that there were many country wives and mothers of quite important families who had neither the know-how nor the inclination to see their daughters through a fashionable season, steer them in the way they ought to go—a satisfactory match with a wealthy husband. They needed nothing more or less than a professional duenna. And she, Arabella, proposed to offer that service, for a suitable fee.

And the future chaperone forthwith became immersed in a bewildering array of costly silks and satins and brocades, drapes and curtaining for her new home. Clara Fairley had been a frequent visitor to the Bellemy household ever since Saranne had first met with her accident. The two youthful matrons had much in common and plenty to gossip about, falling upon one another's necks at sight like long-lost friends. Saranne gathered that they had known each other since childhood, but time, life itself, had separated them.

Despite Arabella's, and now Clara's, urgings, adding her plea, Saranne refused to go out much into society at all, putting forth as her excuse the recent death of her natural father—even if she had scarcely known that gentleman.

"But, my dear, you can't remain a hermit for the rest of your life," Arabella said in alarm. And Clara added her quota, seriously:

"Think of all the beaux of Bath who are dying to make your acquaintance, Saranne!"

"Or of her fortune," Arabella corrected with a wicked smile.

But Saranne was adamant, strong in her purpose not to give way or accede to their demands. Yet there did eventually arrive an occasion when she was forced to capitulate for shame's sake, a big charity ball for some unknown good cause that was to take place in the Assembly Rooms at Bath one evening. She could not easily refuse and so agreed, though with some uneasiness, misgivings.

Arabella was in the seventh heaven of delight at this news and enthusiastically threw herself into the task of helping Saranne to choose a gown for the evening. Accordingly, Saranne gave way to Arabella's importunities, the latter eager to show off this new Saranne who remained remarkably like the old one.

Saranne suffered Arabella's choice of a gown in soft green satin encrusted with seed pearls. It set off her slender figure with its long, flowing elegance of line, while her red hair was fashionably dressed for the night high on top of her small, shapely head, a cascade of auburn curls falling over one shoulder. At the last moment, on the impulse of a whim she could scarcely explain even to herself, she clipped into her ears the long drop emerald earrings old Mrs. Arundale had given her long ago.

She looked very beautiful in the light of many wax tapers set in sconces along the walls of the Assembly Rooms, as the ball got under way. And many present thought so, too, none more than one man in particular, whose dark blue eyes watched her yearningly from across the length of the room that separated them. On the excuse of weakness still in her damaged ankle, Saranne danced only once or twice, then retired more or less from the brilliant throng. She sat out the rest of the evening among the dowagers and other "wallflowers" who were ranged upon chairs on the sidelines, as it were.

She presently found the ballroom growing too hot for her and sought refuge beside a full-length glass door giving on to a small balcony overlooking the ancient Roman pool, from which bubbles still rose infrequently from the slightly steaming warm water, breaking lazily upon the surface as they had done for two thousand years. She started and would have dropped her fan as a man's voice said in her ear, gently:

"May I add my congratulations, too, Miss Markham? As, I am sure, many others have already done!"

It was a voice she would have known, recognized, anywhere, above all others. She turned then, slowly, to find Jerome DeLacey gazing down at her from his superior height, the blue eyes grave, kind for once, belying the lightness of his tone. Nevertheless she stammered foolishly, taken aback, at a loss what to say, "C-congratulations, sir?"

"On your inheritance, of course, your great good fortune, Miss Markham." And then his manner changed, became warmer, less impersonal as he said with what seemed utter sincerity, yet with an underlying sadness that she did not understand: "I hope with all my heart, Saranne, that you make the important grand match you so richly deserve!"

And he was gone, with a formal little bow that was almost like a gesture of dismissal, of farewell. One moment he was there and the next he had gone and dimly, as in a dream, she saw his tall figure mingling with and then evading the dancers upon the ballroom floor. Then he disappeared through the nearest exit. She finished the rest of the evening with a heavy heart, a sense of loss, emptiness, an aching void that his going had left in her breast, like a black cloud overhead.

Nothing now awaited her, no future, save that of the gloomy Paton Mansion in London, under whose garret roof she had slept as a child, banished there by her stepmother, Adeline.

"A staff of idle servants awaits you there, Miss Markham," the Bath lawyers urged, impatient for her to either take up her residence or give them orders to dispose of the property and thus tidy up the estate. "A carriage in the stable, horses eating their heads off for lack of exercise!"

Clara Fairley furnished Saranne with a personal maid, a necessary fixture of her new status in society, Arabella said airily. She accepted this as she accepted so much more in those days, in silence, and with no deep interest, shrugging.

"A likely young girl," young Mrs. Fairley reported her protégée warmly. "Clean and honest—you'll like her, Saranne," she urged.

Chloe, for that was her name, was daughter to one of the Fairley's tenant farmers, had been brought up on the estate and now worked as dairymaid for the "big house." She wanted to better herself in the service of some lady of fashion, Clara said, learn all she could, travel and see the world. Saranne saw the girl, liked her, and engaged her on the spot, to Clara's relief and Arabella's satisfaction.

Chloe flung herself into her new duties with enthusiasm, untutored but able and willing. Under Arabella's wing, who taught her, Chloe seemed to spend more time attending to Mrs. Bellemy than her real mistress, to Saranne's secret amusement.

"We will come and visit you in London often," Arabella promised earnestly, when the question of Saranne leaving Bath came up once more, finally. "Enjoy the season with you, see the sights—won't we, George?"

Saranne smiled wanly in return, thanking Arabella for her offer in the spirit in which it had been given. Arabella would not hear of her friend booking seats for herself and her maid upon the normal stagecoach between Bath and London, but insisted that Saranne take the loan of the Bellemy equipage for the journey, make it in comfort. But on the morning of the actual day when they were leaving, when Saranne had made all her final arrangements, said her brief adieus, Arabella, as the

French would say, again "threw a *sabot* in the works" of the other's plans.

"Wretched woman!" she moaned, prancing into Saranne's room before the latter was barely awake, forestalling Chloe by carrying a cup of hot chocolate. She sat down, ruffling up the counterpane upon the end of Saranne's bed. "Tiresome of her—my dressmaker, I mean," Arabella pouted. "She promised faithfully a fitting for my new ball gown, the blue one! I am afraid I will have to borrow the carriage just for a teensy-weensy bit, Saranne, go see her," she wheedled. "I will be back in no time at all!"

What else could she do, Saranne asked herself? She sighed and agreed, for like most travelers of that age she was anxious to make as much of her trip as possible during daylight hours. Dressed in her outdoor clothes, a soft gray velvet cloak, a fur-trimmed bonnet to match, with shoes and gloves of finest black kidskin, she sat down in the Bellemy parlor to await Arabella's return with as much patience as she could summon up. Her trunk, also, was standing ready packed in the entrance hall.

But the tiny ormolu clock upon the mantlepiece struck ten silvery notes presently, then eleven, to be followed by its ultimate twelve, before she stirred uneasily, going to the window to stare out. It was the normal dining hour, but still there was no sign of the errant Arabella. George and she presently sat down to a midday meal at the former's insistence, but Saranne only nibbled at the food set before

277

her. It was nearly three o'clock before a repentant Mrs. Bellemy put in an appearance.

"Now, don't be cross," she begged, before they could start questioning her. "It wasn't my fault—I was delayed!"

"How?" her husband demanded grimly. "Or should I say, by whom?"

"Clara Fairley," Arabella said simply, taking off her bonnet and flinging it upon the nearest chair. "A glass of wine, George, and then I will tell you all!" she cried gaily, giggling.

It transpired that Arabella, after her visit to her dressmaker was successfully concluded —"I gave her a piece of my mind!"—had had the madcap notion to go over to the Fairley place on the spur of the moment. There she had procured a basket of "goodies" from the kindhearted Clara for Saranne to take with her on her journey. There was a cooked fowl, a small bottle of wine and a game pie among other things, all wrapped up in a clean white napkin and country fresh from the Fairley's home farm.

"Clara sends her love," Arabella continued, "but Giles was not at home. He had gone over to the next town with Jerome De-Lacey, as witness in a court case held at the Assizes there. Some poaching affair, I believe —Clara does not expect him back till nightfall."

Moonlight diced the empty road ahead some time later, as the Bellemy coach carrying Saranne and her maid attained a lonely stretch of the highway, running between lonely moors. At any other hour she might have reveled in the quiet beauty of the countryside, the stillness, stars overhead glittering like points of steel.

It was almost dusk before she left Bath at last, snug in its hollow, the lights beginning to spring up everywhere, looking like a jewel set in a golden ring. The two girls hugged one another tearfully when it came to the final parting, swearing renewed eternal friendship, vowing to keep up a voluminous correspondence. And then the coach with Saranne had gone, driving off into the night. They would make good time, she piously hoped, so as to reach a serviceable inn before it was the wrong side of midnight.

Yet the landscape, had she only known it, was not entirely empty of human beings other than themselves—Saranne, the coachman, and Chloe. In the shadows cast by a black thicket of leaves a horseman waited, tall, motionless, sitting in the saddle on his powerful, well-trained black mare, a mask upon his face and a pistol in his hand. Waiting there, the figure had the tenseness of a coiled spring, a cat, all its muscles flexed, about to pounce upon a mouse. As the Bellemy carriage, with its deceptive crest upon the panels promising rich pickings, came into view, the highwayman acted.

"Halt—stand and deliver! Your money or your life!"

The next few minutes were a confused, frightening melée of rearing horses neighing shrilly, and the imprecations of the driver high upon his box seeking to regain his reins, bring the horses under control once more, and in the end, succeeding. He sat holding them tightly in, not daring to move, staring straight ahead as he had been ordered to by the robber, afraid to glance down at the little drama being enacted upon the ground below.

Saranne screamed once as the gentleman of the roads, as such men were called, appeared upon the scene, her blood turning to ice, and then was silent, trembling, her head in its dove-gray bonnet pressed up against the cushions of the carriage seat. Chloe, the maid, was whimpering, shrinking closer to her mistress. The masked highwayman had dismounted by now and approached the open window, which Saranne had lowered at the first sound of this disturbance.

"Come, ladies, there is no need to feel alarmed." His cultured tones were not wholly the surprise they might have been. Many men of good family took to the roads to gain a living when their fortunes were at low ebb. The reins of his mare looped over one arm, he held a pistol in his right hand, ready-cocked and quite obviously he would not hesitate to use it, should the necessity arise. He held out a gloved hand to Saranne, summing up the situation at a glance and ignoring the maid. "Your jewels, ma'am, if you please? And any other valuables you may have."

This was the tableau Jerome DeLacey and Giles Fairley saw as they came over the moor upon a bridlepath, slowly, barely at a walking pace, for they were tired after a long day spent in the hot, stuffy atmosphere of a country courthouse. The hooves of the horses made little sound upon the loose, springy turf interposed with bracken roots and so they were able to approach the road almost unobserved. There was an element of surprise in their appearance, too, and so they were able to rein in their horses and survey the situation undisturbed.

In the clear black-and-white of the moonlight, the tableau was etched as starkly as if it had been limned in India ink by the hand of some skilled craftsman.

"A hold-up, as I live!" Giles exclaimed softly under his breath, as DeLacey warned him to silence with finger on lip. "A villianous highwayman!"

But Giles Fairley was not to be so easily thwarted. Master of the local Chase, an ardent huntsman with foxhounds, all his sporting blood rose as he scented the prey, his nostrils smelling an imaginery "kill." He lifted himself in his saddle excitedly, standing in the stirrups and then, without giving it another thought, Clara's husband bellowed a stentorian "View Haloo!" and putting spurs to his horse, thundered forward in a wild gallop. DeLacey groaned aloud.

The bandit turned, startled, as Fairley came level with him and then it was all over within seconds. The gun he held went off in his hand in pure reflex, the report echoing loudly, reverberating over the moors. The bullet hit the coachman in the shoulder, winging him.

And again the horses began to rear and plunge in terror until the lawyer, who had arrived in time, jumped off his mount and seized the nearest bridle, as the reins slipped from the wounded driver's grasp.

The highwayman, his mischief done, was as swift in bounding into his own saddle and galloping away, with Giles Fairley in hot pursuit. DeLacey released the carriage horse he was soothing down and helped the coachman from his lofty seat. The man's fawn-colored livery coat, a harmless foible of Arabella's choice, was streaked by blood and he was breathing heavily. Supporting him, DeLacey cast a quick, worried glance into the carriage.

"Are you all right, Saranne? He did not harm you?"

She shook her head without speaking, and apparently reassured by that, he turned away, helping the coachman into the interior of the vehicle, ranged along one seat. Saranne and her maid were making him as comfortable as was possible from the limited means at their disposal when Giles returned.

"Dang me, if he didn't get away!" he reported indignantly, in high dudgeon. "His mare was too good for me—she beat my horse hollow!"

"Yes." DeLacey nodded absently. "Part of his stock-in-trade, the tools of the trade," he said briefly, "a good horse." He changed the subject abruptly. "We must get this man to a surgeon, he's bleeding badly," the lawyer said curtly. "My home is nearer than the next inn —we will go there."

And so it was, later that night, that those two found themselves together at last in the library at Lacey Place. The surgeon had come in his carriage and extracted the slug from the coachman's arm, seen his patient put to bed in a fellow ostler's room over the stables. Chloe was the heroine of the lawyer's servants' hall belowstairs, breathlessly recounting for the hundredth time (and each recital leaving nothing in the telling), the whole thrilling adventure. The physician had taken a glass of wine with them, and now was gone, DeLacey accompanying him to the front door to see him out into the night.

He returned to the room and stood with his back against the closed door. Saranne sat in a great carved chair of oak by the fireside. She had taken off her cloak and bonnet by then and made an appealing picture seated there, the soft light of the candles glowing upon her red hair. She raised her head as he entered, staring at him in turn. It was there they found each other at last.

In two swift strides he had crossed the room to her side, had lifted her to her feet, enfolded her, unresisting, in his arms without a word being said—or needed to be said, on either side, holding her tightly, fiercely clasped to his heart, her flushed, joyful face pressed up against the cloth of his somber coat. It was then he spoke, asking her quietly:

"Why did you run away from me, Saranne, that day back in the winter?"

"It was Mrs. Seaham," she murmured shamefaced, held fast within the warm, protective shelter of his arms. She murmured uneasily: "She said that you and—and Undine—" She choked, unable to go on, then rallied, lifting her serious face to his. "That you had bought the bracelet for Undine and when she refused it, passed it on as a sort of second-best to me!"

"She did, did she?" he exploded wrathfully. "Couldn't you recognize an interfering, mischief-making woman out to cause trouble, my darling?"

Once more he groped in his pocket and drew out a small box that she recognized, having seen it before: the jeweler's case holding the bracelet he had purchased in Bath that fatal day. DeLacey opened it now and firmly placed the ornament it contained into her hand —that bracelet that had been the innocent cause of so many tears, so much heartburning between them.

"B-but—?" she stammered, taking it.

"Go on, Saranne, read the inscription inside it," he ordered sternly. "It was being engraved, hence the delay, the reason why I did not give it to you at once. I could not. It only came by messenger on the morning of that day when the Seahams called."

In utter confusion she held it up to the light of the nearest candles, twisted it so that she was able to read the lettering inside—"To S.M. With All My Heart. J.DeL." She felt ashamed then, longed with all her soul to beg his forgiveness, ask his pardon. Watching her face, his own softened as he took her downcast chin in his strong yet sensitive hand, lifted it up, forcing her to meet the question in that ardent glance, the compelling fascination of those dark blue eyes.

"I love you, Saranne, more than anything in the world," he said earnestly. "Want you for my wife. Will you marry me, dearest?"

But he read the answer in the starry happiness of her gray eyes even before she spoke. Eyes full of trust, unquestioning love for him now, whereas in the dark past there had been only fear, hate. . . . And Saranne, as his lips met hers in the first true kiss of passionate, undying love, somehow managed to murmur softly that "yes," she would.

ROMANCE...ADVENTURE...DANGER...

PHILIPPA
by Katherine Talbot   (84-664, $1.75)

If she had to marry for money, and Philippa knew she must, then it was fortunate a member of The House of Lords was courting her. It would be difficult, though, to forget that the man she really loves would be her brother-in-law. . . . A delightful Regency Romance of a lady with her hand promised to one man and her heart lost to another!

DUCHESS IN DISGUISE
by Caroline Courtney   (94-050, $1.75)

The Duke of Westhampton had a wife in the country and a mistress in town. This suited the Duke, but his young wife, whom he'd wed and tucked away on his estate, was not pleased. So being as audacious as she was innocent, she undertook to win his attention by masquerading as a lady he did not know — herself!

WAGER FOR LOVE
by Caroline Courtney   (94-051, $1.75)

The Earl of Saltaire had a reputation as a rakehell, an abductor and ravisher of women, a dandy and demon on horseback. Then what lady of means and of irreproachable character would consider marrying him — especially if she knew the reason for the match was primarily to win a bet? When he won a wager by marrying her, he never gambled on losing his heart!

SWEET BRAVADO
by Alica Meadowes   (89-936, $1.95)

Aunt Sophie's will was her last attempt to reunite the two feuding branches of the Harcourt family. Either the Viscount of Ardsmore marry Nicole, the daughter of his disgraced uncle, or their aunt's inheritance would be lost to the entire family! And wed they did. But theirs was not a marriage made in heaven!

LILLIE
by David Butler   (82-775, $2.25)

This novel, upon which the stunning television series of the same name is based, takes Lillie Langtry's story from her girlhood, through the glamour and the triumphs, the scandals and the tragedies, the 1902 and Edward VII's accession to the throne.